D1707164

Halfway to Midnight

LARRY LEN PETERSON'S OTHER BOOK PUBLICATIONS

Charles M. Russell, Legacy

❦

A Most Desperate Situation

❦

The Call of the Mountains: The Artists of Glacier National Park

❦

Philip R. Goodwin: America's Sporting and Wildlife Artist

❦

L.A. Huffman: Photographer of the American West

❦

Charles M. Russell: Printed Rarities

HALFWAY
TO
MIDNIGHT

Dr. Larry Len Peterson

WITHDRAWN
BRIDGER PUBLIC LIBRARY
BRIDGER, MONTANA

Copyright © 2011
by
Larry Len Peterson

First Printing, May 2011

FRONT DUST JACKET
© by Beau, *Halfway To Midnight*, 2010,
10″ x 7″, oil on canvas,
courtesy of the Big Sky Collection

PRODUCTION AND DESIGN BY
Mountain Press Publishing Company

Library of Congress Cataloging-in-Publication Data

Peterson, Larry Len.
 Halfway to midnight / Larry Len Peterson.
    p. cm.
 ISBN 978-0-87842-580-8 (pbk. : alk. paper)
 1. Physicians—Fiction. 2. Totalitarianism—Fiction. 3. Montana—
Fiction. I. Title.
 PS3616.E84296H35 2011
 813'.6—dc22

                                    2011018545

PRINTED IN THE UNITED STATES

For my cinnamon girl,
a unknown legend in her time,
and a better friend
than I could ever imagine

There is solace in the solitude of written words
filled with reflections that outlive a lifetime or civilization.
Written words are a sincere invitation
into the shadow of the author's soul
and are the true fishers of men.

❦ AUTHOR'S NOTE ❦

IN 1952 *HIGH NOON* HIT THE BIG SCREEN and garnered Montanan, Gary Cooper, his second Academy Award for best actor. Shot in black and white, the movie with its stark, arid, realism showed how a good American, though fearful and alone, was driven by his conscience to stand up for what was right. At the time, our country was dealing with its own fearful challenge combating the evils of communism and McCarthyism.

Even though the term, high noon, can be traced back to the fifteenth century, the movie forever ingrained in our nation's conscience that high noon stands for a time of decisive confrontation. Unlike the fifties, today we perhaps face our biggest opponent, confusion on what America stands for, from within our own borders and minds. In the last sixty years much has changed in our country. It appears that a veil has fallen over this nation where nothing is clear, and we no longer hold other countries like communist China morally accountable as long as they keep buying our treasury bonds, and we can save a fistful of dollars on a flat screen TV. We're definitely living east of Eden.

High Noon is a great morality play and allegorical masterpiece that just happens to be set in the days of the Wild West, a time dismissed as insignificant by today's elitists. But much can be learned from men of simple convictions and true grit. Several years ago, I dissected every scene from the movie and eventually incorporated the symbolism of many of them into this story. Halfway to midnight is high noon.

There are fond memories of the northern plains region composed of eastern Montana, eastern Wyoming, North Dakota, and South Dakota. It's an area more foreign to the coasters than Oxford, Tuscany, or Normandy. Perhaps that's one reason why this country is in such trouble. But the heartland is what made America great and its enduring values will make America great again. There are no finer and wiser patriots than you'll find in small towns like Plentywood, Montana. That's why the setting for this story had to take place in northeastern Montana in Cottonwood, a fictitious town of the future imagined West.

The great American philosopher, Jimmy Buffet, once said, "If the phone doesn't ring it's me." I would like to lift that line to tell all my friends that if they haven't heard from me in awhile it's not because I haven't been thinking of them. Their love permeates and defines each one of my good characters. However, the unforgiven are totally fictitious. They are an amalgam of the dark side of human behavior that I have unfortunately encountered over the last six decades. I have to admit that some of their traits are hidden inside me. We are all sinners.

This is definitely a book with a message. Along the way socialism; health care; religion; China; Indian reservation life; evolution; dinosaurs; tuberculosis; politics; western art, history, and Rembrandt; rock and roll; and much more are hashed over.

Hearty thanks to my living family, LeAnne, Haley, Lara, Linda, and Cathy and those no longer here for all your love. Minnesotan Charlie Johnston, taught me about Hell Creek and paleontology.

Much appreciation goes out to Mountain Press Publishing who gave me my own imprint, Tumbleweed Reflections. Publishers John Rimel and Rob Williams; editor Caroline Patterson; designers James Lainsbury and Jeannie Painter; and publicist Anne Iverson were invaluable.

Hopefully soon, America will circle the wagons and have a change in attitude since we can't change our latitude. Maybe, in a small way the message in these pages will add to the conversation. But we can't take ourselves too seriously, and you'll see that there's lots of zaniness as you turn the pages. Jimmy also said, "If we weren't all crazy we would go insane." He's one sharp cookie.

I can turn off the lava lamp now and pet our two vizslas.

≈ PART ONE ≈

INDOCTRINATION

Cottonwood, Montana
Friday
September 21, 2020

✐ ONE ✐

IOPENED MY EYES and stepped into darkness. I searched for the light. Why was it always so hard to find? My hospital sleeping quarters were a brisk thirty-second dash from a dying patient. The nurse's call didn't tell me who he was, who loved him, or what dreams he had. I rushed down the stairway and bolted through the dimly lit hallway. My heart pounded and my breathing turned shallow and rapid. Pick up the pace, Don. Pick up the pace. Finally, I reached the emergency room, the arena of quick decisions and fleeting memories.

A jolting, antiseptic smell and blinding lights greeted me. It had been years since I'd seen Lightfoot, an elderly Sioux living off the reservation in Cottonwood, Montana. He lay motionless on the exam table with a heavy cloth wrapped around his right forearm, the stench of stale booze rising like smoke.

"What's going on Nurse Weiz?" I asked wishing I could grab a paper chart instead of an electronic record. "Why doesn't this thing turn on?"

"Dr. Lewis, we've been having problems with our electronic records," she said.

In a brief summary she told me that two months ago Dr. Dennis Anderson biopsied a lump on Lightfoot's chest, and the pathology showed breast cancer. Dennis was going to send him to Billings for surgery, but a tuberculosis skin test came up positive so he exiled him instead to Galen Tuberculosis Hospital run by the state in western Montana for treatment. It was the Trinity Health Plan's policy to keep resistant cases of T.B. out of their hospitals.

"Why in the hell he's back here is a puzzle to me," she said. "He mumbled something about a badger chewing his hand off and evil spirits. He shouted every swear word in the book."

"Mr. Lightfoot," I said. "I'm Dr. Lewis. Can I take a look at your hand?"

Since there was no response, I removed the wrap. Lightfoot leaped up and punched me, and I fell back into the cabinets. Bright red blood gushed from a cut on my thumb.

"Holly shit," I said. I pressed down on the wound.

"Get the hell out of here," Lightfoot said as he suddenly collapsed.

I wrapped a towel around my hand and turned him over. There was no carotid pulse. His pupils were fixed and dilated. He was dead.

Nurse Weiz cleaned my wound "It's more important now to get you fixed up," she said. "We can't afford to lose another doctor in this one-horse town. Looks like there's no tendon damage, but I think you're going to need some stitches."

"Just Steri-strip it," I said.

"Don't trust me?" she asked. "I remember when you were five years old and got stuck here in a hospital bed for two days with a broken bone sticking out your right arm."

"Yeah, I still have nightmares over that one," I said. "My dad felt awful. He had me up on his shoulders when I slipped off and fell like a rock. I discovered that the ground is harder than my bones."

"Don, you sure were a good kid," she said. "No crying or complaining came out of you."

Old Doc Peters was out of town at a bowling tournament in Kalispell when I landed in the hospital. That poor soul almost never got out of town to do anything.

"You let me take care of you then," she said. "Even though I was just sixteen and didn't know what I was doing. That nurse's aid job was my first."

That was a long time ago, but I still remembered how good she made me feel.

"You haven't lost your touch," I said. "We've only worked together for a few days, but I can tell. When are you going to retire? It seems like you've been working here for a century."

"I've got till the end of the year before I call it quits," she said. "It's hard to believe that Sheldon has been dead for twenty years. Work was the best medicine for me. Are you sure it was a good idea coming back home to deal with Doc Dennis the menace?"

"So far, so good until tonight," I said as I shrugged.

Doc Dennis and I never got along. Since the Trinity Health Plan took over Cottonwood five years ago and made him director, I had heard he was a little Hitler. That didn't surprise me. Even though poor Doctor Peters hired him, he treated his father-in-law like shit. After Peters drowned last spring, Dennis got worse. Some say his arrogance was from stress, but I knew he'd been cocky all his life. Why Abigail married him was beyond me. Doc Peters told me once that he wished his daughter and I had tied the knot.

"Seems like Dennis always one-upped me, but things work out for the best," I said. "Abigail got two wonderful children out of the deal, and I got Anne. Hey, I want to take a look at Lightfoot's chest."

Nurse Weiz unbuttoned Lightfoot's blood-soaked shirt. She gasped and stepped back. Maggots feasted on a deep wound on his chest and pus drained into a beefy, red cavity the size of a lemon. It smelled like vomit and cat piss.

"Oh my God!" She said as she put her hand over her nose.

"Look at his stomach," I said, stepping back as well.

"It looks like he carved a triangle," Nurse Weiz said. "He must have been really tanked up. It looks like a tipi. Maybe that's supposed to represent his final resting place in hell."

"Why do you say that?" I asked.

"He never went to church and got saved," she said.

"He was a good man," I said.

"Well, your wife is a good pastor, but she sure isn't getting through to you," she said. "I guess preaching is like parenting, you're one one hundred percent responsible for the process, but zero percent responsible for the outcome."

"I believe in second chances and forgiveness," I said.

"Sometimes you don't get a second chance," she said. "This is one of them."

There were no animal bites on his arm or hand, but there was a deep abrasion on his wrist. It looked like some sort of bracelet was the culprit.

"Hey, it's 2020, and you're no Sherlock Holmes," Nurse Wiez said. "Look what the chief was grasping in his right hand."

I extracted a small folded piece of paper from his clinched fist. As I unfolded it, the lights went out in the exam room. Someone gripped my wrist like a vice and pried the note out of my hand. Weiz and I were shoved into the corner of the room, and the culprits escaped down the hallway.

I chased them, but my bad knee slowed me down. They ran through the hospital kitchen, knocking the pots and kettles on the floor. I high stepped it through the clanging metal like the time I attempted tire drills in high school football practice. By the time I opened the side kitchen door, they were driving away in what looked like a border patrol car. It was hard to tell from the dim street lights. I blinked my eyes and looked again to make sure I wasn't dreaming, but by then the car had vanished.

When I returned to the exam room, I asked Nurse Weiz how she was doing.

"I've been through worse," she said. "What happened to chief's friends?"

"They drove off," I said. "It looked like they were in a border patrol car!"

"Wouldn't surprise me," she said. "They think they run this whole area. The sheriff is just a lackey. We had a couple of journalists from back East snooping around here a year ago trying to write an article on the Trinity Project. I talked with them a little until I was told by Doc Dennis to shut up. Last time I saw them they were heading north in a border patrol car. You know those border guards are all on loan from China.

"That's more than bizarre," I said.

"Well, someone needs to control the illegals," she said. "They're doing a fine job of it."

"We need to get back to work," I said.

When I got the electronic record up and going, I noticed there were no entries before Lightfoot's trip to Galen Tuberculosis Hospital. Scrolling back, I didn't find any documentation that he had a breast biopsy or pathology results. There was just an entry noting a positive tuberculosis skin test.

Bacterial resistant tuberculosis was sweeping the country and made the swine and avian flu epidemics look no more serious than a common cold. Panicked health care communities around the country responded by reopening old tuberculosis hospitals to treat and isolate the infected. Cottonwood was especially hit hard even though the prairies of northeastern Montana seemed an unlikely place. The locals liked to blame it on the illegal farm workers from Mexico.

"Quite a night, right Nurse Weiz?" I said. First, I was called in for a car wreck at two in the morning and decided to spend the night at the hospital since it was a long drive home. Then there was poor Mr. Lightfoot. Thankfully, my wife, Anne, was very understanding.

"Let's have a cup of coffee." I said.

We walked quietly into the break room.

"You've been doing the night shift all your life," I said as I took a sip.

"I know what you're going to say," she said. "'How could you do it?' Well, Sheldon was an understanding man. Of course, he was lucky to work for your father at the hardware store. Your dad and grandfather were wonderful men, just the best. Your dad used to tell Sheldon to leave early so we could have some time together before I went to work. I will always be grateful to him for his kindness."

"I was lucky to have them in my life, but I never felt I measured up to them," I said. "I think they didn't like my decision to leave home."

I grew up in an era of heroes, and I didn't need to look outside the family for mine, but it isn't easy living up to expectations. Maybe, that's why I didn't stay and become the third generation to run the hardware store. At the time, I thought I was too smart to stay home.

"I think they were disappointed, but hey, it was the Vietnam era and the dawning of the Age of Aquarius," she said. "It's not like you headed off to the West Coast and drugged out for the rest of your life. You seem really nervous. "

"Darkness always makes me tense," I said as I popped a handful of Tums in my mouth. "I always hated night call."

I looked at my watch, and it was a little after five in the morning and still pitch black outside, but that was to be expected in late September in northeastern Montana.

Doc Peters wanted me back to help take over his practice that he shared with his son-in-law, Doc Dennis. At eighty-one, he was ready to spend more time fishing, but he died five months before I arrived in town. There was no time to review his patients with him and more importantly, no time to renew our friendship. It had been more than forty years ago since I left town and more importantly since I had dated his daughter, Abigail.

At least he drowned doing what he loved best. A great fly fisherman, he would have wanted it that way. It was bad timing, though.

"Stop day dreaming and get back to being a doctor," Nurse Weiz said. "You need to fill out a report. I still remember your high school days when all you wanted to do was read history books. A lot of good that did you."

"It's still hard for you to think of me as a doctor, isn't it?" I said.

"Late bloomer, I would call you," she said. "Most doctors have a calling to the profession at a young age. You were called to be a college history professor. Well, you came to your senses later than sooner. By the way, Lightfoot had a handgun strapped to his ankle. I think he intended to use it on the good doctor."

"Enough, mother," I said, rubbing my sore jaw. "I think a punch was adequate. Let's call Dave at Halvorson's funeral home in the morning to pick up Mr. Lightfoot. I'm sure Lightfoot's wife will surface at some point. When she does, I want to talk to her."

My mind drifted back to Lightfoot. I knew the old man from childhood but not his current wife who was living in Poplar on the Indian reservation. Nurse Weiz told me that Mrs. Lightfoot grew up in Sidney and wasn't part of the Sioux Nation

"I imagine it'll be after your big wedding today," she said. "Why did you wait to get married to Anne until you got back here? Why didn't you tie the knot in Oregon? She's only been here four weeks. It's not like a lot of her close friends can attend. Waiting for the honeymoon until January isn't the best way to get the marriage off to a good start either. Oh, well, I hear you've been shacking up for quite a while. I guess that kind of takes the excitement out of it."

"I don't know what aches most, my jaw, thumb, or my ears," I said. "Our time together has been eventful, but I need to check in on my friend, Steve. I'll see you later. Thanks again for fixing up my hand."

Everyone wants transparency in a relationship, but Nurse Weiz made you rethink that. However, at six feet, two inches and so heavy she waddled standing still, Nurse Weiz garnered my attention and respect.

∽ TWO ∽

STEVE THOMPSON was found in a heap at the bottom of Hell Creek fifty miles south of town. He had a broken pelvis, six broken ribs, two broken wrists, broken jaw and broken neck. Fortunately, there was no paralysis, but the neck injury prevented transporting him to Billings according to Doc Dennis.

From the looks of it, Doc Dennis must have played hooky the day they taught casting during his orthopedic rotation. The next day he realized Steve was anchored to the hospital bed by gauze and plaster.

Professor Steve Thompson, a renowned paleontology professor from Montana State University, was investigating a dinosaur fossil site halfway up a canyon wall when an avalanche slung his platform and him to the bottom of the ravine. He told me years ago that his days of climbing up cliffs were over—that's one of the reasons he took students on the digs—there must have been something very important up there.

We were close friends when we both taught in Bozeman. His fame sky-rocketed when he was hired as a consultant for several dinosaur movies. The royalties provided him with the financial support to spend every summer hunting for dinosaurs in eastern Montana. Steve, like me, had a wife that left him. She was a demure woman from San Diego.

They had what he called "a slow bleed of a marriage." The first skier with money from California who paid her any attention turned out to be her ticket back to the beach. That was thirty years ago. He never remarried, and his mistress was the badlands of eastern Montana created sixty million years ago.

The professor was still in a full body cast a month after the accident; his jaw was wired shut until two days ago. The body cast bothered me, and I wanted to bring it up with Dennis. It was also too long to have Steve sedated to the point of being completely unresponsive. When I tried to access his electronic medical records, I found only last week's vital signs and medication records. Something was hay wire. For some reason, the records were electronically stored 350 miles south in Billings.

"Indiana Steve, how's my wounded warrior?" I asked.

He responded with a pained blink. That was the only part of his body that could respond. The cast needed to go. "Hang in there," I said as I squeezed his arm. "You'll be out of this cast real soon."

With that I grabbed my jacket and headed to my car. My Waltham pocket watch that my father gave me when I was twelve showed it to be closing in on six in the morning. As I drove away, I looked back at the hospital illuminated by the lights in the parking lot. I knew we were out in the boonies, but the Trinity Project in Cottonwood was supposed to catapult us into twenty-first century medicine. The red brick structure was just five years old and served the entire county population of a few thousand. It was northeastern Montana's finest health facility. There were fifteen beds, an intensive care unit, an attached clinic, emergency room, and living quarters for the on call physician. It was the pride of the community and one of several new buildings built in Cottonwood since the Trinity Project came to town.

As I drove down the hill towards town, it was shocking to me how small it looked. Years in Bozeman, Eugene, and Portland certainly changed my perspective. It seemed just like yesterday when our Cottonwood Wildcats basketball team traveled to Glendive, Glasgow, and Wolf Point to challenge the big city boys. How could we compete with them? The head count of all three towns combined was probably no more than fifteen thousand, tops.

The unending hot, prairie summer days were just a memory now. September was the best time of year on the northern plains with crisp, cold mornings giving way to sixty plus degree days. The hills and prairies browned up after baking in hundred degree temperatures in summer with no rain. The constant wind did its part, too. The leaves on the trees in town had already turned gold and red and were sparse. Overhead, I spotted Canadian geese heading south for the winter and heard the yips of coyotes in the distance.

This land was a desert. Even so, the dry wheat farmers relied on a few inches of rain in the summer that produced at best a few dozen bushels per acre. The price of wheat hadn't changed much in fifty years. The only thing that increased was the cost of farming. That forced the small ranchers and farmers to sell their land to large corporate interests. The county's population dropped like a rock from a peak of sixteen thousand in 1932. There are fewer people on the northern plains now than there were when the Buffalo Bill Wild West show was the rage. It wasn't until the Trinity Project came into town that the downward trend reversed itself.

Cottonwood represented the mythical hometown that affords the opportunity to find your soul. If the Trinity Project proved successful, Cottonwood and the rest of the northern plains would be the template for the entire country to find its soul that was lost somewhere between the Vietnam War and the 2008 economic collapse.

∽ THREE ∽

B Y SIX O'CLOCK EVERY DAY, I was headed to the Elgin Café, the gathering spot for the bull-shitters and yarn-spinners in the morning. Many of the world's problems were solved over coffee, bacon, and hot cakes. The old wood storefront and hitching post out front made it clear that this restaurant had been around for awhile.

A few chapters in western history were written in Cottonwood. Following Custer's defeat in 1876 at the Battle of the Little Big Horn, Sitting Bull and his band retreated to Canada. Starvation conditions brought them back across the border in 1881 to the spot they now call Cottonwood. They surrendered to Captain Clifford at Fort Buford not too far from town.

Things really took off after the Great Northern Railway was deeded land in 1909. Dust bowls, locusts, and low wheat prices were also part of its less colorful history.

These days we could visit the Elgin Café where the coffee was just as bad as it had always been. The four most important things to know about small town life on the prairies is that almost everyone had a nickname, weather dominated small talk, gossip never let up, and most burgs had several bars.

The Elgin was lined on one side with booths where you could still play a tune for a dime at your table. Opposite that side was a dark maple bar and a back bar sporting a mirror twenty feet long above it. Stuffed heads of antelope, deer, grizzly bear, and buffalo peered down from their perch. In the back were card tables, two pool tables, and a dart board. Big dough changed hands back there.

In the middle of the Elgin, at the round tables, Shorty held court. At ninety-one, he still was the best story teller in eastern Montana and my dad's best buddy before he died. He motioned me over to join his audience of twelve old men. They were in their seventies, eighties, and nineties, and all were friends of my father. Even though their faces were wrinkled from age and sun damaged, they were like windows to the past. It was a past where little changed and that made a child feel safe and loved. The past was also a time and place where no one had much materially, although they were rich in family, friends, love of God, and patriotism. It was sad to think I was going to see these men dwindle away after leading such hardy, fruitful lives. They were all that was left of the tough, rough stock. Those that couldn't take this harsh climate had long ago drifted away.

But for now, it was time to enjoy the moment. Shorty delivered the same string of yarns and jokes that I laughed at years ago. There were the North Dakota jokes, the Norwegian jokes, and the city slicker jokes.

"It's darn good to see you again, Donny," Shorty said. "How do you like our Indian summer? It's supposed to be seventy-two degrees today."

"It's great to be back," I said with a big smile and hand shake. He and I were very close. I was the younger tag-along with his three sons, a fourth son in many ways. More time was spent down at their place than at my home since the hardware store kept my dad busy fourteen hours a day. Their home was filled with the kind of fun boys love: basketball, softball, volleyball, and trips to the lakes for swimming and waterskiing. Shorty, a plumber by trade, never let work get in the way of joining his boys for fun. Thankfully, Florence, his deceased wife, had a steady job as a teacher before retiring years ago. When we were kids, he was an athletic, handsome man with a jaw chiseled in such precise angles you would think an engineer had some say in his profile. In the winter, which usually drug on from October until May, we built model cars and planes, played pool, and watched cartoons and cowboy shows on television. *The Lone Ranger*, *Paladin*, and *Roy Rogers* were my favorites.

It was good to have Shorty on your side. He was a legend in these parts. Shorty said he lived to play and was still playing. He was the mayor throughout my childhood. Known to enjoy his whiskey, he installed a liquor room next to the mayor's office. When some of the local women stormed the office, he made a truce and agreed to have the liquor room removed but only after he was out of office. Much to their dismay, that didn't happen for quite a few years. He now delivered free fire wood and food to those same women, most of whom were widows.

The locals were definitely suspect of outsiders who were defined as anyone who left town for more than a vacation. I was in that group. It didn't help that I never came back for school reunions or the mandatory, fall pheasant hunting trips, which I'm sure disappointed Shorty and his sons. However, his warm welcome made me feel like I was part of the community again.

Joe Pesci, the owner of the Elgin Cafe, delivered my hotcakes and bacon on a plate covered with a shiny metal dome just like he did fifty years ago when my dad and I ate breakfast at the café. The steam and aroma filled my senses. It was good to be back home. Some things never changed.

"You damn doctors tell us to watch our diet and then you're munching down on pig's meat," Shorty said as he looked at my plate.

"I only eat this once a week," I said. "Everything in moderation, you know."

"Bullshit," Shorty said. "I'll moderate my visits to the doctor so I have more time for whiskey at Happy Hour."

"Whatever you're doing, keep doing it." I said.

"Big day today for you," Shorty said. "It's been fun getting to know Anne over the last month, although I still haven't set foot in a church. She's a good woman. A looker too."

"I appreciate all you have done to make her feel so welcome," I said.

While wrapping up my primary care practice in Portland, Anne moved out to our family ranch to start making it a home for us. Many in town pitched in to help her clean it up. A fresh coat of paint inside along with our furniture made it feel like home. She then started working at the Trinity Cornerstone Church as an assistant pastor. Pastor Luke treated her with respect and gave her a title that was off limits to many women with leadership roles in churches. Never had I seen her so happy and content. Her divorce, even after counseling, left her depressed at times, but her new life in Cottonwood removed that cloud just as quickly as light from a candle disappears after being blown out.

"Too bad your dad isn't alive to see you get married," Neil Odegard, the pharmacist, said.

Neil was one of my dad's closest and most trusted friends. Every fall dad and his buddies headed north to Canada to go goose hunting.

"I imagine your mom can't come down from the nursing home," said my cousin Rich who owned the Chevrolet dealership. "I don't think she's been out of that place in four years. Her health problems have really thrown her for a loop."

"Is old Pastor Tim or Pastor Luke marrying you?" Stu "Boy" Bacon, the editor of the *Cottonwood Herald* asked. "No one in town seems to know anything about the big day. Don't forget next week.

Stop by the office, and I'll interview you for an article in the paper. We're devoting the whole issue to the completion of the Trinity Project here. Anytime someone returns here is big news, especially when it is a doctor."

"Pastor Luke's been out of town," I said. "And I asked Pastor Tim, but he hasn't been feeling well. Our neighbor, Ray Koler, will do the honors."

"Good choice," Shorty said. "Ray was one of your dad's best friends and a darn good lawyer."

"Choteau Coans, Munchie and Two Moon will be the witnesses," I said. "We wanted to keep the marriage low key since it's the second one for both of us. We'll have you all out for a big reception once we're more settled."

"That's a nice touch including Two Moon," Shorty said. "He's been taking good care of your ranch forever."

"I wouldn't have it any other way," I said.

"I'm glad you're tying the knot," Shorty said. "This shacking up has to go."

"It's strange, this town used to have a lot of churches, but now it's down to one," I said as I changed the subject. "I never thought I'd see the Lutherans and Catholics put their swords down and stop fighting each other and follow someone from out of state, even if Pastor Luke's famous."

I thought that would get a rise, but there was silence. The men looked around the table as if they'd seen a ghost. I'd been back in town for just a week, but I sensed things were a little sideways in Cottonwood. Eventually, Shorty chuckled.

"Did you hear what we pulled on that little shit Munchie 'Jigsaw' Ladow?" He asked obviously trying to change the subject.

"Poor Munchie," I said.

Munchie Ladow was the meter reader and grave digger in town. Shorty liked to call him Jigsaw because whenever there was a problem, he fell apart. Frail and nervous, Munchie had a fear of the dark and ghosts. Shorty recounted how one time he got in a coffin in the basement at the mortuary. Unfortunately for Munchie, he had to read the electrical meter in the casket room. After he entered the room, one of Shorty's cohorts turned out the lights right before Shorty jumped out of the coffin. It took five whiskeys that night to calm Munchie down.

"Well, I've got to get going," I said. "I need to review patients with Doc Dennis before I take the next week off."

"Warm your hands up," Shorty shouted as I left the Elgin. "Who would have thought that damn little Lewis kid would some-day be seeing me with my pants down, and he gets paid to do it!"

A small town doctor's life was a mixed bag. Wives were generally miserable, either became alcoholics or got divorced and left town. The only two to stay in Cottonwood over the years were Doc Dennis the menace and Doctor Peters. Often, the doctor's high income led to overindulged children who were resented by the other kids, but I never felt that way. It was their money, and they could do what they wanted with it.

A referral to a specialist meant a 350-mile-drive to Billings that angered the patient. If a patient died without a referral, then there were rumors around town that questioned the doctor's judgment for not obtaining a second opinion. It was hard to win. On the up side, someone had to do it. It was difficult getting enough family practitioners in the cities let alone out here on the prairies. But I knew that the call of medicine was no greater than in a place like my home town.

I was looking forward with some anxiety to meeting with my new partner, Doc Dennis, who was anchoring health care in Cottonwood with Doctor Peters before he drowned. Dennis's trip to

Minneapolis to meet with Project officials was unexpected. That's why I had to fill in for him the last week.

I stepped off the curb in front of the Elgin Café when the roar from a red blur streaking towards me made me jump back. Between me and the courthouse on the north end of Main Street, a 1970 Roadrunner was closing in at high speed. It came to rest in a cloud of dust just a few feet in front of me. Out leaped Choteau Coans, my dear buddy, lover of the Old West and general town rabble rouser. The music was blaring.

"Howdy, Kid," Choteau said. "Great to see ya. It does my heart good to know you're back in town. Now, we can get together just like old times. We are the two amigos. What do you think of my eight-track player? Remember *Bad Moon Rising*? Credence Clearwater?"

"Of course," I said. I gave my friend a hug.

We all said when Choteau died there would never be another like him. In high school he was a teenage broncin' buck with a penchant for mischief in his pickup truck. His muscled upper body was still as trim as a boy's. He loved to be introduced as Ted Turner to strangers since he bore an uncanny resemblance to the Montana land baron. He had no formal education, but what a grasp he had on Montana history. With the enthusiasm of a child and the knowledge of a history professor, Choteau was my "Mr. Montana."

When I was a young assistant history professor, Choteau was my trusted consultant on a number of obscure facts relating to early Montana history. No library, not even the legendary Montana Historical Society, could provide a researcher with more information about the history of eastern Montana. He made a living by doing handyman work and installing sprinkler systems. He was a magician fixing machines. His wife, Fran, was the school librarian and a very understanding soul.

"Just like old times," I said. "I saw you coming from the court-house. Did you have another run-in with the law?"

"I can't believe it, damn it," he said. "Pardon my French. I got a traffic ticket for drivin' on two wheels. Those sons-a-bitches!"

"Were you speeding on your motorcycle?" I asked.

"No!" he said and pursed his lips. "I whipped around the corner in front of the Dairy Queen on two wheels in my Roadrunner, and 'Dick Tracy' Jensen, emphasis on 'Dick,' pulled me over and fined me $125. That's hard to believe. I was just tellin' the judge I'm innocent."

"The only thing that has changed with you since you were fourteen is the size of your traffic tickets," I said.

"I asked for my friendship discount," Choteau said. "But the judge told me I ain't no friend of his."

"Well, you can't charm everyone," I said.

"Can't wait for the wedding," Choteau said. "What time are you gettin' hitched?"

"Ray is marrying us out at the ranch at one this afternoon," I said.

"You're a Cadillac, Doc. See ya then," Choteau said as he gave me a hug before he sped away.

∽ FOUR ∾

HE THREE LOCAL KINGPINS of the Trinity Project were waiting at the station for Dr. Chen, who controlled the Project's financial purse strings. They were huddled together, waiting for the train that arrived at 7:30 A.M., westbound from Minneapolis. The three looked much older than they did in the informational brochures they sent me: Doc Dennis Anderson, my new medical partner; Bruce Deeds, the Washington D.C. lawyer in charge of running the program; and Pastor Luke Hanson, the famous evangelist, author, and television personality who founded the Trinity Cornerstone Church. It was a coup for the Project to snag him. His nationally syndicated show from Cottonwood put our little burg on the map.

Dr. Chen was taking the train because it was more convenient than flying since the closest airport was more than 200 miles away. I looked at my watch. It was 7:40 A.M. It looked like the train might be on time. If the train was less than fifteen minutes late, the local jokes went, it was on time.

Doc Dennis, who arrived late yesterday was supposed to meet with me at eight in the morning at the clinic before patients started arriving at nine. Things hadn't gone as planned from the get-go. After arriving in town, I thought I would have two weeks off before starting to see patients. That was supposed to give Anne and me time to get married and settled in out on the old family ranch. Instead, Dennis took off with Deeds and Pastor Luke to the Twin Cities. Now, I heard the big wig in charge of the whole operation was coming to town to review the project before it ended next week.

Checking out the patients with Doc Dennis Anderson was going to be painful. He was the golden boy of our class. His father was a big wheat rancher and oil man who drove his son to excel. If there was any feeling sorry for Dennis, it had to be the way his wacko father rode his butt.

Fortunately for Dennis, he produced. Golden boy was the starting point guard on the basketball team, and I was his backup. He was valedictorian, and I was third behind Abigail Peters. Abigail, Doc Peters' only daughter, was the prize, and while I was in the running, Dennis Anderson snatched her up. He ended up with Doc Peters' two prized possessions: his daughter and his medical practice.

At little before eight, I drove over to the clinic. My heart pounded. I told our receptionist that I would be in Doc Anderson's office waiting for him. I spent the time reviewing a few charts and absorbing some medical journal articles. At ten minutes after nine, Dr. Anderson arrived.

He entered the room with the presence of a celebrity and did not apologize for being late. Tall, athletic, and still handsome, he reached out to shake my hand. His once blonde, curly hair had turned gray, but he looked good for sixty-one.

"Sorry I put you in a bind last week," he said. "The Trinity Project trial period ends in seven days, and we had to go to Minneapolis for a last-minute briefing. The whole success of the program depends on us delivering the kind of financial statistics that will knock the socks off Dr. Chen, and of course, I'll deliver. I just greeted Dr. Chen at the train station. Now there's an impressive person. Sounds like you did okay in my absence."

Either Doc Dennis had undergone a personality change, or he was trying to be nice to me for some unknown reason.

"Things went well," I said. I glanced around his office and smiled.

The walls were filled with certificates of achievement dating from the seventies to the present. Sports trophies filled the top of his cluttered desk. A certificate honoring him as the past President of the American Society of Primary Care Physicians hung directly behind him. I wondered how well the ASPCP knew this guy.

"That's quite an honor being past President of the ASPCP," I said, trying to be magnanimous.

"Thanks," he said with obvious pleasure. "Some say that you're as happy as your unhappiest child, but for me, I'm as happy as my latest achievement."

"I understand," I said.

Even though I was upset that Steve Thompson was wrapped with two hundred pounds of plaster and sedated to the point of unconsciousness, I sensed this was not the time to wage that battle. Instead, I told him about Lightfoot. What was up with the electronic charting system? Why weren't the electronic records stored on site?

"Sorry about Lightfoot, but I knew you, Don 'Junior' Lewis, could handle anything," he said. "He was a drunk and took off from the ward at Galen. The appropriate authorities were looking for him. You know we don't want that resistant tuberculosis spread any more than it has already. It was a surprise he ended up back here. As far as record storage, the Project decided to keep the records in their computer center in Billings. Privacy, you know. It's been tough with one of the cell towers down. We can't retrieve information, but they've decided to move the storage back here at the end of the program. Did Lightfoot say anything to you?"

"He told me to get out of here," I said. "I thought that was an odd comment. I wonder if he was expecting you and not me. There was also a triangle cut on his stomach."

"He was full of odd comments and actions, especially when he was drinking," Doc Dennis said. "Maybe, he was shocked at how paunchy you've gotten. He didn't know that all the Lewis clan porked out with age. You still have your hair. That's a shock. The triangle thing, don't get too wound up about that. He was probably just trying to kill time. Was his wife there?"

"Nowhere to be found," I said.

"She's drunk most of the time and suffers from significant dementia," Doc Dennis said. "She stayed down in Poplar on the reservation after they separated. He moved up here looking for a job with the Project. I found some janitor work at the high school for him, but he was always flaking off. If you did talk to her, she wouldn't make any sense. Well, enough of that. I heard you are getting married today."

"Yes, I said. "It's at one this afternoon. It's a small one."

"Don't talk about your dick that way," he said as he broke out laughing. "I used to think that when I saw you in the gym shower, but I never said anything. I have discretion."

"Very funny," I said. What an ass!

"Well, you're finally doing man's work being a doctor and making things legal too," he said. "What was the history professor gig all about? Stephen Ambrose already wrote everything we need to know about western adventure. I like risk, and there's no risk in reading about the past. It's a waste of time. But you did show some undaunted courage raising yourself out of the muck of being a history teacher at that second rate college in Bozeman. I heard you have a boy, and Anne doesn't have any. Is there something wrong with her? Is this your third or fourth marriage?"

"This is the second for both of us, and I have two daughters, Lara and Haley," I said. "Anne and I have been together since I graduated from medical school thirteen years ago. My first wife didn't like me going to medical school or the idea of moving to Oregon."

I didn't feel like I needed to go into the details of my first marriage. It was none of his business, and he didn't care anyway. He was acting more like the old Dennis. College at the University of Washington and Stanford Medical School only fueled his ego. "Have you seen Abigail?" He asked.

"No," I said. "It's just my first week back. It's been hectic."

The less said on that subject, the better. After all, I was going to have to deal with this guy for who knows how long.

"Both of our children are at Stanford," he said. "Layla is in law school and Mick is finishing his family practice residency."

"I heard Stanford has a legacy policy where children of past graduates are given a preference in the admission's process. I'm sure Stanford also liked them growing up in eastern Montana. It's all about diversification these days in the admission's process."

"They didn't need to be a legacy," he said with a snap. "When they finish school they plan to stay in the Bay area. I encouraged that. They've accomplished too much to return to this dump. By the way, why did you quit dwelling in the past? Couldn't you cover the alimony and child support on a professor's salary?"

"I just felt like I wanted to help the living instead of spending my life writing about the dead. Abigail's dad was always my role model," I said.

"Noble aspirations, Junior," Doc Dennis said. "I hope you have a few productive years left in you because I'm escaping in the near future. You can run the whole practice yourself. Maybe, I'll even throw in Abigail. She's saggy. And I like tight ass. "

"I appreciate your kindness," I said.

"But we do need another family practitioner here since we found a floater, Abigail's old man, in the Missouri," he said. "Frankly, I wasn't thrilled about having you come back when Deeds told me that you applied for the job, but I didn't want some unknown macho prick coming in here and trying to run my show."

"That's insightful, Dennis," I said. "Really insightful. A fine way to talk about your partner and father-in-law." I knew Doc Peters and Dennis never hit it off, but this was a new low.

"Any hospital or outpatient clinic problems?" He asked, ignoring my comment. "We cancelled as many patients as possible so we wouldn't stress you out too much."

"There were the typical problems: ear infections, high blood sugars, too much alcohol, and too many donuts, but there was one child who was wetting the bed because of seeing ghosts," I said.

"Then, it looks like I can handle things this week," he said. "What about the bed wetter?"

"That's Iver's kid," I said. "He told me that Charlie saw ghosts in the old Riba house. That's pretty original for a six year old."

"Sounds like coach Iver needs to get his kid out on the basketball court a little more and stop spending his spare time at Habitat for Humanity," Dennis said. "That Iver always was a loser. I remember one time at practice when I lapped him in the mile run. Remember, that? "

"He was only in eighth grade. Look, I need to go," I said. "I guess I'll officially start working a week from Monday."

"Yeah, just like old times, Junior," he said. "I'll lead the charge. You follow. Hey, something's come up. Listen, Dr. Chen wants to have a meeting with you at four o'clock this afternoon. It's mandatory, but it won't be long. Bruce Deeds also wants to chat with you before she does."

"Dennis, my wedding's this afternoon," I said. "Can't that wait?"

BRIDGER PUBLIC LIBRARY
BRIDGER, MONTANA

"No, it can't wait," he said abruptly. "Chen is only here today and leaves tomorrow. Important person, you know. Make it work, Junior. You're a company man, now."

"I'll be there," I said.

"Good boy," Dennis said as he shook my hand. "You're predictable. I like that in an employee, and don't forget that you have to work that shit hole clinic on the reservation next week."

I looked down at my watch. It was 9:30 in the morning, but already I'd been punched by an Indian, watched him die, and bantered with the last person in the world I wanted to see, Doc Dennis.

∽ FIVE ∽

LOOKING OUT on the morning light over the wheat fields, I thought of Anne. As long as there was peace inside our home, I could deal with the outside world. The drive to the ranch was through classic American West country: high plains at 2,200 feet where naked hills rose above gulches dotted with Russian thistle. I passed abandoned ranches, collapsed homesteads huddled against the wind in a sea of wheat stubble. In the Great Plains there are less than six people per square mile. Nearly 900,000 square miles have so few people that it would meet the nineteenth century Census Bureau definition of frontier, and I liked it that way.

My ex-wife never liked my idea of becoming a doctor. She wanted the center of attention to be on her, not my aspirations. She wasn't happy in Bozeman even though she enjoyed skiing and working at Bridger Bowl. We drifted apart as so many couples do when they're chasing separate dreams. Friends and lovers don't jump ship until they have another ship to land on. She jumped ship. Before I had time to pack and move out, she took the kids and moved in with her boss. I didn't have a clue.

That time seems so far away now. I grieved. I particularly missed the kids, Lara and Haley, who were so busy with their activities they hardly seemed to miss me. I spent some time together with them when I coached their youth girls' basketball teams, but after that we drifted. I worked hard to stay close to them, but I used the rigors of work to justify my absences. I regretted not bringing my children up in a church, but that only surfaced after I met Anne. Their mother didn't want anything to do with religion. When I quit my comfortable job as an MSU history professor, they were puzzled and felt betrayed that I would want to pursue a career that took nearly ten years of training and wads of money.

When a childhood friend convinced me to head to Eugene for my pre-med classes, I went from teaching cowboys wired on chewing tobacco to walking past pot heads communing on the campus lawns. The campus at the University of Oregon was gorgeous. I was proud to be a Duck. I stuffed all the calculus, biology, physics, and chemistry classes into one year. Money was tight, especially when you had to pay out of state tuition and child support. The alimony was short-lived since my ex married her boss in a ski lodge, with John Denver music wafting through the air, a few months after the divorce.

During medical school, I returned to an empty apartment each night hoping someone would miss me, but no one did. I had my dream. Then I met Anne. She grew up on a farm outside Portland and worked as a medical technologist at the Oregon Health Sciences University. Deeply religious, Anne was encouraged by her friend, Faith, at Garden Community Church to take Christian theology classes. Her marriage went south when she decided to pursue a major in Christian ministries. Her husband who never stepped foot in a church deemed her crazy and moved out. After years of working days and attending night classes, she got her theology degree and hoped that it would qualify her to be a pastor at her church. The church informed her that they wouldn't change their by-laws for her. Women could only hold the title of director and weren't allowed to preach on Sunday. We both thought that was shallow-minded in a church that emphasized love, acceptance and tolerance. Even the guy who ran the lights who never took a religious class in his life had the title of pastor.

We looked forward to joining the Trinity Cornerstone Church in Cottonwood where they openly encouraged women to become head pastors. From the moment she arrived in town, Anne was welcomed into the church and given the position of assistant pastor. By the time I arrived, she was a changed woman brimming with confidence and tranquility.

I fell hard for Anne. If going to church and supporting her schooling made her happy, I was in on her dream. Anne helped me understand the difference between a bold Christian who holds nothing back and an obnoxious Christian who treats non-Christians as if they were projects. The bold, she said, say what they're for, while the obnoxious say what they're against. The bold are committed to righteousness while the obnoxious are committed to being right. It made perfect sense to me and helped me feel more deeply committed to Christianity.

We dated for years, both of us hesitant to remarry. After serving a three-year residency and accumulating big debt, I joined a private family practice group by the Rose Garden sports arena in Portland. I was miserable. Managed care by that point had morphed from cutting reimbursements to patients needing referrals, then to capitation of doctor's fees and finally to increasing deductibles. Health care costs spiraled; malpractice suits still threatened to strip doctors of everything. Health insurance premiums rose at double digits, and the patients complained about their bills, which didn't help the doctor-patient relationship. Battle fatigue set in. I was the poster child for the burned out doctor.

Anne was receptive to my idea of moving out to our family ranch near Cottonwood, especially after she knew she would have a pastor position at the church. Horses, not trips to Nordstroms, made her happy.

Migrating from Minnesota, my Swedish-born grandfather, Len, bought the Spirit of Winter Ranch in the 1930s from a German family who called it quits after living through the dust bowl. They moved across the border to Williston, North Dakota. When the wheat crops failed and cattle prices plummeted, grandpa moved into Cottonwood and took over the Our Own Hardware franchise store. But he never lost the love of ranching and farming and passed the ranch down to my father who kept it going through some really bad times.

The drive to the ranch from Cottonwood passed by quickly as my mind switched back and forth between thoughts of Anne and our new home. As I entered the driveway, I saw the ranch buildings that stood behind a lofty grove of cottonwoods and poplars planted on the north side of the house in an attempt to tame the relentless wind blowing south from Canada. The buildings rested in a small coulee right in the middle of 10,000 acres of wheat fields, badlands, buttes, and cattle country. Even though it was a showcase back in the forties, the wind, sun, snow and ice hammered the structures to the point that there was constant maintenance required.

The bunk house was the first building erected and was the first home on the property. A few years of prosperity led to a two-thousand-square-foot, sturdy ranch house; a house that was meant to be lived in and not just to hold boards off the ground. Grandpa had made extensive repairs to the roof and siding that leaked wind everywhere. The barn where the cats patrolled for mice sat about thirty yards from our three bedroom ranch house. The pole barn, as brown as the plowed earth, weathered the years surprisingly well.

Anne and I seemed closer, somehow, out on the ranch. Her smile was softer and the Montana sun made her long, curly brown hair more beautiful. At five-foot, six-inches tall, she was an athletic, musing girl who loved the rigors of ranch life. Even the thought of the dark, long cold Montana winters brightened when I closed my eyes and thought of her. I didn't need much more. None of my relationships with other women compared to the one with her. Likewise, she knew that if she went my way that I'd be good to her.

I found Anne in the barn spraying down the horses with insect repellant and finishing mucking the stalls and paddock area where a tidal flow of manure and urine greeted us every day. The mosquitoes, wasps, and horse flies found the climate very appealing and bit with glee anything that moved. Winter brought a welcome reprieve from these winged intruders.

We embraced and headed into the house to get ready for the wedding.

It was Anne's idea to get married on our horses. Big Sky was my twenty-year-old, palomino, quarter horse gelding. Sunny was her seven-year-old bay, saddlebred mare.

Our neighbor, Ray Koler, agreed to marry us outside the paddock area of the barn. Ray, a well respected family attorney, was one of my father's best friends. He never fully recovered after his wife, Jeanne, died eight years earlier but worked hard at maintaining a positive attitude. His two sons, like most children of the plains, fled Cottonwood to work elsewhere. Few grandparents in Sheridan County had the pleasure of watching their grandchildren grow up.

After being up all night, I smelled pretty ripe so I headed to the shower. Unfortunately, the well water was brown and alkaline so bathing was not a totally enjoyable or successful endeavor. The odor from the water would repel a skunk and often you smelled worse after bathing.

Ben Two Moon, our ranch hand since before I was born, agreed to give Anne away. His gray braids roosted upon his leathery face and wiry torso. Grandpa took him in seventy years ago when he was seven years old after his parents were killed down on the Fort Peck Indian Reservation. Both were drunk when their car plunged off the Fort Peck dam after the bars closed. One of the government agents forgot to put up a "road closed" sign. Living off the reservation brought ridicule from his tribe and frequent heckling from red necks in Cottonwood. However, the only time he ever showed any emotion was when his wife, Alma, died five years ago. I flew back for the funeral. Even though it was only late October, the temperature dropped to forty below and froze the grave site deep enough that she couldn't be buried until the next April.

Two Moon was honest, hard-working and one of my best friends. His loyalty and work ethic allowed our family to keep the ranch going at a time when my father was struggling at the hardware store to make enough money to feed us. Even though his world didn't extend past northeastern Montana, Two Moon taught me more about life than anyone. Two Moon always told me when I was growing up that I could learn anything that the Ivy Leaguers knew, but I would know many things that they would never understand. And he was right.

Ray Koler was fifteen minutes early, but Choteau didn't arrive in his Roadrunner until ten minutes after one o'clock. It was a cloudless day with only a light breeze from the north. Meadowlarks and magpies serenaded us as we greeted each other in front of our home. We headed over to the paddock area where Big Sky and Sunny awaited us. They acted as if they knew this was an important event. After we mounted our horses, Choteau insisted playing "Here Comes the Bride" on his fiddle. Yo Yo Ma, he wasn't, but we appreciated the effort.

"Before you exchange vows, we have something to show you on the other side of the barn," Ray said with a big grin.

Behind the barn, there sat a beautiful, vintage doctor's buggy with a black doctor's bag on the seat. It looked like it just came from the factory.

Anne said. "How wonderful! Don can really impress his patients now!"

"I'm trading in my Chevy tomorrow," I said. "Thank you so much."

"It was Choteau's idea," Two Moon said.

"I found it, and we all chipped in to pay for it," Choteau said. "But Ray paid the most. I believe in socialism where you screw the hard workers. That's why I took it easy all my life."

We all laughed. They insisted on taking a picture of Anne and me sitting on the buggy seat.

When the picture had been snapped, Ray held his hands up to talk. "Two Moon restored it," Ray said.

"Yeah," Choteau said. "It looked like shit before the chief got a hold of it."

"Well, let's get back to the ceremony," Ray said, as we all walked back around the barn.

"Keep it short," Choteau said. "I'm getting hungry for weddin' cake."

"Yeah, keep it short," Munchie said. "After about a couple of minutes, I drift off to Jack Daniels country."

"Rest assured that Anne and I are not long-winded pontificators," I said.

"That's true," Anne said. "We just have a short thought to share with you and God."

"What the Sam hell is pontiacators?" Munchie asked.

"Thems are those fancy hood ornaments that go on a Pontiac Firebird," Choteau said. "I had a set back in the eighties. Paid a shit hole for 'em, and they still looked like crap."

We all chuckled. "Are you ready, Blue Jean Baby?" I asked.
"You bet," she replied.

I held Anne's hands and looked her in the eyes as I spoke. My voice was quiet, her fingers lay still against my palms.

> I look at you, and know I love you.
> Love can be painful, and love can cut you.
> Before you, Anne, I walked away.
> But our love has healed me,
> and your teaching has led to my salvation.
> I know today is not like the past.
> I hear what my soul says.
> I will love you for eternity.
> I feel your embrace around my spirit.
> I look at you and know I love you.

Anne's cheeks were wet, her eyes shining when I finished. There was a brief silence. Then Choteau said, "Holly shit, Kid, I didn't know you could talk like that, "Thems are the prettiest words I ever heard. Maybe, I could get um from you and say um to Fran tonight. We'd be headin' for the bedroom faster than crap down the shitter."

"You have such a way with words," I said to Choteau dryly. "I'll be happy to share a copy with you."

"Anne, your turn," Ray said. "Are you ready?"

She nodded. She squeezed my hands and shook her long hair.

> I'll never forget the day we wed.
> I love the words you just said.
> From this day on we have a new start.
> My love for you is deep in my heart.
> God is good, and God is fine.
> Our lives together will be gentle and kind.
> Jesus says, "Yoke yourself to me."
> His love will set us free.

My love for you is timeless and true.

Together, there's nothing we can't do.

This time, Munchie, poor Munchie who'd fall apart in a second, was crying. "I wish I had a little woman who talked to me like that," he said. "If I did I'd be President of the United States. Behind every good man is a better woman, and I just made that up."

"Hell. If you'd stopped hangin' out at them whore houses down in Livingston in the seventies, maybe you'd a found a good woman," Choteau said. "Pokin' ain't fallin' in love,"

"Gentlemen! This is a wedding ceremony," Ray said. "Please watch your tongue. Now let's proceed."

Ray sat on the top paddock railing as we exchanged traditional vows. Two Moon then beat his drum and pranced around us chanting words I didn't understand.

In closing, Ray asked if anyone wanted to say something. These were words I'll never forget.

"I will always keep our lives and love for each other close," Anne said. "But I will keep my love for God closer."

That statement haunted me for the rest of my life. She had her priorities in the right order. Before I met her, those words might have offended me.

Ray looked at me and smiled and gestured that it was my turn to speak.

"Through you Anne, I finally know what that means."

∽ SIX ∽

W E INVITED OUR GUESTS IN for wedding cake that Anne had made. Two Moon serenaded us again with an old Indian drum song. Small talk about the weather and the local football team eventually led to the Trinity Project.

"How do you like being a doctor under socialized medicine?" Ray asked.

"So far, so good, although I've only been here a week," I said. "They told me that everyone's health insurance is covered under this pilot program so I'm sure the residents of Sheridan County are thrilled with that. If they're happy, I'm happy."

"What's the pay like?" Ray asked. "They must be skimping somewhere. I don't trust them."

"I get a salary I'm happy with, and I don't have as much paperwork or have to worry about overhead," I said. "It removes the temptation to do more procedures to get reimbursed more. But I don't have a good feeling about how easy it's going to be to access specialists in Billings. Doc Dennis assures me that won't be a problem. We'll see. They let me know they wanted to keep referrals to a minimum. That part of the health plan reminds me of the capitated plan popular in Portland where we got a fixed amount of money to take care of each patient. If our services were over-utilized, then the clinic was on the hook financially. That led to fewer referrals and more primary care doctors holding on to their patients."

"I bet that made your patients real happy," Ray said.

"They weren't pleased," I said. "Angry patients finally revolted. Quite a few clinics around Portland went under trying to guess how much the average patient was going to cost them to manage. The insurance company geniuses put all the risk on the doctors who were too scared about losing patients to fight it. The doctors lost most of their savings including all their retirement. A good day was when no one showed up."

"That's the shits," Choteau said.

"That system wasn't right," I said. "At least with this plan, Dennis and I aren't on the hook financially although I don't know who's figuring out the money side of it. The health plan's just one part of the Project that also includes financial aid for businesses and farmers, and support for the Trinity Cornerstone Church. That support is exciting to us, but why would they support religion? Socialism and religion seem to be opposites. What do you make of it, Ray?"

"In one way it's been nice to have everyone in Sheridan County covered by health insurance, but some of our seniors are being denied services," Ray said. "Once you get a certain age, there are no elective surgeries and only generic medicines are covered. It has covered the poorer families in town, but also a lot of dead beats who won't work and spend most of their time at the bar. The weekly online newsletter from the Project continually emphasizes the fact that the latest National Institute of Health studies have confirmed that after age seventy, preventative care is unnecessary. Not cost-effective. What they're saying is the quicker you die, the less money they have to spend on you, but with the

Project hanging out the money carrot, people have signed on. With how bad the economy is, they really didn't have any choice."

"That's crappy," Munchie said.

"They've worked with Galen Hospital to send those infected with the new resistant tuberculosis strain there for treatment," Ray said. "A bunch of friends my age were sent there. I haven't heard from then since they left. Is cutting off communication with folks outside the hospital part of the therapy?"

"I don't understand that," I said shaking my head.

"The T.B. strain has really hit the elderly, disabled, and impaired children around town hard," Ray said. "The infection has left only the strongest living in Cottonwood. What does Doc Dennis say?"

"I really haven't talked to him much about what we can do under the plan," I said. "I got a feeling they don't want me doing much until I got my official orientation from Bruce Deeds. I meet with him today at five. I wasn't given a choice. I hope that's okay with you, Anne."

"I'll have you the rest of my life," Anne said. "I guess I can let them have you for an hour even if it's our wedding day."

"I'd watch Deeds," Ray said. "Maybe I'm just a small town attorney, but I don't trust those big-city lawyers. At the University of Montana law school, they taught you how to do the right thing for your clients."

"Ain't the East where most of the politicians that end up in jail go to school?" Choteau asked. "Course, I think anything on the other side of Minot is back East."

"Aren't you a little disappointed they called it the Trinity Project?" Ray asked Anne.

"No, Pastor Luke likes the name," Anne said. "He said it emphasizes unity. What they're accomplishing here is so wonderful that it's hard to believe."

"Well, I'm going to have to work with them for at least awhile," I said. "Even with the restrictions, I still don't know how they're paying for it. I've heard that some of the specialists in Billings are outraged at Trinity's low reimbursement rates. There are no negotiations and they have to comply if they want to keep their medical licenses. The governor rammed that through the state legislature."

Just then the phone rang. Neil, the pharmacist, was on the other line.

"Don, I was just up at the hospital delivering medications, and I think your dinosaur hunter friend is getting over-sedated on IV valium," Neil said. "He's ended up in the ICU, and I don't know if he is going to pull out of it."

"Shit, Neil," I said. "I ordered to slowly taper the dose. Have you gotten hold of Dennis? He's on call for the next week."

"I'm sorry," Neil said. "I thought you were still on call. I'll give him a jingle."

"No. Don't," I said. "I'll be there in a few minutes."

Ray caught me looking up at the clock and knew it was time for him, Munchie, and Choteau to leave.

When the door shut behind them, I turned to Anne. "I hope tonight the light of love is in your eyes, and I feel the magic of your sighs," I said and took her hand, pressing it warmly.

"Don't get too California with me," she said, pecking me on the cheek. "Remember, I married you because you are a Montana boy."

As we took the dogs, Beau and Lexy, for a short walk, I promised her I would be back from the five o'clock meeting as soon as possible. Our wedding night menu included T-bone steaks from one of our Black Angus cows and a bottle of wine we bought at a Yamhill County winery in Oregon. That sounded good to me as long as I didn't let anyone around town find out I was drinking wine.

As I drove off and waved good-bye, I knew I finally found my hard-headed woman, and thoughts of her made the time traveling the miles of rutted, dusty dirt roads zip by.

There were still areas where the cattle grazed in the open range with no fences, and towards evening it wasn't uncommon to hit a stray one. It was twilight, and as I turned onto the pavement, I noticed through the sunset that there was a strange blue light in the fiery autumn haze. I'd seen it only once before. It was the night my father committed suicide.

∞ **SEVEN** ∞

STEVE WAS COMATOSE, but his vital signs were stable. I ordered the IV valium tapered and asked the nurse who ordered the increased dosage. They showed me the electronic record that indicated it was approved by me! How could that happen? I had given verbal orders to the nurse to slowly lower his dose. I told her, emphatically, that no more order changes were to be made.

I needed to speak with the nursing staff and Dennis. The medical errors had to stop.

"Steve," I bent down to whisper in his ear. "I'll come by in a few hours to see how you're doing. Hang in there, buddy."

My next stop was the Trinity Project's main office, perched high above the valley floor on Big Sky Point. Its granite presence loomed large not only on the landscape, but also on the psyche of Cottonwood. The glistening glass front faced west and welcomed in the setting sun. An American flag on the roof of the second story flew alongside those of the state of Montana and the Trinity Project's flag which was highlighted with a prominent, red triangle.

The wind always seemed to pick up in the late afternoon on the northern plains, sending the fields of golden prairie grass moving in rhythmic waves.

I was eagerly anticipating meeting Bruce Deeds, the alternately charming and pugnacious fifty-eight-year-old who was head of the Trinity Project.

A national celebrity who had graced the cover of *Time* and *Newsweek* magazine, Bruce Deeds was a rock star in a business suit. The magazines chronicled his meteoric rise from growing up as the son of a North Carolina mill worker to receiving his health economics undergraduate degree at Yale and attending Harvard Law School, where he finished first in his class. After landing several high profile jobs in Washington D.C. where he advised presidents from both parties on health care issues, Deeds worked as a consultant. He helped the Canadian and British governments make their national health plans more cost-effective.

Both political parties, in panic mode over the escalating federal deficit, wanted Deeds to solve the health care problem. The conservatives waved the white flag but demanded a pilot project that controlled medical costs. Thus, the Trinity Project was born in 2015.

I parked my '58 Chevrolet Impala station wagon and headed into the building for my meeting. Upstairs, I passed three statisticians hunched over their computer terminals in Deeds' bright, orderly outer office. His secretary, Louise Darling, asked me to have a seat. She was a wonderful childhood friend of mine. We chatted. Five minutes later she gave me a nod, indicating that it was time for me to go in.

The window of Deeds' second floor office overlooked the Cottonwood Valley. His oversized desk was covered with stacks of papers. Plaques honoring him lined the walls, as did framed *Time* and *Newsweek* magazines featuring him on the cover. Pictures of Deeds with Clinton, Bush, Obama, and our current President were prominently displayed on his desk.

"Have a seat," he said, looking at me with what can only be described as a pirate's smile. "I'm so excited about you joining our team. I'd like to explain to you in more detail the miracle that is happening in your hometown and across the northern plains. All our data show that this pilot project should be able to be adopted nationally just in time to save our country from terminal decline. Sorry we had to call you into service earlier than planned."

"Thank you and no problem," I said. "It's been a dream of mine to come home."

It was easy to understand his success. His intelligence and charm were a marriage made in corporate board room heaven.

"We've worked hard to make this project a big success, and with this being the last week before I present our data in Minneapolis, we want these last few days to run smoothly, if you know what I mean," Deeds said. He arched an eyebrow.

I didn't know what he meant. What could I do to disrupt it, and why would I want to anyway? He motioned me over to the window.

"Don," he said, putting his arm around me. "What do you see when you look down on our town?"

"Well, I see the place where I grew up, where I have known wonderful people and have wonderful memories," I said.

He suddenly and unexpectedly fell back in his chair. His eyes gazed upwards as if summoning strength from a higher force. "Do you remember when you grew up here and how everyone said Cottonwood was thirty years behind times?" He said.

"Yes," I said. That was one of my favorite things about it. Nothing really changed as a child, and that gave me a sense of security.

"When I look out across this beautiful valley, I see America's future," he said with passion.

The President appointed Deeds as the Trinity Project czar to develop a model for universal health care that was deficit-neutral. Unlike the more than three dozen czars appointed by the President who only answered to him, Deeds had another boss who he told me I would soon meet.

"Sit down," he said.

I sat down.

After the stock market crash of 2008 and the financial bail-outs, he recounted, pressing his hands together and looking across the desk at me, the progressives launched a health care reform effort that eventually fell short. Much to the distress of the liberal or progressive wings of the party, it was a watered-down version of their dream. Several party members contacted Deeds to come up with a pilot project that could be initiated on a regional scale—then adapted to a national one.

Deeds nicknamed the pilot region, "SEN," (South Dakota, eastern Montana, eastern Wyoming, and North Dakota). Statistics on economics, religion, age, and quality of health care were taken into account. The powerful Senators from Montana, Wyoming and North and South Dakota on the Senate Finance Committee steered the Project to their states. Amazingly, Cottonwood won out over Billings, Fargo, Casper, and Pierre as the Trinity Project headquarters. The reason it did was because of Bo Hart.

Senator Bo Hart, head of the Senate Finance Committee, Deeds continued, played a pivotal role in bringing the Project headquarters to northeastern Montana. He'd spent summers out on his uncle's ranch south of town and loved the area. It probably didn't hurt that he now owned mineral rights and lots of land throughout northeastern Montana.

A pilot project on the northern plains was ideal: it was isolated, had a relatively stable population, and it was easier to avoid scrutiny from the media centers that were located on the coasts. Seasoned, liberal investigative reporters had no interest in critically examining the Project and instead sent rookie interns out to report progress. They were no match for Deeds.

A more spiritual reason for the Trinity Project arrival on the northern plains, Deeds explained, was that the region symbolized the Garden of Eden, an untainted and unfettered area, the paradise that existed before Satan arrived to ruin mankind.

"This great experiment needed to happen in a rural area," Deeds said. "Urban areas in this country are beyond decay. This Project had to be born in the Garden, a start over, if you know what I mean."

Using what Deeds termed "compression statistics," he developed computer software programs that made a five-year study of a few million people as accurate as twenty-five-year study. With that information, he would be able to predict the success of a national universal health plan.

"Look, from the get-go I envisioned a three-headed plan resembling the Trinity in the New Testament," Deeds said with confidence. "I'm no Biblical scholar, but that's how I came up with the name. As CEO of the Project, I'm like father God overseeing my flock. Dr. Dennis Anderson is like Jesus, the son who heals human disease. And Pastor Luke, the head of the Trinity Cornerstone Church, is the Holy Spirit, instilling God deep into the hearts of people. Those are hearts that yearn for health care for the masses. He is an apostle, profit, evangelist, shepherd, and teacher all rolled up in one. Listen, health care is a right, not a privilege. Even your friends on the reservation agree: whole in the body, then whole in spirit, they say."

Doc Dennis, I'm sure, delighted in being likened to Jesus. How much resistance would there be to yet one more government takeover in a country stuck in downward mobility? The government already controlled the banks, the automotive industry, energy, commodities, education, and most of health care.

"Was there any resistance to the Project?" I asked. It was hard for me to believe that independent westerners signed on without a fight.

"Not much," Deeds said, once again flashing me his confident smile. "It's a different world since you grew up here. It's more like how socialist Cottonwood was in the 1920s. Small businesses in town were on life-support before we arrived. Independence stops at the wallet. A starving dog doesn't have principles. He'll take the meat from a stranger without growling."

"Yeah, but I thought he might bite along the way," I said. It was hard to think of this place I loved as so down, so desperate.

"Not even a whimper," he said. He shook his head, and then brightened. "We have subsidized them with tax credits and write-offs so their bottom line is positive for the first time in decades. Bailouts shouldn't just go to the Wall Street fat cats. With every-one's health care covered, they couldn't wait to join up. I'm a populist. Americans are angry. The greedy Wall Street bankers made sure their politicians took care of them while ignoring Main Street. The Project hasn't. Washington spent hundreds of billions of dollars supporting the bank crooks, and then to make it look like they're populists, they trickled a few bones to Main Street mutts.

"We have strong support from Independents and many Republicans. Extreme right-wingers are hiding in their closet with gold bullion in one hand and an assault rifle in the other. We have marginalized them. It hasn't been lost on us that there are more Independent voters than Republicans and Democrats com-bined. They want results. No more lip service. No more political infighting. We already have experience controlling the farmer's attitudes. We've paid them for decades not to farm. You know how much they embraced the soil bank plan."

"They sure did," I said. "They all moved to Arizona and had their government checks sent down there. Soil bank subsidies wrecked small-town America. The small business owners had no one to buy their goods. That sealed the demise of most every farming community on the northern plains. Every government program has its unexpected consequences."

"Sounds like I hit your hot button," Deeds said. He gave me a stern look, drawing his eyebrows together. "Listen," he said. "The country is a mess. Do you think our best days are ahead of us? Unemployment is too high, health care is out of control and our military and economy are crumbling. Inflation is eating us alive. Most of the federal budget is funded on borrowed money. We have the power in this project to show Americans a way out of this downward spiral and set the world on fire."

"I thought fire was the Devil's only friend," I said.

"Cute, Dr. Lewis but not amusing," he said. "You know what I mean. With health care eating up twenty percent of our gross domestic product, we can't compete with the rest of the world. Our rivals spend half that amount. Besides, we have a moral obligation to help our people. Go to church on Sunday, and you will hear Pastor Luke preach from the Bible about what Jesus said. Jesus wanted to help the poor not the rich. President Obama said 'For our country to be a success, every individual needs to be a success.' That's about the only statement he ever made that still resonates with Americans."

"What about change?" I asked. "He liked that slogan too. You don't hear too much about that anymore. With inflation, the dollar is worth just a little change."

"Let's not dwell on the past," Deeds said. "I'm a visionary not a historian. Maybe, it's not back to the American glory years, but at least we won't go the way of the Europeans. We need to stop licking the earth, looking for satisfaction and drink from the cup of universal health care."

"Where's the money going to come from to pay for universal health care?" I asked wanting to get to the bottom line.

"Dr. Chen who arrived today for a short visit will explain that," he said his eyes boring into mine. "Dr. Chen will talk with you and go over the data to make sure everything is in order before the formal presentation in Minneapolis. She also wanted a photo taken of her with me in front of the grain elevator to use in our promotional material. We all assumed that you would embrace the project, especially since you've been living on the West Coast.

"Socialism is alive and well on the coast, but once you head east of the mountains it's a different story," I said. I figured that's all I'd say. I wanted to see everyone covered by health insurance too. Who wouldn't? But how, I wondered, could we ever pay for it?

He motioned me over to the window. When I neared him, he grabbed my arm in a grip that was slightly too tight. He pointed to the western sky now lit with brilliant reds and yellows.

"The West has always captivated American imaginations," he said. "You know that, with your history background. Look past Montana and Oregon across the ocean to China. America is east of Eden. They are providing us the funds for universal health care. This country has benefited greatly from our association with China. Americans are living better lives because of the inexpensive goods we import from them. Who wants to work on an assembly line? No one does. Let them do the grunt work. I will stop there."

"I must be honest with you," I said. "I don't like our dependence on China." That's all I said to him. I didn't want to get fired on the spot.

"You're wrong, doctor," Deeds said. "The best thing America can do is have closer ties with our Chinese brothers. Our standard of living is much higher because of our trade agreements with them. Get your head out of the sand. I don't want you talking like that, especially to Dr. Chen. You need to turn down the volume dial, compartmentalize your concerns and throw them in the River of Doubt."

"We get their poor quality products, and they get our treasury bonds," I said. "They own this country."

"They do, so why fight it?" Deeds said. "If they cash in their US Treasury bonds and other securities, our military will be eating dog food and asking our friends down on the reservation how to use a bow and arrow."

My temper was getting the better of me. I stood up and headed for the door but then hesitated. I knew I shouldn't burn any bridges and turned back. I had to learn to work with them. Anne was warmly welcomed by church members and was pleased with the prospect of her future role as head pastor when Luke moved on. She wouldn't be happy with me if I screwed things up now. Yet, as much as I wanted to keep quiet for her, I felt like a whore for being so submissive. "Cream puff," I could hear Doc Dennis say.

"Look. Sit down," Deeds said as he pointed to the chair. "Politics are not your expertise. Stick to treating patients if you expect to stay employed here. It's obvious that the medical profession has done nothing to help the situation. Let lawyers handle it. As long as doctors can rack up high incomes, they don't think much about the uninsured, the poor, and the suffering."

I reluctantly sat back down. "Please continue," I said. "I'm sorry I interrupted. My mother's Irish temper is getting the best of me. It won't happen again, but why would the Chinese care about our health care?"

"Ironically, even the communist Chinese have private insurance, but it's not working," Deeds said. He pressed his hands together, prayer-style, on the desk in front of him. "They're investing in our Project in the hope they can adapt our model to use in their own country. They realize they can't continue to treat their people with herbs and spices."

"Really?" I said. That didn't make much sense. So we were outsourcing our health care financing to the Chinese? After the

Soviet collapse, I thought Marxism was a relic only found in China, Cuba, North Korea, and in the liberal arts departments of expensive private American universities.

"They know I have a proven record of getting the job done," Deeds said. "I have spent years studying health care, so you're not going to be able to tell me something that I don't already know. Medicare is broke."

"Private insurers don't have the answers either," I said in a conciliatory tone.

"You're right," Deeds said. "Most insurance is still stuck in the obsolete fee-for-service model. Premiums are now going up twenty to sixty percent a year. We need to reward doctors and hospitals for good outcomes and not for running patients through like sheep. Under the Trinity Health Plan doctors will receive a monthly allotment for patients regardless of whether or not they get sick."

"That's like the old capitated program," I said. "That didn't work."

"Yes, but with one caveat: a bonus for meeting quality-of-care targets," he said. "Under the old capitation program, a good day for the doctor was when no one showed up. There was no emphasis on preventative care. But when the patient did show up they were often a train wreck and ate up money faster than a slot machine in Vegas. Doctor's clinics went bankrupt."

"Who's going to pay for medical education costs?" I asked. Since I was strapped with student loans, it was a major concern of mine.

"The educational debt of young physicians will be eliminated by the government paying for their medical education," Deeds said.

"Great idea!" I said. Oh no, was I buying into it now?

I knew they did that in countries with socialized medicine. No politicians seemed to even talk about that in this country. The average student debt is close to $300,000. If that didn't change, only kids with rich parents would be able to afford to go.

"The Trinity Health Care Project has come in on budget by cutting waste, installing electronic medical records, instituting preventative care, changing procedural guidelines, and improving quality of care," Deeds said, his face flushed with passion. "Go over to your old high school and see what's happening. It's a model for every school in the country."

"I'm planning on doing that next week," I said.

Deeds cleared his throat. "One more thing—to make this work we have changed the focus of care," Deeds said. "The Hippocratic Oath's admonition to 'use my power to help the sick to the best of my ability and judgment' as an imperative to do everything for the patient regardless of cost or effect on others will be removed from the oath by government mandate."

"Wow, that sounds radical," I said.

"It's key to our ability to rein in costs," Deeds said. "Doctors will serve two masters, the patient and society. Health services covering individuals who are irreversibly prevented from being or becoming productive, participating citizens are not basic and will be restricted. For example, there's no coronary bypass surgery for someone who is mentally impaired or eighty years old."

"Sounds like eugenics, where the undesirables are essentially eliminated from society," I said.

"Your hero, Teddy Roosevelt, didn't object to eugenics," Deeds said. "One hundred years ago eugenics was given great credence throughout America. Back then government run eugenics offices were opened all over the nation. Thirty-two states adopted laws that allowed the sterilization of defective humans in support of what was called 'Social Darwinism.' Over 60,000 Americans were sterilized in the early twentieth century because they had epilepsy, stuttered or were mentally challenged. Look at Ota Benga."

I knew about the tragedy of Ota Benga, a well known tale in historical circles. An African Pygmy, Ota Benga was caged with the monkeys in the Bronx Zoo as a teaching exhibit on the descent of man. William T. Hornaday was the head of the Zoo and a close friend of President Teddy Roosevelt. Eugenics was so popular in America that the Nazis came to this country in the 1920s to learn how to eliminate the weak in their society.

"Let's move on," Deeds said as he sat down again. "What about malpractice reform? We have standard-of-care manuals in the clinic and hospital that Dr. Anderson will review with you. If they follow government guidelines, doctors will be legally protected."

"Then the opposite is also true," I said. "Doctors will risk lawsuits if they stray from federal guidelines, even if the guidelines aren't in the patient's best care."

"Correct," Deeds said. "But the guidelines have been approved by the American Medical Association and the American Bar Association, so as long as the doctor doesn't stray, he won't be in trouble."

"The AMA doesn't represent most doctors," I said. "The trial attorneys will sue doctors if they stray."

"Don't be facetious," Deeds said. He waved his hands as if to dismiss my objections.

"Doctors are just going to be technicians and lots of patients will get hurt when the guidelines are found to be ill advised," I said.

"Big deal. Adjustments will be made," Deeds said. "Now it's time to move on. I think you'll be more convinced after your next meeting, which will be short since it's close to supper, and I'm hungry. Dr. Anderson, Pastor Luke, and I are taking Dr. Chen to the Blue Moon Night Club. We want to show her a little western hospitality."

∽ EIGHT ∽

I WAS GLAD to have a break before meeting Dr. Chen. I was exhausted and took a seat in the waiting room. The room was quiet, filled with the sweet scent of sage-perfumed air drifting in from the open windows. I closed my eyes and rested.

Suddenly, I was jolted awake at the sound of splintering glass. Two more shotgun blasts shattered windows. In the clinic, alarms blared and people ran for the exits from the parking lot below. I heard shouts. I peered out and saw Lightfoot's son, Banner, behind his old Ford pickup, holding off several Chinese guards with a shotgun. I hadn't seen Banner for years, but I recognized the nasty scar on the left side of his face.

"The Trinity killed my father," Banner yelled from behind his pickup truck and fired two more rounds.

The Chinese guards returned fire. Gun smoke obscured the street lights. Suddenly, he was blown over the top of the hood of his Ford and landed in a bloody heap on the asphalt. A sharp shooter on the roof nailed him. Half of Banner's head was blown off. The side with the scar remained, a scar that two rednecks inflicted on him in a bar fight years ago.

Within a few minutes the alarms were silenced, and the air was filled with gun smoke. Two orderlies placed the body on a stretcher and took Banner away, and everyone returned to the building. Louise came by to ask me if I was okay, and I told her I was just fine. I headed to the restroom to wash my face. When I looked in the mirror, my face was ghost-like, glistening with sweat. Minutes later I was called in to see Dr. Chen.

"Have a seat," an attractive Asian woman said shuffling papers while not looking up at me. "Sorry for the parking lot inconvenience."

"Hi, I'm Dr. Lewis," I said. Was she Dr. Chen's private secretary? I pressed my hands together in front of me to keep them from shaking. "Where's Dr. Chen?"

Dr. Chen looked up and smiled, giving me her full attention. "I am Dr. Susan Chen. I am the one who will approve the funding for the Trinity Project when it's expanded to include all of America. I want to welcome you to the team. The exciting results of the Trinity Project will bring this town even more national attention, and we want you to be a convincing spokesman for us."

"I'm sorry," I said. "I'm very upset about Banner Lightfoot getting shot."

"Please have a seat. Don't you Americans say that the only good Indian is a dead Indian?"

"That saying was objectionable when it was used over a century ago," I said, looking at her steadily.

"I believe General Sheridan said it in 1869 when he was in Indian Territory, now Oklahoma," she said. "Too bad your county is named after him."

We looked at one another, each taking measure. Both of us understood that she had one-upped me. She was smart, scary smart.

"I always travel here with extra security, and it looks like today it paid off," Chen said. "I think your country is more violent than when Butch Cassidy and the Sundance Kid roamed the West, but enough of that. I'm sure you are familiar with my writing."

"I am," I said. "I've admired your writing for years. I apologize for not recognizing you."

"Thank you," she said. "This may sound like lecture number two, but I want to communicate a lot of information in our short time together. First, I want to tell you a little about myself."

"Please do," I said.

She told me that she was born in San Francisco but grew up in China and received a doctorate in behavioral psychology at the University of Southern California before returning to China and taking a position as a trade negotiator with the United States. She worked on various projects over the years with Deeds. They negotiated many of the trade agreements between our two countries. She let me know that the Chinese government was very excited about supporting the Trinity Project.

"You may wonder why we would care about universal health care in America," Chen said.

"I do," I said. "Mr. Deeds touched on it."

"I'll be frank with you," she said. "Our interest is not totally altruistic."

"It makes sense that it wouldn't be," I said.

"China owns a vast amount of U.S. securities," she said. "It is in our best interests to keep America strong and stable. Currently in 2020, America spends five trillion dollars a year on health care. In five years, it will be eight trillion dollars. We plan to give back eight trillion dollars in U.S. government securities to launch universal health care in America as long as the Trinity Project Health Plan is deemed successful. We look at it as an investment in the future of both countries. That's why we want to see fiscal responsibility, a value absent in America today, and an end to deficit-spending."

She noted that the American government promised the Chinese they would significantly cut U.S. military expenditures and that the Chinese would be their partner in policing the world and America's domestic borders. Locally, ten Chinese border patrolmen were already manning the Montana border with Canada, north of Cottonwood. In addition, the Chinese wanted the Americans to stop pressuring China to float their currency, the yuan, on world markets. They wanted to keep the yuan's value low so their overseas exports remained attractive. They also wanted the global warming hysteria ended. There was absolutely no room for cap and trade in a vibrant Chinese economy.

"Is that all?" I asked, trying to keep the ironic edge out of my voice.

"Actually, there's more," Chen said. "We need your government to control inflation. If your government can guarantee that, then it works for us financially. If American inflation escalates any more, then we'll lose trillions of dollars in value in our U.S. Treasury holdings."

I really didn't know what to say, so I said nothing, which seemed like the best policy at the time.

"Look," Chen said. "I have studied you Americans for years. You may be familiar with some of my books I've published on what makes Americans tick."

"One of your books was required reading in our psychiatry class in medical school," I said. "You did a great job."

"That was probably *On Being an American*," she said.

She went on to explain her theory that America lived by the unexamined belief in the superiority of its historical moment over all other countries. The heritage passed down by city dwellers in America was mostly the sense of entitlement and not values. Chinese money made American politicians not even talk about human rights anymore. Why should they? The only green policy the Democrats and Republicans cared about anymore was how to stuff more in their pockets.

The Chinese wanted a successful Trinity Health Plan in America to be their model for Chinese health care. Right now, most health care providers in China had little more than a stethoscope and a thermometer. Few had medical degrees and learned about new drugs by reading package inserts. The Chinese government understood that they needed to upgrade their health care system to prevent civil unrest. The Chinese government hoped to adopt the Trinity Plan by 2025. Chinese liked adopting American innovations. It's one of the few things the Chinese respected about our country.

"Well, I'm glad you had at least something nice to say about America," I said.

She ignored my comment and continued, explaining that we needed better preventative health care in both countries. Resistant tuberculosis had ravaged China because most of their people worked in factory settings where they were forced to be in close quarters—the perfect breeding ground for spreading disease. Ten million people around the world were currently infected with tuberculosis, and with rapid spread of the new resistant strain, the number was going to go up exponentially. She projected that China would be hit the hardest.

"Time is short, and I don't want to overload you," she said. "Do you have any other questions?"

"Yes, one more," I said with some reluctance. "Why are the Trinity Project and the Chinese government funding Pastor Luke's Trinity Cornerstone Church?"

"That's an excellent question. I was hoping you'd ask that," she said as she stood up and walked over to a screen. "I'm a pragmatist, not an idealist. My mission is to achieve universal health care in China, and if Christianity will help me achieve my goal, then I have no problem using it to my advantage. Besides, there's not that much difference between socialism and Christianity."

"There isn't?" I asked feeling even more spiritually inadequate. "You're the expert, but I thought they were opposites."

She then projected a picture of Chairman Mao as a young man and one of Jesus.

"Let me read you a quote out of a book I didn't write," she said. "'There were no needy persons among them. For from time to time those who owned lands or houses sold them and brought the money from the sales … and it was distributed to anyone as he had need.' Is this a passage from a book on socialism written by Mao?"

"It kind of sounds like it, although I admit I haven't read any of his writings," I said.

"You should," Chen said. "I left out that they brought the money to the feet of the apostles. It is from Acts 4:34, NIV version of the Bible. Let's see, Apostle Luke wrote this line telling the masses to bring them all their wealth so he could distribute the way he saw fit. That sounds to me like socialism. Our communist leaders would say the same thing. The message is that the common man isn't wise enough to know what to do with his wealth."

"Oh," I said somewhat stunned.

"My studies reveal that there is no group in America with a greater sense of entitlement than Christians," Dr. Chen smiled to herself. "Missionaries are the worst. They'll eagerly travel to Africa on someone else's money to save the poor savages, but show no interest in going across town to feed their fellow citizens. Evangelists have become counters of men instead of fishers of men, and most weren't good at math. Many Christian leaders believe since they plant churches and have a special relationship with their God that they deserve good fortune for themselves. That's narcissism. America's Manifest Destiny was shameful."

She shook her head, smiling sadly. Then she looked up at me, brightening.

She continued, "Our goal is to channel that sense of entitlement into a national movement for health care for everyone. The Chinese look back to America's 2008 economic recession as the watershed year when the United States finally came to its senses and turned into a socialist country.

"Wow," I said.

"It obvious," she said, shaking her head. "That Americans are capitalists as long as they have more money than their friends and neighbors, but when they don't, they turn socialists real fast. America's persistent economic recession has made the change to socialism easy. Without that change there would be no Trinity Project funding by the Chinese."

She folded her hands neatly and looked at me again. "I know how the rich, middle, and poor classes in America think and what makes them tick," Dr. Chen said, cooly. "You can't get into their pocketbook without getting to their spirit. Most Christian clergy have failed to grab their congregation's heart, which has resulted in poor attendance and low tithing rates. Liberals, however, failed to pass universal health care because they didn't care about the conservative Christian vote."

"You really know your subject," I said.

"The Christians, the very group that champions helping the needy, were ignored by the liberals," she said. "They even made fun of Christians. Devalued them. The success of the Trinity Project is characterized not by self-centeredness but by mutually self-giving love. Americans call it Christianity, and the Chinese call it socialism. That's where the Trinity Cornerstone Church comes into play."

"You've certainly done your homework," I said. "I used to think communist's hated religion because Karl Marx said 'religion is the opiate of the masses.'"

"Marx didn't understand American Christianity," she said. "America is a deeply Christian country longing for a connection with Jesus. I don't understand that, but I'll go along with it. Liberals and socialists don't like Christianity because they want the government to control people, not religion. This is our way of achieving that end. The Chinese government realizes that in this age of information imperialism from the American internet, the appropriate Christian message can work to our benefit."

Christians, she said, were absent from the arenas in which the greatest influence in our American culture is exerted. The most obvious one was universal health care. That would change with the Trinity Cornerstone Church leading the fight for the adoption of the Trinity Health Care Plan. Christianity no longer will be marginalized.

Seven hundred billion dollars a year, she explained carefully, is wasted in taking care of patients who will die in two months. What a waste. The Trinity Project wanted to remind Christians that it was okay to die whether it's your child, spouse, friend or parent. When Lazarus was dying, Jesus didn't rush to his friend's side, but went elsewhere for several days. When heaven awaits, the message should be that death was no big deal. Jesus came to save souls, not bodies.

"The great Christian apologist, C. S. Lewis, stated, 'The only place besides heaven that is free from pain and suffering of relationships is hell,'" she said and smiled. "But he was only partially right. Look around you. The Trinity Cornerstone Church has effectively removed pain from Cottonwood and soon the rest of the country. Notice everyone gets along here—no more fighting over religion, the divorce rate is close to zero, rates of illicit drug and alcohol consumption are plummeting. Heaven is here in Cotttonwood."

"I always thought I was in heaven growing up here," I said in a clumsy way.

"Deeds told me Pastor Luke has done nothing short of a miracle here," Dr. Chen spoke slowly, carefully, spreading her hands on the desk. She smiled, if you could call it that, her lips lifting up on each side. "Wait until America has the same opportunity, and we know Christians have to have miracles to keep their faith. Well, I need to go. Work hard and keep your nose to the grind stone. It's harder to rock the boat when you're rowing. We'll be watching you."

Her veiled threat made my throat tighten, but I had enough presence to smile back, stand and shake her hand as she escorted me out to the parking lot.

As I drove off, I looked in my rear view mirror. Anderson and Deeds stood next to Chen on the gray asphalt, watching my car wind down the road. I don't think my performance pleased anyone. The light of the harvest moon was the only bright spot to this dark day.

Was the Trinity another Cerberus, the three-headed mythical hound that guarded the gates to Hades, the underworld? Or was I off base? They were passionate and believed they were doing what was best for our country. I thought of Matthew 16:18 and hoped that it was right in this situation: "Thou art Peter, and upon this rock I will build my church, and the gates of hell shall not prevail against it."

What a wedding day. I just left the twilight zone. My dream of returning home and finding my soul was turning into something of a nightmare as each hour progressed.

∞ NINE ∞

A T THE HOSPITAL, Steve was coming out of his Valium stupor. His eyes were somewhat bright as if his mind had cleared, but he couldn't speak yet.

"Steve," I whispered. "Are you hurting?"

He gently shook his head no, but I could tell he was troubled and wanted to say something. I held up a cup and watched him sip ice water through a straw. He gestured toward me to come closer. I bent down toward him.

"We found human bones, fresh human bones." he whispered. "They pushed boulders over the cliff on top of me, Chinese border patrol. It wasn't an accident."

With that he fell back into a coma exhausted from uttering just a few words.

"Nurse Lindsay, have any friends or relatives visited Steve?" I asked.

"No," she said. "He's the first patient I've taken care of in a long time where that's the case. Dr. Anderson wouldn't allow visitors. He said it would slow down his recovery."

"Thank you," I said.

It was odd that Dennis wouldn't allow visitors. If anything, they always helped the healing process. Things just didn't add up.

The ride back to the ranch was a blur as I tried to make sense of Steve's words. Was he delirious when he told me the business about government agents trying to kill him? After the parking lot shootout, it didn't seem that far-fetched. Did he really find human bones? What did that mean?

The northern lights pulsed with color.

At the door, Anne greeted me with a big hug and smiles but stopped, dropped her arms and looked at my face, sensing something was wrong.

"Honey, what happened this morning?" she asked.

"An Indian in the E.R. punched me in the jaw, and then I fell backwards and cut my finger on a glass container," I said. My voice was flat and quiet. "He collapsed and died right after he cold-cocked me. I don't know what hurts more, my hand, my jaw, or my pride. And the day got worse."

"Please tell me," she said.

"The Indian's son, Banner, had his head blown off in the parking lot of the Trinity office by a Chinese sharp shooter," I said.

"Oh, my dear Lord," Anne said, brushing a hair from my face.

"Yeah," I said shaking my head in disbelief. "His son said that the Trinity people were responsible for his father's death. Then, when I checked in on Steve at the hospital, he said his injuries were no accident, that the Chinese border patrol was responsible. Maybe the drugs confused him. I don't understand what's going on. Maybe, his confusion is confusing me."

"Surely, he's not thinking right," she said. "Why would federal agents want to hurt Steve on a dinosaur dig? It doesn't make sense. You're overly tired, Don, and when that happens, you get depressed and paranoid. Let's be proactive. Let's drive out to Hell Creek tomorrow, and find out, first hand, what happened to Steve on the dinosaur dig. Besides, it's a nice drive, and I've wanted to see that area. But now, let's forget about it. I've got steaks for you to barbecue. And it's our honeymoon."

She knew I loved beef, but I wasn't hungry. I was thirstier for the truth but settled for a whiskey.

"You're right," I said.

"How were your meetings at the Trinity Project Building?" Anne asked.

"Deeds and Chen are interesting people," I said. "They gave me quite an earful. Tomorrow we'll talk more about it. C'mon sweetie, let's enjoy what's left of our honeymoon night."

With that, I took her in my arms and kissed her.

The pinot noir went well with the dinner, a nice finish to a wild day. As I relaxed, I listened to the comforting clatter of plates as Anne washed the dishes, and afterwards, she cut up cooked chicken breasts and added it to some dog food for Lexy, who was at an age where she didn't have much appetite. The next thing I knew Anne was waking me up. I'd been out for over two hours. Not exactly how I planned my honeymoon night.

In bed, of course, I lay, wide awake, looking out the window at the stars, while Anne slept soundly and our two dogs snored at the foot of the bed. How tiny and insignificant I felt, especially living on this ranch outside Cottonwood, nowhere for some people, but it was everywhere for me. One of my patients, a Horizon Airline pilot, told me that every time he flew cross country and saw the lights of Cottonwood, he thought of me. He called Cottonwood a bright spot in a sea of darkness. Little did he know the impact this small town was going to have on America if the Trinity Project was successful.

≈ PART TWO ≈

INVESTIGATION

Saturday
September 22, 2020

∾ TEN ∾

I T WAS A CRISP SATURDAY MORNING, and the thermometer read twenty-one degrees. Before I left for the hospital, I went out and fed the horses. Normally when they saw me, they whinnied and moved toward their stalls, easy as flies on honey, but not today. Restless, they stared toward the hill north of the barn. Perhaps they saw a deer or antelope. Finally, I got the horses in their stalls and fed them.

Driving over the dusty roads in autumn reminded me of bird hunting trips when I was a kid with my father and his buddies. Minnesota Vikings football games blared on the car radio and the air was thick with the smoke from the unfiltered Camels they smoked. The only reprieve was a breath of fresh air from the front window wing vents. From then on, motion sickness was my constant companion. Today, like then, the clouds in the sky mimicked towering whipped cream like those painted by my heroes, Charlie Russell and Maynard Dixon.

Dennis's shiny new BMW was in the hospital parking lot. His vanity plates read "THEMAN." I looked at my watch, eight o'clock, he was early.

The nurse told me I could find Dennis in our on-call room, the sleeping quarters we used if we wanted to stay overnight after a middle-of-the-night emergency. It didn't make much sense to go home and turn right around in an hour or two and head back to the hospital. I asked her if there was a car accident, and she just shook her head and gave me a sour look.

I didn't catch her meaning until I unlocked the door to the sleeping quarters. There was Dennis making out with the youngest nurse on the staff, twenty-three-year-old Bonnie, the daughter of a classmate of ours. Bonnie quickly dressed and brushed past me as she walked out the door.

"Hey," I said, any other words escaping me. I was disgusted.

"Junior," Don said. "What the hell are you doing here? I thought you and your little bride would be whooping it up out at the ranch or can't you get it up anymore."

"I came in to see how Steve is doing," I said. "What's with the Valium dosage?"

"Sorry about what you just saw," he said unconvincingly. "Let's pretend you didn't see anything. You know Abigail's been a little fragile and frigid since her dad died. I wouldn't want to make things worse."

"I have a feeling this hasn't been the first time," I said. "You should give Abigail more credit than that."

"Don't tell me how to treat my wife, asshole," he said. "Anyway, your buddy Steve took a turn for the worst last night and died a couple of hours ago. I've already sent him to the funeral home. Anchors away."

"What in the hell happened?" I slammed my fist on the desk and kicked the chair. "He was improving last night."

"Cool down, Junior," he said. "I've never seen you act like this before. Look, we had to increase the Valium later. He was very agitated and in lots of pain. His blood pressure sky-rocketed from all the pain and so did his pulse. I gave him an IV bolus

70

of morphine. It was the right decision at the time, but then he tanked. Trust me. Did you see the knockers on Bonnie? What a babe."

"I'm upset about the negligent care you've given him," I said. "And stop the dirty talk. I'm sick of it."

I started to hyperventilate and knew this conversation was going nowhere.

"Shut up," Dennis said. "End of subject. I don't want to fire you before you officially get started."

"And Bonnie?" I asked. "What's with Bonnie? She's your daughter's age."

"I admire risk-takers," Dennis said. "She wanted a promotion. One thing led to another, and here we are. You know me and women. My motto is no harm, no foul. Just like in sports. She's not complaining. She'll probably volunteer for more night duty, if you know what I mean."

✑ ELEVEN ✑

I RETURNED HOME WITH MORE BAD NEWS.

"I don't know what the hell is going on," I said as I walked through the door and shut it behind me. I rested there, facing Anne. "But here's the bad news up front. Steve is dead. I'm concerned that Dennis overdosed him on Valium and made it look like an accident. I'm convinced he killed my friend."

Anne held me tight, and I could feel her soft body press into mine. She said, "Maybe, you're jumping to conclusions. Pastor Luke thinks Dennis is a wonderful and competent physician. He says he's the best anywhere. I value Luke's judgment."

"Thanks for your support," I said and stepped away. "You make me feel like one of my paranoid patients."

"Honey, I'm not trying to do that," she said and took my hand. "I just hate to see you in so much pain. How could there be evil in a place blessed by God with the Trinity Cornerstone Church?"

I began to cry. I felt leveled. Suddenly I was overwhelmed by sorrow of losing a friend, and also the fragile happiness of our new life together. Anne seemed to be turning on me. A vortex of evil swirled around the entire community, and my wife couldn't see it.

"Hey," Anne said brightly. "Let's go down to the Hell Creek and get to the bottom of this. We owe it to Steve and ourselves."

I wiped my eyes.

Vintage Anne. My spirits were rising.

Within minutes we were in our Chevy station wagon, heading out on the one hour trip to Hell Creek in the Missouri Badlands.

"Looking out at this rugged country makes me wonder," I said. "Do you think the world is only six thousand years old like it says in the Bible? A lot of the fundamentalists believe that."

"No," Anne said, over the rumble of the engine. "Science says it's much older. Christians lose credibility when we ignore science."

She told me that Dr. Francis Collins, who was the head of the Human Genome Project and later the National Institutes of Health, did a wonderful job of explaining creation in his book, *The Language of God*. Collins, Anne explained, believed in theistic evolution, as did the Trinity Cornerstone Church.

"What's that?" I asked. "I hope it's more convincing than the religious fundamentalists who take the Bible literally. Continue, professor."

"The theists believe the universe appeared out of nowhere about fourteen billion years ago," she said. "The origins of life are unknown, but evolution and natural selection occurred over the years. Humans share a common ancestor with the great apes, but are still unique from all other life forms."

She explained that man's uniqueness includes the adherence to moral law (the knowledge of right and wrong) and the search for God.

"So when did humans show up?" I asked.

"Homo Sapiens showed up about 190,000 years ago, but that date isn't in stone," she said. "They find new evidence about that all the time."

"We'll call today a day when the dinosaurs and humans meet," I said.

"Sounds good to me, Don," she said as she smiled and rubbed my neck. "From what you've told me about this area, there's no better place anywhere for that to happen."

Years of drought scorched the plains and forced ranchers and farmers to look for more lucrative crops: the bones of Triceratops, Tyrannosaurus Rexes, and Velociraptors that could be sold to museums and private collectors. A Triceratops skull could go for $250,000 while a complete T. Rex skeleton could top $8 million. Those numb ers certainly made wheat farming pale in comparison.

Amateur dinosaur bone hunters angered the academic world who claimed the locals destroyed valuable specimens with clumsy handling. Steve and other paleontologists at Montana State University also accused the ranchers of digging the specimens up too hastily without taking proper field notes. Heated debate and occasional confrontations at dig sites broke out. I wondered if that's what happened with Steve. Someone must have really wanted those bones. But why did he mention the border patrol?

One ranch that still allowed academic excavations was the old Sieber ranch. In my youth, I hunted pheasants in the gullies not far from there. Max Sieber's grandson, Laton, made just enough money from his cattle and dry wheat operation to squeak by. Water was the issue. To find water, you had to dig a well so deep, few could afford it.

As we approached the ranch, a dog barked. An old windmill spun a few feet from the ranch house. If there had been paint on the outside walls, you couldn't tell now. The dogs barking let our friends know strangers were approaching. Laton was outside working on his old Ford pickup; his wiry frame belied his ninety-three years. His wife, Edna, waved from the front door. They recognized our old car from our hunting days.

When we pulled up, Laton limped toward the car.

"Howdy, Don," Laton said wiping off grease from his hands with a towel. "I heard you were back in town. Your dad would be happy to know you came home."

"It's great to be back home," I said. "You and Edna look terrific. It's so good to see you. This is my wife, Anne. We just got married yesterday and are living at the Spirit of Winter Ranch. I'm practicing medicine in Cottonwood."

Anne and I sat in the car, listening to their nonstop chatter about all their friends dying of cancer.

"There's no doubt in my mind that we have a higher cancer rate here than anywhere else," Edna said.

"You betcha," Laton said. "We are positive there have been radiation leaks from those dam ICBM missile silos. When the Glasgow Air Force Base was open, they were flying in shit that glowed in the dark. I doubt it was a crate of fire flies."

"I remember my mom worried about the high cancer rate around here when I was growing up, but the government never has done any studies to confirm it," I said.

"That's 'cause they don't care about us," Laton said. "The only attention we get from the Feds is when they mail us our tax returns. Otherwise, we don't exist. I sure hope Bo Hart can change that. We've never had a Senator like him."

"He looks like Tom Selleck," Edna said. "Tom's my man."

When I got around to Steve's accident, Laton was shocked when I told him that he had just passed away. I told him we were out today to look at the accident site as a way of bringing closure to the tragedy.

"It's been a funny summer around here," Laton said. "Lots of vans were coming and going, and I just assumed they were working at the dig sites. I talked to Steve about all the activity, and he said the government workers told him that they were marking dig sites with GPS units. He thought they were preparing for future digs, but they never got my permission. I guess I really didn't care. As long as they don't screw up the hunting, it's fine with me."

"Why would they need vans to do that?" Anne said.

"I don't know that much about GPS gear," Laton said. "Maybe it's big equipment."

"I don't think so," I said. "They make watches and cell phones with GPS."

"You know me," Laton said. "I don't have a cell phone or the internet."

"Well, Anne and I should probably head out to the site," I said as I looked from him to Edna. "Is the rest of the team still out there? I'd like to say hello to Lee, Steve's paleontologist friend."

"You're too late," Laton said. "They packed up and left about the time you arrived in Cottonwood. No more vans either. I guess they got all the bearings they needed. They still have border patrolman out there drivin' around. Don't they know where the border is? No wonder this country is so God damn screwed up. The war on terrorism isn't takin' place in a big dirt hole a thousand miles from nowhere. They're Chinese or Japanese lookin' fellers. I can't tell the difference. They stand out like a sore thumb. I don't like foreigners on my property."

"That's too bad Lee left," Anne said. "We'd like to know more about what happened the day Steve got injured."

"Not so fast," Laton said. "You young folks always react too fast. Lee left you Steve's log book, and Lee filled in some details of the accident. He told me not to give it to them Feds, and it was only for you to read, not me. He knew you'd come callin' at some point. He said you were a true friend. The Feds came by asking lots of questions, but I told them I didn't see nothin' or know nothin' about the accident. They seemed pleased with that."

"I'm glad you didn't tell them anything," I said.

"Lee said he was going to drive up to Cottonwood and contact you," Laton said. "Actually I'm surprised he didn't. He also said he was going to send me a thank-you gift for lettin' them dig on my property. He did before—I usually received somethin' within a week of them leavin'. Not this year. I figured the accident shook him up so much that he didn't get around to it. In fact, after Steve was hauled away by Doc Dennis, I thought they would have showed up to investigate. Maybe, they talked to Lee in Cottonwood. They put up 'No Trespassing' signs on my property, and by federal order I can't even go out to the dig site. That's bullshit. Stay right there."

Laton went into the kitchen and eventually returned with a tattered, leather journal book layered with dust. There were dark blood stains on the cover that sent chills through me. Paging through it, I could tell Steve took meticulous notes.

The daily entrees were clear and straight forward. Steve and a group of eight—two scientists and six students—were excavating a Triceratops skeleton. He noted that they were working on the old Sieber ranch. In his introductory notes, Steve recorded that this was his twenty-third year working the area.

They had been working below Browny Butte. Steve's notes described their daily routine. They got out of their tents at six in the morning for breakfast which generally included bananas, cornflakes and coffee. Work started at the creek bottom in the crustacean formation. After two students located some unusual specimens in a cave and brought several down to him, Steve traced the formation up the side of the cliff to evaluate the bone fragments. Something must have been out of the ordinary, I realized, for him to go up that cliff. He was scared of heights. The other people spread out to work the creek bed. There were always at least two in a group in case someone got hurt.

It had been a rewarding summer. In past years it was not unusual to take out twenty or thirty specimen crates with each containing three or four bones. But this past summer, they hauled out even more crates. The day of the accident, a semi truck had just collected most of the crates and was about to head back to Montana State University.

The day was scorching. The crew was dressed as usual in jeans, red wing hunting boots, and T-shirts, wearing hats and sunscreen. Steve was perched on a ledge one hundred feet above the dry bed, brushing dirt off several skull fragments when he realized they were human bones. These, he noted, seemed especially fresh, not fossilized. As he removed the fragments, he discovered a small piece of a metal bracelet. He made out the letters "ale." On the next line were the numbers 12/46. He couldn't make out anything else, his notes said, in the shadow of the cliff.

At that point, Lee took over the journal. He wrote that Steve yelled down to him about the bones just as a few pebbles started showering down from above the ledge. Shortly, a rock slide was underway. A four-foot boulder hit Steve and sent him and his journal tumbling down the cliff.

Lee rushed to his side. Both of them served in Vietnam so they were used to trauma. Blood was everywhere. Steve, Lee wrote in the journal, looked as if he'd been hit by a mortar round. Steve looked at Lee with a weak smile and asked him if he was still a male. Looking at Steve's groin, Lee assured him that he was. Steve smiled, turned his head, and passed out. Lee thought he was dead.

Lee drove back to the Sieber ranch and called the Sheriff who said he'd send out the coroner. It was routine in rural Montana for the county coroner to show up at death scenes. Two hours later, the county coroner showed up with Doc Dennis, who explained his presence by saying he came because he was teaching the new county coroner how to evaluate patients.

Still, Dennis showing up this far from town just didn't fit, I thought as I read. The coroner was elected over a year ago and altruism wasn't one of my partner's virtues. He was after more than a teaching opportunity.

Next, the journal noted, workers took off their shirts and laid them together to cover Steve. Steve was conscious but in severe pain. After giving him a shot of morphine, Dennis determined his pelvis was broken in two places as well as bones in his jaw, neck, ribs, and both wrists.

Lee noted in the journal that Dennis seemed more concerned about what Steve saw up in the cave than about how Steve was doing.

I read on. The morphine soon started relieving his pain to the point where Steve thought he might not be injured at all. They assured him he had severe life-threatening injuries.

Doc Dennis asked Steve again what he saw in the cave. Steve never uttered a word to him. Lee acknowledged in his notes that they were warned at the beginning of summer by the border patrol not to go up the cliffs because of the potential for landslides.

Odd, I thought, I never remembered border agents patrolling the Hell Creek area, which was a long way from the Montana–Canada border.

When Lee wrote that Steve determined the skull bones in the cave were human and not from a dinosaur, my attention sprang into focus. Steve said the slide was started by the border patrolmen who'd been seen earlier in the area in plain clothes. Lee wondered if Steve was delusional. Steve then handed him the bracelet, and Lee placed it between the last two pages of the journal.

I picked it up, and examined it, touching the rough pointed knicked metal. It looked like it had been through a meat grinder. I put it in my pocket.

Dazed, Anne and I drove out to the accident site, but it was fenced off. We were parked about ten minutes when a border patrol vehicle pulled up alongside us. The Chinese officer told us to leave immediately or we would be arrested. I let them know who I was. The officer told me in no uncertain terms that that information and three dollars would get me a latte at the Glendive McDonald's restaurant. Rude, but we got the point. His strange cologne haunted me, bringing back the memory of the chase scene in the hallways of the hospital.

If Steve was right, why would federal agents try to kill him? What was the significance of the bracelet?

Anne and I were quiet as we drove back to the ranch. As we bounced along the bumpy road in the station wagon, I knew it was time to tell her about the disturbing lectures I had from Deeds and Chen.

"Anne, I hate to bring this up, especially after just what's happened, but I think you need to know some things about the Trinity Project," I said.

"I'm a big girl," she said. "I think I can handle it."

"The Chinese are footing the bill for most of it," I leaned over and looked at her, gripping the steering wheel. "One of the ways they're going to control costs is by denying patients care using health panels that determine when a person is no longer productive. Basically, it's the renewal of the old eugenics policies from the early twentieth century. Do you know much about Dr. Chen?"

"I know she's from Beijing and one of the foremost authorities on American life," she said. "Her books are best sellers."

"She controls the purse strings for the whole project!" I said. "One of her goals is bringing a universal health care plan to China based on our experience here. Even more important to the Chinese is gaining total control of this country. First, they hook Americans on the Trinity Health Plan by pouring trillions of dollars into it. After that, our government will be totally dependent on them for almost everything in our society. We'll go the way of Europe."

"Maybe you're being too negative," Anne said. "Their health panels might just make the right decisions. Does a ninety-year-old with Alzheimer's need a hip replacement or do we spend those health care dollars on preventative care for hundreds of God's school children?"

"When money's involved, how often is the right thing done?" I asked. "Chen said that there's not much difference between socialism and Christianity. Can you believe it?"

"Pastor Luke agrees with that," Anne said. "He says both groups champion looking out for God's lambs while the capitalists only look out for themselves."

"Anne, you're rejecting our parent's values—you know—reaping the rewards of hard work," I said.

"I'm rejecting their idols of money, big homes, and fancy cars," she said. "Pseudo sacrifice for the less privileged is almost worse than doing nothing. God hates lukewarm. He can tolerate cold people better, but he really longs for us to be hot and passionate about loving our fellow man."

"I sure hope Pastor Luke isn't involved with those border patrolmen," I said.

"There you go again, Dr. No," she said tersely. "Steve's head injury probably had him saying a lot of things that weren't true, but you're the doctor. If there's anyone who needs to get to church more, it's you. Don't ever talk to me about Pastor Luke again like that. I'm very happy with our life here in Cottonwood so don't screw it up."

"I'm not trying to," I said. "That's the last thing I want to do, but the Project has changed everything that I value."

"Are you including me in that ridiculous statement?" Anne asked.

"No," I said. Actually, however, I did.

It was eight in the evening by the time we arrived home. When we entered the house, the dogs were covering in the corner. My office desk drawers were open as was the door to our little closet safe. As far as I could tell, nothing was missing. "Well, it looks like the border patrol was here looking for illegal aliens," I said.

"Don't even try to be funny," Anne said. "This is really scary. Some transient must have been looking for sustenance."

"You think they'd take the stereo or TV," I said. "I think someone was trying to send me a message."

"Are you hearing voices, too?" she asked. "You're paranoid. Look, it was probably some poor soul looking for enough money to buy some food. After we pick up, I'm going to bed and read."

This wasn't just the shoulder, but the entire cold body I was getting. From the bathroom, I heard Anne yelling.

"Oh, Lord!" she screamed. "Don, come quick. Don hurry."

"What is it?" I asked as I ran into the room.

She pointed down to the toilet. The bloody head of our pet goat, Sarah, was stuffed in the toilet. Just because you're paranoid, it doesn't mean someone isn't out to get you.

∽ PART THREE ∽

INSPIRATION

Sunday
September 23, 2020

✐ TWELVE ✐

THE LARGEST STRUCTURE IN THE COUNTY, the Trinity Cornerstone Church was a three-story, L-shaped building with tan brick and a vaulted shake roof. Half the L was classrooms and the other half was the 666-seat worship center which also served as venue for community gatherings and concerts. To the left of the front entrance rose a thirty-five-foot tower topped by a thirty-foot spire that dwarfed the homes around it. The expansion of the old Lutheran Church into a showcase of faith was truly amazing.

There were four services, two on Saturday night headed by a rotating group of assistant pastors including Anne, and two on Sunday morning when Pastor Luke preached. The youth ministry was outstanding and eagerly attended. Junior high and high school students not only took part in Sunday school but also joined their parents for the church service. Anne said Pastor Luke believed that this was very important in reversing the downward trend of church attendance among young Christian adults.

The services were televised nationally. This was Pastor Luke's fifth year in the pulpit in Cottonwood, and you could tell he was

85

very comfortable. As he preached, high-definition television cameras were strategically placed around the worship hall and viewers around the country saw him silhouetted by a map of the world, with a massive wood cross to his left.

After an opening prayer, amen, and several worship songs, Luke started his sermon. He had an appealing, everyman delivery style with a slight southern drawl without one iota of arrogance or elitism. Tall and handsome, he was considered one of the most charismatic figures in the country.

"I have never felt so strongly that God is with us today," Luke said from the pulpit. "I want to welcome all of you from around northeastern Montana and also our national television audience to what will be my last regular sermon at the Cottonwood Trinity Cornerstone Church. Also, I want to extend a special greeting to our armed forces overseas and our good friends in China who are watching on our television broadcast. We're also streaming live on the internet.

"I hope in the future I will be welcomed back occasionally to see you all. The experience here over the last few years has been more wonderful than I could have ever expected. My beautiful wife, Verlane, and I have felt right at home. God has really shown his love to all of us. I would like to thank the Trinity Project for inviting me to take part in their transforming project that has provided the foundation to take our message nationally and then globally."

Pastor Luke wiped his hand across his brow and looked out at the pulpit, then to the cameras. "I have some very exciting news for you about what God has called me to do next, but first I would like to present a brief history of Christian theology that will make the news more meaningful. You may feel more like you're in the classroom at school than receiving my normal sermons based on the Bible, but, if we don't understand our religious past, then how can we understand how to make our faith grow in the future? The foundation of modern warfare is based on our understanding of the strategies employed by past, great military leaders like Alexander the Great, Washington, Grant, and Patton. We all know that every day Christians are battling their own war with Satan. This is a sermon that for sure none of you have heard before. Sound understanding is God's gift to the enlightened."

I definitely agreed with him on that point, but I hoped he kept it short.

"One of my greatest regrets over the last twenty years with many Christian churches is that they have ignored the power of Satan and his influence on sin in our lives," Luke said. "Much of our Christian history has been unfortunately influenced by him. Often the lessons learned from Adam and Eve, Jesus, and Job about how to deal with Satan are glossed over. Most of our time is spent on love. Caution, the Evil One needs our full attention. In the Old Testament God was with us. In the New Testament Jesus was for us, and since his death the Holy Spirit is within us, but Satan is ever present and all around us like a cloud of choking smoke. He has played a key role in destroying Christian unity! There are over three hundred different Protestant denominations, thanks to him."

There was some rustling in the pews, a few coughs, then stillness.

"All of you, hopefully by now, know our view on those subjects since we have dug deep into each one of them over the years," Pastor Luke said. "Satan worked on Christians through pride. Amen?"

"Amen." The congregation said in unison, voices rising.

Pastor Luke explained that over the centuries great thinkers and armies battled over Christian theology, and by the dawn of the sixteenth century, Christianity was in real trouble. The Catholic Church was faltering. That was in no small part due to corruption and to the belief that the only way to get to heaven was with Church assistance.

"Satan worked on Christians through pride," he said again. "Amen?"

"Amen." The congregation said in roaring voices.

He continued, describing how Martin Luther, who was an Augustinian monk and professor of theology at the University of Wittenberg in 1520, was excommunicated from the Roman Catholic Church for his beliefs. That was the beginning of the Reformation. Martin Luther and protestant reformers had three major principles: salvation by grace through faith alone, scriptures above all other authorities for Christian faith and practice, and the priesthood of all believers.

"Our church agrees with these principles that unite and make every member a missionary for God," Pastor Luke said.

He went on to explain how the Trinity Cornerstone Church believed that everyone has a chance to go to heaven by accepting Jesus as their personal savior. He, Pastor Luke, believed in free will. There was evil and chaos in this world brought on by Satan, but Jesus came to save us from the great Tempter. He reminded everyone that God is in control of even bad things, and that God is the only uncaused thing because he causes everything else.

"Satan worked on them through pride," he said. "Amen?"

"Amen." The congregation roared.

All right, I get the pride thing. Let's move on I thought as I gazed around the room filled with folks who had the appearance of hungry puppies.

Pastor Luke now went on to discuss Christianity in America. How pre-Revolutionary organized religion rested on government support: Congregationalists in New England and Episcopalians in New York, Maryland, Virginia, North and South Carolina, and Georgia. The state collected tithes from every citizen even if they didn't attend church. The money was used to build and maintain church properties. Clergymen were hired, paid and fired by the state also. Amazingly, in some colonies, church membership was a qualification for holding government office, but the pastors became lazy.

"Satan worked through the sense of entitlement," Pastor Luke said. "Amen?"

"Amen." The congregation roared methodically.

He told us about the importance of George Whitefield, the Oxford educated English minister and close personal friend of Benjamin Franklin, who founded the evangelical movement, and came to the colonies on several occasions to champion the colonies' independence from England. Many historians believe if it wasn't for Whitefield's influence, there never would have been a Revolutionary War and thus the United States. That's the type of Christian leadership we need today, Pastor Luke emphasized.

Pastor Luke stated Thomas Jefferson said to "keep Christianity simple, but keep it moral." Jefferson supported separation of church and state because the Baptists were being persecuted by the state supported Anglican Church in Virginia. Luke said he didn't agree with Jefferson's statement "we are saved by our good works which are within our power and not by our faith which is not within our control." He didn't like the Jefferson Bible either that generally only had quotes from Jesus and not his miracles. My friend Boots Carter, who didn't care for Jefferson, told me once that Jefferson wrote his own Bible so he could be accountable only to himself.

After the Revolutionary War there was shift from personal faith to fulfilling social obligations during the Second Awakening. "At that point," Pastor Luke said, "It wasn't about me but about the community." Satan was on the run, Pastor Luke said, but that all faded during the Industrial Revolution, when manufacturing replaced agriculture. The revivalist movement, which sprung up, greatly emphasized the individual experience. It returned the emphasis to 'me' and led to the worship of money, success, power and glory.

"Satan worked through idolatry," Pastor Luke said. "Amen?"

This was his most passionate amen yet. Idolatry was a common theme I'd heard from many evangelists in the last few years. The same ones that lived in big houses, took missionary trips around the world on their follower's money, and built shrines to themselves. I could hear in my mind the Commies saying "dirty capitalist pigs."

Our faith, Pastor Luke went on to say, must be anchored in the knowledge of the Bible. If the passionate work of a Boston shoe clerk, Dwight Moody, can lead to one of our great centers of Biblical teaching, then anything is possible. The Moody Bible Institute also trained women to lead church worship.

And on that note, Pastor Luke paused and gestured toward Anne. "I'd like to introduce Anne as our new pastor. Anne will do a terrific job leading this congregation"

Everyone in the room turned to us and applauded. Anne blushed, red as a rose hip. I felt very fortunate to be her husband.

When the applause died down, Pastor Luke continued to talk about the Christian evangelical movement through the late twentieth century, which perpetuated the celebrity pastor and its emphasis on enormous memberships, which meant larger Marriott-style churches and greater disillusionment from younger folks and the poor. Now more nonbelievers behaved by the golden rule than Christians whose divorce rates were higher than those that didn't have a personal relationship with Jesus. Religious passion had faded. He emphasized that we have to work hard to reach the heart, but also educate the individual mind to learn the teachings of Jesus.

"Satan works by placing a schism between knowledge and the heart," Pastor Luke said sternly. We can't gain our hearts and lose our minds. Amen?"

"Amen." The congregation roared.

"Most of you know my story," Pastor Luke said as he slowly moved from one side of the stage to the other. "I was a dirt-poor Oklahoma farm boy born in 1963 and early on preached the 'prosperity gospel.' God has a special purpose and plan for you, but now I'm more spiritually mature and believe God has a plan for all of us together. Remember, God chose us to love. We didn't choose him to love. There's a big difference. God controls everything."

He said Christ instructed him to found the Washita Cornerstone Church in Oklahoma City. He had received many accolades, but he made it clear that they weren't for him, they were for Jesus. He was especially honored to be the only pastor inducted by the prestigious National Cowboy and Western Heritage Museum into the Hall of Great Westerners.

Pastor Luke's weekly television show, now on the air for twenty-five years, had humble beginnings, being aired on a few stations in oil towns in Oklahoma and Texas, but by God's hand, he said, it now had the highest viewing audience of any religious show not only in this country but the world thanks to the support of the Trinity Project. By 2012, God had worked miracles in his life. Pastor Luke was recognized by ninety-two percent of Americans.

Critics, he warned, would try to discount the success by pointing to Cottonwood's small population, but the longings of the people of our fine community reflected those in the rest of the country. Look at the national TV and internet ratings. It was the longing for God. This is our test tube baby, he said. It's a winner.

With applause still ringing out, the covers of *Time* and *Newsweek* were projected on three large screens behind him.

"See our church in little old Cottonwood on the cover of both magazines," he said as he smiled. "They wanted me on it, but I told them that it's not about me. It's about God and our country. Recently, in Minneapolis I also gave interviews to the *The Wall*

Street Journal, *The New York Times*, and *USA Today*. Several TV shows including *60 Minutes* and *20/20* will soon be airing features about our vision."

"Listen, this is the most exciting news," Pastor Luke said as he held out his hands for silence, and a hush spread over the congregation. "This Friday Bruce Deeds, Dr. Dennis Anderson, and I will board the train to Minneapolis to present our experience here with officials who will decide the worthiness of a national movement that will soon bring a unified church and universal health care to our great country. Isn't that exciting? Pray for us. With all our success here in this fine community, we will launch the National Trinity Cornerstone Church. Simultaneously, Presidential candidate, Senator Bo Hart, will introduce a bill on the floor of the Congress for a universal health care plan based on the Trinity Health Plan. God does not want sixty million American souls without health coverage at the mercy of Satan."

Pastor Luke announced the opening of the Wright Bible Institute in Minneapolis next month to train future pastors. Because of the importance of separation of church and state, the national expansion of the Church was totally funded by non-U.S. governmental sources that were in place and ready to unite Christ's children for the first time in more than 2,000 years.

"Finally, God's people will be fulfilled through mutual love and caring and hearing one voice, the voice of our Savior," Pastor Luke said. "No American will ever be left behind or unhealthy. Satan will be packing and heading back to Hell once and for all. Amen?"

"Amen." The congregation repeated, applauding thunderously. There was a rustling of coats and programs as everyone stood to give Pastor Luke a standing ovation.

"We believe our national church concept will be well received," he said. "Christians are disillusioned with organized church mainly because of bad leadership and rigid rules that punish the weakest and most vulnerable in our society. Is there a Christian who hasn't been disappointed by their pastor? My staff and I will personally retrain the pastors of today and train the pastors of tomorrow. In 2020, almost all churches are suffering financially, in no small part due to weak leadership. Last year alone almost 10,000 closed. No wonder more than 90,000 church elder boards have already contacted us."

Wow! Those numbers were hard to believe!

"Pain," he said. "Alas, there will be pain. Some pastors won't pass the training and thus be dismissed, but new and better ones will take their place. The graduates will also be guaranteed a very attractive salary that will be subsidized by the Institute. To attract the best and brightest in any profession, you need to offer an attractive employment package. Say amen if you're listening to me."

"Amen," the congregation spoke, their voices again rising up in unison.

"Thank you so much and God bless you," Pastor Luke said as tears flowed down his cheeks. "I love every one of you. Remember, we have all found God's purpose for us in the Trinity Cornerstone Church. Pray for your leadership and be submissive to them, and God bless America and China too."

With applause still ringing out Pastor Luke hushed the audience once more. "I have more good news," he said. "I would like to introduce to you a Christian man whose vision made this all possible."

The applause began again.

"Brother Deeds would like to take a few minutes to talk a little bit more about health care," Luke smiled, wiping tears from his eyes.

That was odd, I thought. When I met with Brother Deeds, I didn't think God was that important to him. I leaned forward, curious about what he had to say.

Deeds faced the congregation, scanning the room to make sure everyone was listening.

"Pastor Luke and I strongly believe that the church should lead the fight for universal health care," he said sternly. "Remember Pastor Luke's sermon on Dietrich Bonhoeffer, the Lutheran minister who resisted the German Nazis in World War II and ended up being imprisoned and hung in 1945 for his beliefs? He witnessed the complete failure of the German Protestant Church to face Nazism. Will we fail to face the stark reality that the richest country in the world doesn't provide health insurance for all of its citizens?"

"*Nooooooo!*" the congregation roared.

"Where was the church when someone needed to oppose slavery?" Deeds asked. "Where was the church when Native Americans were almost exterminated? And where is the church when the great moral issue of our generation is debated? No where until now. The Trinity Cornerstone Church is not going to stand by as another travesty unfolds. Every American has the right to health care. Our church fight for this goal would be proudly called by Bonhoeffer, costly grace. We may initially suffer for our beliefs, but that pales in comparison to what Jesus suffered for us. I know our suffering will lead to victory."

There was thunderous applause.

I was astounded at this man's wealth of information but my backsides were beginning to go numb. I'd had enough preaching for one day. I shook my head to stay awake.

Pastor Luke came back to the pulpit.

"Our country is one nation under God with liberty and justice and equality for all. Amen and thank all of you wonderful followers of Jesus," Pastor Luke said as he concluded his talk and waved good-bye.

Everyone stood and applauded for what seemed an eternity.

Before I stood to take communion, my beeper went off. I walked outside to answer it. It was one of the nurses at the hospital clarifying orders on a patient. I reminded her that I wasn't on call and to call Dennis. She apologized, lamenting about the ongoing problem with the electronic records. She also wanted me to dictate a summary of what happened to Lightfoot in the E.R. Sighing, I admitted that I had forgotten that one—and it was a hospital rule that dictations needed to be done immediately. I called the automated dictation number and completed my report.

By the time I finished, communion was over.

✌ THIRTEEN ✌

IT WAS IMPORTANT TO PASTOR LUKE that everyone broke bread together after the service. We arrived at the red brick Catholic Church, a sprawling, one-story building that now served as a lunch hall, where lunch tables replaced the old pews. By the time we arrived, the place was packed. The Lutherans and Catholics had argued for years which church was larger—now it didn't matter. The smaller churches, the Methodist, Congregational, Assembly of God, and several others had been transformed into community support centers.

As we gathered at the tables, the room was buzzing with easy conversation about weather, local sports, and produce prices. Everyone seemed content and happy in a weird sort of way. Lot's of smiles. Anne and I traded small talk about settling in at the ranch, and everyone seemed excited that Anne was going to be their new pastor. They all said she wowed them when she gave several of the Saturday night sermons.

After dessert, Judge Bastar announced that we had a surprise guest visiting us. It was Senator Bo Hart, the most popular politician to come out of Montana since Mike Mansfield. The hall erupted with cheers and applause.

"Hi everyone," Bo said as he waved. "It's nice being back in beautiful Cottonwood. Wasn't that an informative talk by Pastor Luke? That man is a visionary."

I didn't know if I would totally agree with Bo about that.

"I'm so excited to introduce the Trinity Health Care bill in Congress in a few weeks," Senator Hart continued. "I wanted to make sure my Presidential bus tour stopped here. Tonight, I'll give a speech in Bismarck and then on to Fargo. I wanted to personally thank all of you for being such great Americans and fine Christians. Bruce Deeds, Dr. Dennis Anderson, and Pastor Luke have done a remarkable job. They asked me to speak at church this morning, but you've heard enough speeches. Besides, I can't take credit for all their wonderful efforts. I want to assure you my run for the Presidency will be bold and faith-driven. I'm running not for me, but for you and for God. I've prayed, and he has told me to go for it, and I am."

Applause rang out, and after a few minutes he left the stage to mingle. The crowd kept applauding, men slapping one another on the back. Anne and I were far enough back that I knew we wouldn't get close to him for nearly an hour. Anne wanted to meet him, but I needed to take a walk before we met with Pastor Luke. Politicians didn't excite me that much even if it was Bo "Charisma" Hart. It was hard to pull Anne away, but I needed some down time.

We strolled through neighborhoods where I rode my bike and played with friends, along cracked sidewalks past houses that seemed smaller and the yards a little more packed together than I remembered. Freshly painted homes of my youth were now drab reminders of tough times. The Project brought money to the community but just enough to keep it afloat. Bicycles and swing sets were replaced by rocking chairs, a sign of an aging America. Anne showed much-appreciated patience as I reminisced about fond childhood memories, but before we knew it, it was time for our meeting with Pastor Luke.

Back at the church, we entered Luke's second floor office. The walls were lined with honorary certificates and photographs of him standing with presidents and religious leaders. On the wall behind his desk was a dark, monochromatic image with haunting overtones of an old man who had his hands on the shoulders of a kneeling young man as several others looked on. Their faces were mesmerizing.

Luke was sturdy and handsome with thick black hair combed back and held tight in place. His teeth were slightly over-bleached, but he had a genuine smile, disarming eye contact and a firm handshake that seemed to signal the fact that he had it all. I smelled Old Spice cologne.

"Please sit down," Pastor Luke said with a fixed smile. "I guess I'm the last of the group to talk to you. Dr. Lewis, I hope you're settled in. We are so happy Anne is joining our team. Please forgive me for wearing this heavy makeup. It embarrasses me. For HD TV they insist on spraying it on an inch thick. The producer wants to minimize my flaws which are many. Anyway, how did you like the service, Dr. Lewis?"

I was fixated on the image behind him.

Pastor Lewis turned around to glance at it, then back at me. "Dr. Lewis, I can tell you admire my picture," he said. "You have good taste. It is my favorite print and is filled with Christian symbolism. Are you familiar with Rembrandt?"

"Very little, I must admit," I said. I was ready, instead, to impress him with my knowledge of western art. "Coming from Montana, I have art books on western artists and love authors like Rick Stewart and Brian Dippie. My favorite artist is Charles M. Russell, who lived in Great Falls. He is the only artist honored in Statutory Hall in Washington."

"If there's one thing men of the plains have in common, it's a love for Charles Russell," Pastor Luke said. "I don't think he painted any religious scenes, did he?"

"Not many although he did paint a few. Wise men on camels I believe," I said. "His most famous painting that alluded to a higher power was *When the Land Belonged to God*."

"Interesting. Well, the original of this image, *Return of the Prodigal Son*, hangs in The Hermitage in St. Petersburg, Russia," Pastor Luke said. "It was acquired by Catherine the Great in 1766 for that great museum. The young man kneeling is the younger son of the father who has his hands on his son's shoulders. His older brother is standing on the right. If you look at his face, you can tell he isn't happy with his brother's return. Are you familiar with the story?"

"I'm not," I said. "My Biblical knowledge isn't what it should be, but I'm trying."

"I like your honesty, Don," Pastor Luke said. "All of us have a lot to learn about Christianity."

The painting, Pastor Luke told us, was painted late in Rembrandt's life after three of his children and his wife had died. He was declared insolvent and his possessions were sold off. From that point on, Rembrandt was never free of debt and died in 1669, a poor and lonely man.

"Rembrandt related to all three men, as I think every human does," Pastor Luke said. "The younger son was brash, self-confident, a spendthrift, sexual, and arrogant. He betrayed family values, and by asking for his inheritance early, shamed his father. His story is one of redemption. Our goal is to bring back those that have left the church so they can accept Jesus as their personal savior. The great rebellion started with Adam and Eve and will end when everyone is united under one church. No matter what anyone loses, they need to know that they are still their Father's child, and God is enough."

"Amen," I said eager to earn brownie points with him and Anne.

"I like your enthusiasm, Don," Pastor Luke said. "Well, many stop there, but this is also a parable of the Father's love, tenderness, mercy, and forgiveness.

"Please go on," Anne said passionately.

"To me, the elder son represents traditional churches and lack of concern for each other," Pastor Luke said. "The elder son is inwardly lost and is wandering away from his father, but won't outwardly admit it. The elder son is unhappy and unfree. He is resentful, proud, angry, selfish, and jealous."

"I could have never understood all that on my own," I said.

"All of us have a lot to learn about Christianity," Pastor Luke said. "More than any other in the Gospels, this story expresses the boundlessness of God's compassionate love. It's what the Trinity Project is all about. You two weren't here five years ago for my first sermon series, but it was a ten-week teaching dissecting this parable. All of our members need to appreciate it. I just love sharing this passage, Luke 15: 1-3, 11-32, with new believers."

"I'm sorry I missed it," I said with conviction feeling almost mesmerized by his charismatic powers."

"Just as Jesus is the cornerstone of the church, let this church model be the cornerstone of a new religious awakening in America, the Third Great Awakening," Pastor Luke said. "God is love. Our church is love, and we are altogether in love. We Christians need to stick together. No one should be denied what another

Christian has. Health care is a good example. Power to all Christian people, just not the rich."

"Well, Pastor Luke, this sounds like an odd mix of religion and socialism." I said in reflex response that I regretted the moment I blurted it out. I guess the spell was broken.

Anne grimaced, shaking her head.

"I note a hint of resistance," Pastor Luke said, glaring at me. "Are you a doubting Thomas? " He shrugged and instantly switched to his 100-watt smile.

"Maybe, a little," I said reluctantly, but I was trying to be authentic.

"In time, we will win you over," Pastor Luke said confidently. "As a Christian, don't you embrace socialism and equality for all? Look, my father was a capitalist and womanizer who struggled with an internet pornography addiction. He eventually left our family to fend for ourselves in a small shack in Oklahoma. We had a strong sense of abandonment. He lived for the pay check, and at the same time he was a church elder. His life was consumed by meetings. He especially liked to have them at night. Our family assumed he scheduled them to avoid dealing with us and also to rendezvous with other women. Mom drank at night after she put us to bed. I hate people driven by money and material things. It is the devil in their hearts. It's idolatry. Jesus should be our idol and nothing else. He should be our only treasure, only, only treasure. That's undeniable.

Jesus hung out with the poor. Jesus would champion socialism not capitalism. Capitalism is dead in this country, and it makes God happy. I give 90 percent of my royalties back to the church. No one can doubt my motives."

"We certainly don't," Anne said, giving me a disappointed look.

"I'm just worried about the Chinese getting a stronger hold on this country," I said. "I don't like them funding America's health care. Maybe, I'm just old-fashioned."

"'Gratitude is in the past,' C. S. Lewis, the great Christian apologist, stated, 'love is in the present, and fear, avarice, lust, and ambition are in the future,'" Luke said. "The devil works in the future. Capitalists work in the future through their greed and fear tactics. Dr. Lewis, you fear the Chinese without a rational reason. Satan is working on you. They are intelligent people and will do the right thing. There is no evil in a foreign country that supports our church. In the last five years, the Chinese government has become increasingly tolerant of Christianity. They have agreed to start letting us train pastors at the Wright Institute who will plant churches there. They would much rather deal with Christians than the Buddhists in Tibet and Muslim Xinjiang. When I found out that the Chinese would help fund the Trinity Project, I made several trips to Beijing to talk with government officials. Dr. Susan Chen assured me that their government was tolerant of Christians and were very impressed with my vision for both countries."

"Who wouldn't be?" Anne said as she gave me an irritated look.

Pastor Luke told us that in China there are twelve million Protestants, five million Catholics as well as some three hundred million more Christians who meet in local house churches. The Chinese government realized that freedom of faith is something not even history's most repressive governments could fully snuff out. The leaders in China appreciated the power of Christianity and embraced it over any other religion. Many of them, Pastor Luke added, even watched his TV show.

"Your words are like words from God," Anne said.

He was a greater talker, but words from God? That seemed a bit much. But right now wasn't the time to get into it with her. If she adored this man, then who was I to throw water on her fire? Her happiness was what mattered most to me. I realized long ago I needed to be more flexible about other's opinions, especially someone I loved.

I swallowed hard and cleared my throat. "Pastor Luke, I appreciate all you've done for Anne, this community, and country," I said. "I wish you nothing but success in the future. You have a purpose-driven life like few others, and I know God is pleased with all your efforts."

I figured I better leave on a high note so I didn't get in trouble with Pastor Luke, Anne, and the guy upstairs.

❧ FOURTEEN ❧

L
ATER SUNDAY AFTERNOON, we stopped at the Sheridan County Care Center that rested on top of a hill overlooking Cottonwood. Built in the sixties, it was the pride of the community. It still looked new, especially after the Trinity Project remodeled and expanded it. Unlike some care centers in many urban areas, the staff loved taking care of their elderly residents, many of whom they'd known for years. There was never a concern with patient mistreatment. The smell of freshly baked bread wafted through the air as we walked through the front entrance.

Ann and I came to visit my mother who, despite all her years in the West, still had a southern accent. Her room was modest but neat. On her nightstand were pictures of our family when she was a young mother: I was the youngest. Linda, who was ten years older, lived in Portland, and Cathy, who was five years older, and lived in idyllic Sisters, Oregon. They got back to Cottonwood when they could, but one of the many hardships in rural America is having your children and grand-children live so far away. When you left Cottonwood for the big city there was always a feeling of inferiority, especially back in the seventies and eighties. When people in Portland would ask me where I was from, and I told them Montana, they made me feel like a hillbilly. That's perhaps one reason why rural kids always competed well with their urban rivals. They tried harder.

Mom and Dad met during the WW II, when he was stationed in Georgia. Like many men heading off to the uncertainties of war, Dad fell in love and married her before shipping off to the South Pacific. Shortly thereafter, pregnant, she headed by train to live with her in-laws in Cottonwood. While Grandpa Len was nice to her, mom found little to like in Grandma and my dad's sisters, and this never changed throughout the years. The Cinderella story comes to mind minus the Prince. I liked them all and never embraced Mom's darkness.

After the war, dad and mom raised my two sisters and me in a modest ranch style house in Cottonwood. In the summer we spent more time at the ranch, although Mom was never really fond of ranch life. She never shook her Southern roots. While she was a good mother, she was unable to show affection to the rest of the family, a fact we all came to resent. Her main pleasure in life was smoking three packs of Winston cigarettes a day.

Mom never lost her southern accent even though she spent her adult life in Montana. Alzheimer's disease settled in on her several years ago along with a bad heart and poor circulation. They still caught her sneaking cigarettes. Sometimes she was lucid while other times she seemed far away. This was a lucid day. We both hugged her and exchanged small talk.

I noticed unopened bills and statements. It looked like we'd be taking over some accounting responsibilities. I reassured her that I would take care of everything. Anne and I listened while Mom reminisced in great detail for almost an hour about raising our family. She almost never mentioned dad since his suicide. It was upsetting to me that she couldn't forgive him.

Finally, after Anne and my mother had been visiting for a piece of time, I looked at my watch. Thankfully, it was time to go. We hugged and said our goodbyes. Five minutes after we left, she wouldn't remember our visit. We probably did it more for ourselves than for her.

Down the hall, Pastor Kiser rested in a rocking chair outside his room. Even though he couldn't hunt anymore, I heard he still loved flying his Cessna. Cloudless skies and unlimited visibility made Sheridan County an ideal setting for sightseeing from the air. He said he felt closest to God at 10,000 feet.

Almost everything I learned or should have learned growing up about Christianity, I learned from Pastor Tim Kiser. I still called him Pastor Kiser. The thought of using his first name seemed inappropriate. The Gospel, redemption, sanctification, justification, communion, and baptism were concepts that he preached to me as a child but faded in my adult memory and heart. At the time, church seemed more like a form of punishment. When you're young and death is a concept and not a reality, you don't seem to take Christianity seriously. I didn't look forward to hunting trips with him and my dad because he grilled me on Bible verses. I was more concerned about not upchucking in the back seat of our Chevy Impala station wagon from motion sickness and cigarette smoke.

"I know Anne's been coming by to see you after she sees Mom, and we're both going to make it a priority to come by and see you after Sunday church," I said. "Did you ever think I would attend church as an adult and marry a pastor?"

"Well, I wondered about you at times, but I never lost faith in you," Pastor Tim chuckled. "Miracles do occur. Old men can still dream dreams."

"It sure is exciting to see the Trinity Cornerstone Church so successful," I said. "What a coup to have such an outstanding man of God preaching and broadcasting nationally from little old Cottonwood. If you read it in a book, you wouldn't believe it."

"I champion Pastor Luke's dedication and hard work!" Pastor Tim said. "He is the great spiritual leader in this country today, and even the main stream media is paying attention to the miracle in Cottonwood. Any church is only as good as its leadership. He seems to be a man with true passion to pursue God, and I don't believe it's for his own self gain. Passion is contagious. It seems lately in this country that the different denominations spend too much time fighting over matters that didn't matter to Jesus."

"I got the feeling at the church luncheon that everyone was happy, but I don't know about how passionate they are," I said stirring up the pot once more. "They seemed a little weird."

Anne didn't like that comment.

"You have totally misread things," Anne said. "Dr. Skeptic here can't accept the fact that a community can come together with love for each other. He equates passion with jumping in the aisles."

"Pastor Luke and I are from different times and religious values," Pastor Tim said. "I'm more traditional and conservative. Pastor Luke grew up in an era of social activism filled with doubts about the different organized religions. Today, this country is attracted to those that preach the spirit of love and champion the liberation of the oppressed. Pastors don't like to talk much about Satan. Belief and skepticism are on the rise. I didn't have to address skepticism. His job is tougher."

"Was Jesus a socialist?" I asked. Chen's and Pastor Luke's statements had disturbed me. "I remember the passage about it's harder for a rich man to get to heaven than a camel to go through the eye of a needle."

"You definitely need more Bible study," Anne said and laughed.

"There's nothing wrong with being rich, but most rich men worship their money more than God," Pastor Tim said. "Money is one of many idols. I think he wanted all of us to use the talents he gave us to succeed to the fullest of our abilities, but we also need to help the less privileged."

"Anne won't like me saying this, but I worry that the religious component of the Project is only there to convince everyone to buy into their government control of health care and then every other aspect of our lives," I said.

"You're way off base," Anne said. "I hope you're not talking to anyone else like this. No one will want to be your patient."

"Well, I guess I'm at least consistent," I said. "You're right. I need to work on that. However, knowing that the Project is all about entitlements really bugs me. I think we should only be entitled to life, liberty, and the pursuit of happiness. It seems like everyone has a chip on their shoulder and is looking for a hand-out. That's an America I don't understand or like."

"Give it some time, Don," Pastor Tim said. "You're tired, and I heard about your friend, Steve, passing on. What a waste, but he's in heaven now."

"I totally agree with that statement," I said nodding my head in approval.

"You need to remember human nature," Pastor Tim said. "It's normal to have a little criticism make you angry and a little rejection make you depressed. A little praise raises one's spirits and a little success excites. Often we can feel like a boat being whipped around in the storm of life if we don't stay anchored and committed to our faith. Believe in Pastor Luke until proven otherwise, but remember; only God never needs proving."

"Well said, Pastor Tim," Anne said smiling. "You're wonderful."

"I've got an idea," I said. "Anne's going to Regina tomorrow to visit her friend and shop for some good old Canadian horse tack. Why don't we go up to the cemetery? I need to put some fresh flowers on dad's grave. The dead may be the only conservatives left in this county."

"That sounds great!" Pastor Tim said. "I'll bring your mother. I haven't been up there in at least a year. Some folks find cemeteries scary, but to me it's like being at the Elgin Café with Shorty and old friends. The only difference is that I can preach and no one objects. Two o'clock would work for me. I don't get up and get going very early anymore. I'm not going flying again until Friday. I won't even ask if you want to go since I know you probably still get motion sick and are afraid of flying."

"You're right about both," I said. "See you tomorrow!"

∽ FIFTEEN ∽

THE ONLY SOUND WE HEARD driving down the hill was the scraping of the windshield wipers. It was five o'clock. A light rain showered down on us from the steel gray clouds. The clean, sharp smell of nitrogen from lightning filled my senses and renewed my spirits. Anne and I were quiet as we drove along, both of us thinking. We decided to eat at the Dairy Queen on the way home. It wasn't exactly five-star dining, but I didn't need that experience any more. The dogs had our leftover hamburgers to look forward to when we got home.

After we fed the horses, we had a glass of wine and planned to spend the evening figuring out everything that had happened over the weekend. Could the border patrol be responsible for Steve's injuries? Did Dennis overdose him on purpose? Is God a socialist?

We were just opening the bottle, when the phone rang. It was our neighbor, Ray Koler. He thanked us for letting him take part in our wedding and asked if we could come over. His voice was edged with panic. That was the last thing we wanted to do, but I knew he wouldn't ask if it wasn't important.

Ray's spread was perhaps the nicest one in the county. His home was a rambling five-thousand-square-foot ranch where I used to love hanging out with his two sons. They had a basketball court, swimming pool, pool table, and color TV. When I couldn't get into town to play with the Timmerman boys, I headed to his place. The home seemed incredibly big and empty since his wife, Jeanne, passed away.

Ray was a very successful family attorney in town. My Dad trusted him completely. Ray knew his law and had a disarming, down-to-earth way of presenting matters, due in part to his father being a rancher and farmer. There was no time on a ranch for a big ego, just hard work.

When we arrived, he motioned us to the round pen. I smelled booze on his breath.

"You know there's been a lot of strange activity around here," Ray said, looking from side to side. "I think our houses are bugged. I saw an unmarked white van with a satellite dish on top of it driving around here the day our homes got broken into. Too bad we were gone. I would have plugged the bastards. We haven't had a robbery around here for years. Back then, some old drunk from town just stole a few chicken eggs and pissed on my steps. This time they just threw things around the house and didn't steal anything. They planted bugs."

"What makes you think our houses are bugged?" Anne asked.

"Right now, that van is parked up on Squatter's Butte looking right down on our ranches," Ray said almost in a whisper.

"I was told they are checking out sites for a new cell tower," Anne said.

"Bullshit!" Ray said raising his voice. "They have one tower two miles from here. Cell towers have a range of at least five miles. Nope, they're bugging us."

"Why would they do that?" I asked although that the conclusion wasn't so far-fetched after the weekend's events. "Have you found a bug?"

"No, but it's not hard to figure out after our conversation Friday afternoon," Ray said. "They don't want anything to happen before they can submit their final report on their Project results. It's all about power and money. Be careful what you say to the Trinity boys."

Anne and I looked at each other. Had Ray spent too much time alone on the ranch? Was the alcohol affecting his logic? Isolation can cause paranoia. On the other hand, maybe he was right on target. He was one of only a handful in the entire county that hadn't bought into the health plan, and he refused to attend church. I was going to tell him about the goat head in the toilet, but I figured that would put him over the top.

"I think you're on to something," I said. "I'm having a hard time digesting all the changes. We'll be careful."

"Ray, don't get upset," Anne said. "But I think you and Don have been drinking some bad well water. We'll find out about that van. Don't worry. I'm sure it's nothing. Maybe, they were looking for oil."

"I don't like changes," Ray said, spitting out some chew. "They won't get me to buy in or go to that church. Sorry about that, Anne. Find out what's going on with that van. I'm old and not needed anymore, but I haven't lost my common sense."

We left his ranch, unsettled. In the rear view mirror I could see Ray pointing his 12 gauge Model 50 Winchester shotgun in the direction of the butte. I figured I better get mine out and load it.

∽ PART FOUR ∽

REFLECTION

Monday
September 24, 2020

⚜ SIXTEEN ⚜

I WAS RELIEVED to have a week off before starting my doctor
duties in town. I did have to cover Doc Dennis at the Poplar
clinic tomorrow, but otherwise I had time to do some detec-
tive work. There were lots of questions to be answered.

Anne made sure she had her passport before she drove the
hundred and twenty-mile trip to Regina. The border used to
be a quick stop on the way to Canada, but now it resembled an
Afghani outpost. I heard that the Chinese border guards were
unfriendly protectors of their adopted mother state and enjoyed
dismantling cars and strip-searching drivers, especially women.
When I was a kid, the two border patrolmen were good friends
of my father. In the sixties, the Canadians supported the local
economy in Cottonwood, when their dollar was worth more than
ours. Even when their dollar lost value, they continued to frequent
the local bars where the booze was still cheaper. The alcohol tax
in Canada didn't seem to curb the rate of alcoholism. Many a
drunken Canadian headed for the border only to take their last
breath on dead man's curve. The directors of socialized medicine
in Canada were probably thrilled to have one less on the plan.

I headed to town to confront Olaf about his missing rent payments. Perhaps he had a good excuse. I hoped so. I had time to kill before Stu Boy interviewed me at the *Cottonwood Herald*, where he planned to run a feature about me so the locals could learn about my life outside of Cottonwood. Talking about myself was one of my least favorite activities, but according to my clinic contract, I had to be available to the media.

It was difficult returning back to the store where my father and grandfather had made their living. In grade school, it was my job to sweep the floors before closing time at six o'clock. Every Sunday, Dad and I threw a sticky powder on the oiled wood floors to remove more dirt. That oil smell greeted me when I entered. Dad, it seemed, should be right around the corner.

Olaf was eight years older than me. His blonde crew cut had turned gray, but he was still in good shape. We had spent many hours together delivering furniture and appliances. I liked him, or at least I used to, when I was growing up. He was always a straight shooter, and he didn't resent me or try to brown-nose me just because I was the boss's son.

Built in 1913 by George Bolster, the hardware store was the first two-story building in town and carried Bolster's name etched in stone above the second-floor windows. My grandfather's generosity to the children of the Depression was a public relations bonanza for decades. Every morning he set bicycles out on the sidewalk, paying particular attention to the children who paused to admire them, returning daily to dream about owning one. Grandfather Len gave them pep talks about getting out and earning money by picking rock, running errands or mowing lawns. He believed in relying on yourself and not hitting parents up for money. Kids bought bicycles for twenty-five cents down, no interest, and the rest on time. He never got stuck with a dead beat, and his generosity made responsible citizens out of a lot of poor kids who had nothing going for them except for my grandfather's hope and trust.

The 1930s massive, National Cash Register was still in use. I loved pushing the buttons and cranking the handle to open it up. Old court records were stored in one of the back rooms upstairs, a dark musty room where my love for history was born as I spent hours there reading about crimes that took place in the 1910s and 1920s. Before World War II, part of the upstairs was a mortuary. The pipes that drained the blood were still there. The elevator that used to handle the bodies now carried freight. The upstairs was a great but scary place to play hide-and-seek.

When Olaf greeted me, I was looking up at the beautiful tin ceiling tiles.

"Hi, Donnie," he said, extending his hand and smiling. "I heard you were back in town. I never thought you would be a doctor. I guess I can't call you the little professor anymore. We sure need another one since Doc Peters drowned last spring. That was a horrible shock to the community. Everyone seems to be dying off in this town, just like the economy. The farmers are almost all gone. Business has been terrible. Thank God for the Trinity."

I shook his hand. "It's tough times around here." I sensed he knew why I was paying him a visit, and he was softening me up with the bad news.

"It's hard to make a living on nuts and bolts," he said. "Thankfully, our health care is covered, and believe it or not, I'm going to church. For the first time in my life, it makes me feel good for the rest of the week."

"That sounds real positive," I said. "I'm glad you're going to church. Say, I hate to bring it up, but what's happened to the rent you're supposed to be paying mom? We would have appreciated a phone call."

"I knew your mom's memory wasn't good, and I didn't want to upset her," Olaf said abruptly. "I was just going to call you this morning about it."

"Well, I'm a little disappointed," I said. "I've been here a week. You could have called me sooner."

"The Trinity promised all of us some stimulus money at the first of the month," he said, his voice snappy, indignant. "I was going to pay all of the back rent once I received it. Now, they say it won't arrive until next month. Money isn't heaven sent, you know. I'm telling you the truth. It's hard times all over for small businesses. Without the help of the Project, we'd be sunk. Besides, after all the years of loyal service I gave your family, I expected your mother would've given me a better deal on the store."

"She sold the store to you on a contract for half the assessed value and no interest," I said annoyed about his ingratitude. "No bank would give you a loan because of your credit history."

"That deal doesn't look so good now with the never-ending recession," he said. "She won't renegotiate. She should have just been satisfied with what I already paid her and handed the title over to me."

"Are you kidding me?" I asked incredulously.

"That's reality to someone who hasn't had it handed to them," he said.

His voice shook, angry, unapologetic. It was clear he felt entitled to a better deal. We talked some more, but it was clear that he thought we had enough family money. I guess socialism had also taken hold in downtown Cottonwood.

"What's going to happen when the Project stops the stimulus payments?" I asked.

"The Project guaranteed us at least ten more years of support," he said. About halfway through that I'm going to sell the store and move to Arizona."

"I've counted seven employees on the floor," I said looking around. "Dad used to have only three. Why don't you cut back on the overhead?"

"It works out that we actually get more subsidies by hiring more employees," he said. "The cutoff is seven."

With that, we abruptly said our good-byes.

I walked out the front door and gazed over at the town's one stop light. It brought back memories of the Fourth-of-July parade, when it was turned off. I could still see the grand procession: the school band, tractors, dignitaries, and my dad in his Shriner's garb walking down the street throwing out candy to the kids. When I was four, I played the Maytag family baby, getting to ride in the baby stroller. By the time the parade was over, my buddies complained about the horse shit all over their shoes, but I was sitting pretty.

The grand finale every year was Pastor Tim flying his two-seater plane, dropping paper plates stapled with gift certificates from the local downtown businesses. I fought over those plates as hard as I did trying to catch a home run ball hit by Willie Mays in the 1965 All Star game in Minneapolis. Tim then landed his plane on Main Street to a round of cheers. He always had the mayor, Shorty, in the cockpit behind him who rose and led all of us in "God Bless America." It doesn't get any better.

Now, the organizations my father was so involved in—the Lion's Club, Masons, Elks, and Shriners—were gone. They were too exclusionary and divisive for the Trinity's vision of the new America. The businessmen instead belonged to the Trinity Service Club.

I headed up the street toward the *Herald's* office for my interview.

Walking north, I waited at the curb as the light turned green. One car was stopped there. Wind stirred the dust around, but it never blew away. There was "Abigail's Jewelry Store" run by Doc Dennis's wife, my first serious girlfriend. Doc Dennis wanted the sign to say "Anderson's Jewelry Store," but because Abigail's father set her up in business, Dennis didn't have much say.

Peering through the store window, I could tell that time had treated Abigail well since I'd last seen her at our ten-year reunion. In high school she'd fancied herself as Ali McGraw in *Love Story*. There was a certain resemblance. She smiled and looked at me just like she did when we dated in high school.

We all wanted to change the world back then and take our girlfriends with us. As freshmen and sophomores, Dennis and I waited our turn as the upper classmen courted her. Our junior and senior year, we fought over her.

As young men, we both spent a lot of time at Abigail's home, dreaming someday to go to medical school and marry Abigail. Dennis's dream came true.

"It's great to see you!" Abigail said with a warm smile.

"You look great!" I said enthusiastically.

"So do you!" She said.

"Who would ever think that I would be back in Cottonwood in partnership with Dennis?" I said.

"Not me," she said as we made small talk. Then, she shook her head. "You've probably heard the gossip that our marriage is on the rocks or more like in the sewer. This Trinity Project has consumed Dennis. He's not the man I married. It won't be a secret long so I'll tell you I'm leaving on the train Friday to stay with my children in California for a few months. I may not come back. That's the day the Project concludes, and Dennis and the others take the train to Minneapolis. I'll be heading west. He'll be heading east. I can't wait."

"I'm sorry to hear that," I said. I stood motionless, too stunned to say more. I was amazed she'd made it this long. Her mellow disposition was definitely gone. I avoided talking about the Trinity.

"Dennis is upset with me because I haven't been going to church," she said. "After dad died, I was underwhelmed by the church members' compassion. Also, Dennis and dad were fighting over hospital policies, and you know Dennis, he always wins the battles. Dennis and the Project only care about the bottom line. That made dad and me bitter. I used to go on walks with dad, and he cried the whole time about the way his patients were being treated. They were just a statistic to the Project. Since I'm about the only one in town not attending church services, I've been ostracized. I guess you really don't know about someone until you tell them no."

She paused and looked at me closely.

"It's strange," she said. "It's like that church has a hypnotic control over people. I know Pastor Luke is incredibly charismatic, but things around here have just gotten ridiculous. Even my best girl friends from high school have changed. They've turned on me."

We stared at each.

"Well, I hope I get to see you again before you leave," I said.

She smiled and gave me a hug.

✑ SEVENTEEN ✑

STU BACON was the third generation of his family to run the *Herald*, since it had published its first edition in 1908. His pickle-nose and large belly belied that fact that he was a great editor and reporter. His office was lined with Cottonwood Wildcat team photos which, decades later, were still undisturbed except for being a little crooked on the wall. After a bout with early-stage emphysema, he chewed on stogies instead of smoking them. The conversation was easy, and I gave him a general update on what I'd been doing since high school. I was more anxious to ask him how life in town had changed over the last few years.

"The Project seems to have been real good for the community," I said, watching his face closely.

"You bet!" He said, resting his hands on his belly. "Every element of the Project has been wonderful. The government should be the instrument for the common purpose of free people. The Trinity Project has made a positive difference in the lives of everyone it's touched. We're all in it together, and this town has a long history of pulling for each other."

I couldn't believe what I just heard from Stu Bacon, whose family had fought against socialism years ago in Cottonwood. Up until World War II, Sheridan County had been a hot bed of socialism, and the *Herald* played a big part in ridding the "red" threat. My father told me when he was stationed in Georgia in the army during WW II, other recruits knew Cottonwood was a major center of socialism. The local *Producer News*, an infamous communist paper published by "Red" Taylor, was a bitter rival of the *Herald* in the 1920s and 1930s.

The *Cottonwood Herald* emerged as the leading voice against communism in the mid-1920s by publishing stories critical of Taylor and his supporters. Stu's grandfather purchased the *Herald* in 1928 and continued the battle against socialism. The sheriff, a Taylor supporter, ignored the wrongdoings of the socialists and took every opportunity to harass their opponents.

In the 1930s, the *Producer News* changed its motto to "the paper of the oppressed and exploited." Any entertainment value was gone. The paper stressed militancy and revolution in America. In 1933, students trained by the Young Communist School raided the Red Cross office in Cottonwood and stole winter clothing. Empowered, they planned a large demonstration in May 1934, but were thwarted by a group of angry Cottonwood citizens who met them with pick axes and hoses.

Communists, the *Cottonwood Herald* pointed out, believed that "Christmas is a pagan holiday, that Jesus Christ is only a myth, and the Christian religion is but a superstition fostered by the Bourgeoisie to overawe the masses and keep them in check." As the *Producer News* became more radical, the local folks moved away from the socialist movement. Eventually, the socialist candidates suffered defeats at the polls. Businesses stopped advertising in the *News*, and soon the newspaper went bankrupt. Its last issue was in 1937. The folks at the *Cottonwood Herald* became a united voice, where they've been publishing weekly ever since.

"It's ironic that we won't trade with Cuba because of human rights," I said. "But that's never mentioned in our Chinese dealings. Both the Democratic and Republican administrations are addicted to the narcotics of Chinese money and cheap goods."

I figured that would raise some ire, but someone had to say it.

"You're off base, Donnie," Stu said. "You don't realize how bad the economy got here until the Trinity Project arrived. Their support for local businesses has been critical to our survival. Everyone has health care, and the Trinity Cornerstone Church has been our savior. Folks feel good after the service, Don. That's been missing for forty years. Look, I've got my finger on the pulse of the community better than you do, Doc."

"Don't you believe giving people financial incentives to attend church is inappropriate?" I asked.

"No," he said. "We need to do something in this country to reverse the downward trend of church attendance. The conservatives should be pleased. And we progressives get our universal health care. I know doctor's salaries will be less, but we all need to sacrifice."

The Project's momentum, I could see, would be harder to stop than a Great Northern freight train. Stu and I switched subjects, and Stu asking me the obligatory background questions, and I told him how happy Anne and I were to be here. We said our good-byes, and I left, Stu patting me on the back as he showed me out the door.

The wind almost pushed me back into his office. With time to kill, I headed to the high school to see how the Future Socialists of America were doing.

✌ EIGHTEEN ✌

JUST AFTER ELEVEN IN THE MORNING, I stopped by my old stomping grounds. The school building was unfamiliar—the original one was rebuilt by the Trinity Project five years ago. The windows were downsized to preserve energy, which gave the building as much architectural appeal as the Montana State Prison. Gone were the floor-to-ceiling windows that let in natural light but leaked too much warm air in the frigid winters. I'm sure the new building was more economical, but it still didn't feel right.

The basketball gym, fortunately, was saved. I headed there first. The gym felt like a smaller version of Butler University's gym where *Hoosiers* was filmed. Was that Gene Hackman coming through the door? No, just the janitor. School banners from my years in school were still proudly displayed reflecting a real sense of community.

As I walked down the hall, I studied the class photos. You could differentiate the eras by the hair styles. Crew cuts of the fifties gave way to longer hair in the sixties. The girls went from curls to bangs and back to curls. The school administration didn't allow boys' hair over the ears back then—too rebellious—so we had to settle for Beatle boots from J. C. Penny.

Walking past my old math classroom, I flashed back to the days of stale ale. Our math teacher was Hawk Jensen, an Army Sergeant during the Korean War. We all knew he was a little off-center. He threw erasers at screw-offs and dragged them to the second floor window where he threatened to throw them out. My dad was the president of the school board and gave Hawk slack because the mathematician had experienced some pretty bad shit during the war. The problem, however, was that the screw-offs usually ducked and some poor innocent soul took the eraser hits. Maybe, that's why they made the new windows so small.

The strongest hallucinogenic, at the time, was beer: Oly, Grain Belt, Great Falls Select, and Schmidt. It cost fifty cents for a six-pack, which even then seemed reasonable. One time I borrowed the answer key from Hawk so my buddies and I could review some algebra problems before the final test. A bunch of us were over at my friend's house drinking, shooting baskets and going over math problems. I popped the top of an Oly, and the foam shot out and soaked the answer key. The pages all curled up when they dried and smelled like week old beer. Panic hit me. What would happen to me when I handed the key back to GI Joe? I could see Hawk throwing me out the window and yelling "I like the smell of napalm in the morning, not stale beer." Hawk never said a word. He was an alcoholic and my dad was the head of the school board.

As I was strolling down the dimly lit hall, I bumped into Delia, Abigail's best friend in high school. She was blonde and beautiful, but unfortunately fell in love with a senior her freshman year. He sealed the deal early with her, and they got married within a month after her graduation. They were still married.

"Hi, Delia," I said as I gave her a hug.

"Don, it's great to see ya!" She said with exuberance only she possessed. "I heard the great news that you were back and have listened to your wonderful wife at the church. What do you think of the new school?"

"It's beautiful!" I said, hoping she didn't detect the lie. I didn't want to let her know that I thought the building sucked.

There was a pause as we looked at one another.

"How often do you get together with Abigail?" I asked. "You two were inseparable in high school."

"I feel so bad for her, but I hate to tell you that I hardly ever see her anymore," Delia said, frowning. "She quit going to church after her father's death and has been severely depressed. Dennis is so concerned. Don't tell anyone, but he said that they may have to sedate her and have her committed if she doesn't snap out of it."

"I just saw her, and she seemed fine to me," I said.

"She puts on a good front, but you can't judge a book by its cover," Delia said as she shook her head. "She's not the same gal we knew in school."

"I'm sad to hear that," I said. "She sure fooled me."

"Do you want a tour of the school?" she asked, brightening. "That's one of my specialties. I want to make sure to get you on our mailing list. We're always having fundraisers. Email me the information."

She handed me her card.

"I heard you were head of alumni functions and the booster club. I'll give you our address, but I may have to take a rain check on the tour," I said. "I wanted to say hi to Bob Lowe, and then I have to run. Great seeing you!"

Bob Lowe was one of my favorite students at Montana State University, but I heard he was disappointed when I went into medicine. I helped him land a job teaching history in Cotton-wood, and he didn't forget it. A varsity football and basketball coach, Bob, at five feet, ten inches," was the point guard on a Wolf Point basketball team that won several state titles. His father was a legendary coach. Bob was also an all-state quarterback. Still athletic and trim, Bob was a natural leader and teacher of young people. I greeted him in his room where he was eating a light lunch of carrots, celery, and almonds.

"Coach, now I see why you stay so skinny," I said as I gave him a hearty hand shake.

"Great to see you, Professor," Bob said. "I've heard you've been getting settled in. I've enjoyed listening to Anne's sermons. She's so fit that she looks like she could start on our girl's basketball team. Intelligence, spirituality, and athletic ability are a winning combo."

I beamed. "I'm very proud of her," I said. "She said she might talk to you about assisting with girl's basketball."

"I'd love to talk to her about that," Bob said.

"I doubt you need help," I said. "I hear you've won the state basketball and football championship three years in a row. That's an incredible record!"

"Well, thanks to great kids, committed parents, and the financial support of the Trinity Project," he said. "We have the finest athletic facilities anywhere in the state, and our athletes are so focused that if you didn't know better, you'd think they were on something."

"Hey, how are Julie and the kids?" I asked.

"They're just fine, thanks," Bob said. "We all love it here. You were right when you said everyone was friendly. I'm glad the Trinity brought you back home. I can always use coaching tips."

"With your record, you don't need any help, but if you want some, I think you better get them from Dennis," I said. "He was the star, not me."

"Sometimes, stars aren't the best teachers," Bob said. "They can't understand why everyone else isn't as good as they are."

"Well, I hope you're teaching the students history, because that doesn't seem to be emphasized anymore," I said. "The liberal media would rather remake history than let teachers teach it.

Some are even touting Mao as someone who championed individuality and trusting one's own choices. Where do they get off? You know that Mao was the greatest imposer of mass uniformity in modern history. He created a slave society of a billion drones wearing Mao suits and waving the Little Red Book."

I knew I had a supporter in my redneck friend. We had many conversations at Montana State about the evils of communism and the greatest mass murderer of the twentieth century: Mao. Sixty-five million Chinese died during his reign. In fact, nearly one hundred million people were killed under communist rule worldwide in the twentieth century, a fact all but forgotten today.

"Wait a minute, Don. Socialism scared the hell out of me when I was younger," Bob said. "We agreed it was a pit stop between capitalism and communism. Every time we had a nuclear bomb drill and hid under our school desks, I cursed them, but we can't dwell on the past. I was wrong."

"What?" I exclaimed. "You didn't have a problem with New York City lighting up the Empire State Building with red lights to celebrate Mao and the anniversary of communism in China a few years ago?"

My protégé flushed, a red blush rising in his cheeks.

"No," Bob said. "I thought that was great. We were brainwashed growing up. Look how socialism has transformed Cottonwood over the last five years. We are all family. Capitalism didn't do it. That group stole our oil, screwed our farmers and left us to blow away in the wind like tumbleweeds."

I couldn't believe what I was hearing. Was I going to be converted like everyone else in town? Was he going to hand me my own Mao hat or was that the responsibility of Welcome Wagon?

"It's called maturity. Taking ownership of our social problems," Bob said. "Dennis may not have told you, but I'm the head of the teacher's union and the Trinity Youth Health Program, which is going to make your job a whole lot easier and waste fewer health dollars. We're targeting the obesity rate of youth in this area—nationally it's more than seventy percent—it's even higher in rural areas. By changing the environment, we can help kids live healthy, active lives."

"How'd you do that?" I asked.

"We've had our students eat lunch after recess rather than before which gives them more time to understand what they're eating," he said. After each sentence, he paused and wadded up a piece of paper and threw it for a three-pointer in the recycle can. "It's not about them eating less, but about having them eat a more complete nutritional profile. They're more attentive and focused in class, and their test scores have risen dramatically. We're also posting calorie counts in the cafeteria, where all students have to eat. The Trinity Project uses the Sunday meal after church to teach adults how to prepare wholesome meals for the family. The Trinity also hands out cook books and discount coupons for healthy foods. The whole town's losing weight!"

"Wow, Bob that sounds terrific!" I said. "And you were six for six!"

"That's the beauty of a progressive approach to social problems," Bob said.

He was a changed man. I knew that a college education often leads to liberalism, but the Project outshone that. By the time we finished some small town gossip, it was time for Bob to head to class and for me to head to the cemetery. Hopefully, things would make more sense among the dead.

∽ NINETEEN ∽

On my way to the cemetery to meet Pastor Tim and mom, I pulled off the dirt road. As I stared out at the gray dirt, I thought about my day. Almost everyone I talked to embraced the Project. Maybe, I needed to chill out. Steve's death may not have been caused by foul play. Could his memory be trusted after his fall? Perhaps Ray was drinking again.

There was nothing attractive about the Cottonwood Memorial Cemetery. Prairie grass interrupted by grave markers on a treeless horizon made for a dreary setting especially on a gray day. Pastor Tim was already at my father's grave bent over kneeling and rubbing dirt off the marker. The swirling wind blew it in every direction. A few grasshoppers kept him company.

Mom was seated next to my father's grave with her head down dressed in all black. Wiping the dust from his hands, Pastor Tim looked as if he were surveying the area, counting how many of his followers were buried here. I didn't want to burden him with the details of Steve's death or Ray's concerns, but I did want to discuss more about the Trinity Cornerstone Church. It would be hard to bug a cemetery, and dead men tell no tales. The staff at the care center told me he didn't partake in the communion that one of the assistant pastors provided there once a week, so I knew he wasn't sold on the concept. Maybe, he put on a positive face at the care center for Anne's sake.

"Great day Pastor Tim," I said after I hugged him and mom. "Hi, mom. It's nice to see you out in the fresh air."

She looked up momentarily with a blank look but said nothing. Her mind seemed so far away.

I turned to Pastor Tim. "How are you feeling?" I asked.

"We all deserve hell, and anything else is a great day!" he said and smiled. "I'm feeling much better. Thank you."

"I wonder if dad would have embraced all the changes in Cottonwood over the last five years," I said. "I'm seeing things differently than most people I've run into since I've moved back. There's even an underlying tension between Anne and me."

"I wish your father was here to join us," Pastor Tim said, as if he were far away in thought. "Seeing his grave here reminds me that he was a fine Christian man. My mind gets confused between my memories of the dead and the sleeping."

"What do you mean by that?" I asked.

"I can't remember who died and who is still living," he said. "I can't recall when things have happened either. Sometimes I wake up, and I think I'll go down to the hardware store and shoot the breeze with your dad. Other times, I see friends that I thought were dead. When you get old, the line between reality and imagination blurs. Maybe, it makes moving on to heaven easier. I miss Borgne so much. She was a wonderful wife and put up with all my quirks. I can't believe she's been dead for ten years."

"That must be really hard," I said in a soft voice.

"Well, enough feeling sorry," he said. "Pastor Luke is impressive. I think your father would have enjoyed the services, but he may have been a little suspicious of outsiders coming to town and changing his world so much. It is definitely a move toward socialism.

I've been surprised how little objection has arisen over the Trinity Project. We have times when we think we've found the truth, but there should also be times when we know we're wrong."

Tim was amazing. Without asking, he knew what I wanted to talk about. His words affirmed my gravest doubts. Standing next to him, my mother nearby, was the first time I could handle seeing my father's grave. His suicide had rocked the town and our family. The stress of running a faltering business left him with anxiety attacks. Pressured by being the one in charge of the family business when it was failing, he was hospitalized with a bleeding ulcer. The night before they were going to send him home, he swallowed a bottle of tranquilizers

"Remember, your Christian faith is all about redemption," Pastor Tim said sensing I was thinking about dad. "Starting over, sinless, with a clean slate in God's eyes is what Jesus offers us. When you are saved, God sees Jesus when he looks at you."

"Those are very comforting words," I said.

"No two clergymen think the same on all matters, but it worries me when Pastor Luke talks about the church as a destination," Pastor Tim said, graciously changing the subject. "We've all seen what's happened to overbearing churches. They've controlled Christians by preaching to them that they can't get to heaven without the assistance of the Church. It's all about control for them."

"When did he give that sermon?" I asked.

"After they remodeled the old Lutheran church," he said. "His passion for a physical structure was a little unsettling to me. The million-dollar sound system was topped by the two million-dollar television control center in the basement. The emphasis was on bringing more people to church at any cost. So many ministers today are obsessed with numbers. But it doesn't matter how many people walk through the church doors. What matters is the quality of the person who walks out of the door every Sunday. The church is our reference point, just like a parent on the beach is for the child who is swimming in the Missouri River. Without a reference point, in no time the child will drift downstream and tumble over the waterfall. Without a reference point, our souls drift. But there is so much more than the church."

"Most nonbelievers see mega-church pastors who want to be idolized as narcissists," I said emboldened. "They want to control your life, mind, and wallet."

"There may be some truth to that, I regret to say," he said. "Pastors are just imperfect messengers from God bearing a perfect message, nothing more and nothing less. Just like doctors are imperfect healers," he said and smiled at me. "Neither deserves to be placed on pedestals. Reserve the pedestal for Jesus, the only perfect messenger and healer."

"You're so right," I said, nodding my head in agreement.

"You know when I was talking about Satan with you and Anne yesterday I didn't want to say much," Pastor Tim said, looking down. "Keep our conversation just between you and me. I know my generation probably preached too much on him, but now he's hardly ever brought up, especially on the coasts. I call today's followers: John Wooden Christians. Remember the great UCLA coach?"

"Of course I do," I said. "He's the greatest of all time in any sport. I've read all his books and used his writings to teach deep Christian values to my youth girl's basketball teams in Bozeman. However, I've never heard that terminology before."

"That's because I made it up right here in little old Cottonwood," Pastor Tim said and smiled. Wooden, he explained, never worried about his opponent's offense or defense. He only was concerned with preparing his players to play to the best of their ability. That's what most Christians do today. They study Jesus and prepare themselves for Heaven without regard to their opponent, Satan. Their offense is good deeds and their defense is grace. It's all about love and community. Talking about hell and damnation is taboo. Not in Pastor Tim's day. That's why today's Christians believe that everything good is a miracle from God, but everything bad is quite unexplainable and a mystery. That makes the unconvinced, cynical. They see Christians handling pain worse than non-Christians.

Pastor Tim said that Wooden didn't need to worry about the other team because he was the best coach of all time, and he had the best players in the country. Christianity doesn't have that luxury, Pastor Tim warned. The church takes all comers.

"*The Screwtape Letters* by C. S. Lewis is the most important book on Satan ever written," Pastor Tim said. "It shows how Satan works to win us over to his side. Most people today only know that Lewis wrote *The Chronicles of Narnia*."

"It seems like Pastor Luke would want to teach more about Satan," I said. "His talk today was very effective."

"Drilling folks on the evils of Satan doesn't exactly instill hope in someone who is down and out," Pastor Tim said. "Besides, he talked about Satan today, I think, because a couple weeks ago I came down on him pretty hard on the subject. Looks like he took my advice today, but he's obviously someone who is wildly successful following another path. Those types go with the show that got them there. I don't think you'll hear much from him about the ultimate bad boy once he moves to Minneapolis."

"Did I tell you my electric football theory of life on why bad things happen?" I asked Pastor Tim. I knew I was probably on shaky Biblical ground, but I forged ahead. God, I explained, gave us the free choice to play out our lives on many different fields. We choose the field. Some fields were inherently riskier and carried a greater chance of colliding with, Screwtapes, Satan's helpers. Mountain climbers and bull riders are examples of individuals who have chosen dangerous paths. Once we pick our field the game is on, and the players and Screwtapes vibrate in haphazard directions. Riskier fields have more evil players whose contact cause pain and possibly death, but even the least risky fields still have some bad players vibrating around. Choosing to live at the beach seems to be a low risk life style until the tsunami player hits you. I think Satan tried to pack as many of his players on our field of life as he could. Bad choices, of course, increased the Screwtapes.

"My theory is a work in progress developed by someone who is immature in his faith, but trying to improve," I said in the spirit of modesty.

"Your theory is provocative, and you are humble. I like that. All I can ask for is that you keep seeking," Pastor Tim said.

Suddenly, Pastor Tim was interrupted by Munchie and Choteau and the two labs that bounded along beside them. Munchie told us that he was digging a grave and called Choteau to join him to crash our party.

"What the hell are you fine folks shootin' the breeze about?" Choteau asked.

"Looks like you two and your dogs are on a Montana double date," I said. "Those are beautiful labs."

The dogs, as if on cue, stared up at me, tongues lolling.

"We're talking about hell, the devil, and how you two are lost souls," Pastor Tim said as he laughed. "Come join us. I know religion is high on the list for both of you."

"Not on mine," Munchie said. "I was born in the mud, and I've been getting' dirtier ever since. Prayer ain't for me. How do you know there is a God?"

"No human could place such a deep faith in my heart," Pastor Tim said.

"I don't pray either, but maybe I should," Choteau said. "Deer seasons comin', and I need the big boy upstairs to send some bucks my way."

"We all know you are a horrible shot, but you can still enjoy the beauty of nature when you're hunting," Pastor Tim said with a grin petting the labs.

"Hey," said Choteau. "Since me and Munchie don't go to church, I brought some beer and pizza so we could have our first communion. What do you think, Vicar? It's not that fancy wine like them folks serve at the church in town, but it does the same thing don't it? Heck, I think the wine is the main reason everyone is goin' to church. I hear they serve it every service. It sure picked up after they switched off the grape juice. I call beer and pizza a Cadillac communion."

We all laughed. After Pastor Tim presided over communion, we made small talk about the weather, hunting, and football.

"Why are some Christians so passionate about Jesus and others ain't?" Munchie asked. "I guess it's kinda like me and whiskey. I have the passion for it and some don't."

"Cause they don't want to go hell," Choteau said.

"Let me give you a different reason, Munchie," Pastor Tim said. "Remember that time when you were kids, and we all went rabbit hunting years ago? That first night we all sat around the campfire with our dogs."

"Another Montana double date," Choteau muttered.

"Kind of like that," Tim said. "Remember when Don's dog, Rick, took off into the dark. He had a real nose for rabbits. He had a rabbit cornered, but the rabbit escaped. Soon, the other dogs joined in the race to catch the rabbit. The next morning all the dogs were back in camp except one. Remember who was still chasing the rabbit?"

"Yes, my dog, Rick, was," I said.

"Do you know why?" Pastor Tim asked.

"Cause he was the smartest and fastest?" Munchie asked.

"The farts made him keep goin'?" Choteau asked.

"No," Pastor Tim said as he laughed. "Rick was the only dog that actually saw the rabbit. The other dogs lost the passion. It's like that with humans, too. Some have seen Jesus and have a personal relationship with him. Others think they do until something goes wrong. They tire and leave the chase. You have to believe. I hope someday you two will believe."

"How can I believe in someone who lived over 2000 years ago?" Choteau asked. "Seein' is believin' in my book."

"You have to trust him," Pastor Tim said. "Remember Einstein?"

"Don't he sell those fancy pickles?" Munchie asked.

"No, he was a Princeton physicist, probably the most brilliant man of the twentieth century," I said giggling.

"They once asked Einstein's wife if she understood her husband's theory of relativity," Tim said. "She said no, but I know my husband, and I trust him."

"That's kinda heavy for us two, Vicar," Choteau said.

Munchie shrugged. "I better get back to diggin' that grave," Munchie said. "Once it starts turnin' dark, I'm out of here. I can't believe I do this to make extra dough. This place gives me the creeps. Besides, Shorty starts servin' drinks and snacks around five. You guys take care."

"See ya old boy," Choteau said. "I sure hope they get the dam project done soon. They're screwin' up my fishin'. It's nothing like it used to be when me and Don used to hook 'em. That pork barrel project has been goin' on too long. Typical government bullshit. Pardon my French, Vicar."

"What's going on over there?" I asked. "It looks like a huge project."

"They're installin' a hydroelectric plant," Choteau said. "They're goin' to blow out part of one side of the dam to install them turbine generators. They've spent a hell of a lot of time buildin' a retainin' wall on the lake so when they blow out the old dam the lake water don't flow down the River of Doubt and wash out the old town site again. We'd lose all the fish too. Remember, back in the fifties before the big dam was built? That river flooded the old town site almost every year. That's why they didn't build any homes down there after the Riba House. That was the grandest home ever built in these parts."

I recalled that the mansion was built around 1912 by Adoph Riba, a successful pioneer banker, who spared no expense when constructing his seven-thousand-square-foot masterpiece. The millwork and woodwork were fabricated in Minneapolis. It received national attention when it was featured on the cover of the *Ladies Home Journal*.

"Is someone living there?" I asked. "A little kid in my clinic told me there were lights on inside and ghosts walking behind the curtains. Doc Dennis didn't tell me it was inhabited."

"It ain't public knowledge," Choteau said. "A few border patrol officers live there. I don't know why them foreigners sack out there. It's drafty in the winter and God damn hot in the summer. I know about it cause I rode along one time when Munchie was readin' the electric meter. He said that they sure use up the juice. I thought the Feds stressed cuttin' down on consumption. Green, my ass, I guess that holds for only non-government buildings. They're goin' through lots of green supplied by the tax payers. They ain't very friendly either. Foreigners. Lots of frowns and security."

"You do have your opinions," Pastor Tim said with raised eyebrows.

"I ain't goin' to church either," Choteau said. "I got better things to do like huntin' birds and fishin'. Nature's my church, and I don't have to put dough in an offering plate. They just want my bucks. Sorry, Pastor Tim, but I find God in the great outdoors."

I knew Pastor Tim had heard all kinds of excuses for not going to church over the years. I had mine. At this point in life, he was satisfied to have fought the good fight. He started coughing uncontrollably.

"That cough don't sound good," Choteau said.

"Doc Dennis is seeing me later today," Pastor Tim said. "It seems like so many at the care center have come down with that resistant T.B. strain and have been shipped out of town. I hope I don't end up in Galen. Once you end up there it seems like you never come back, but I know where my real home is."

"I want to go home," Mom said.

Until now, she had been sitting quietly, staring blankly at dad's grave.

"This place depresses me," she said. "Where's dad? He needs to take me to the Dairy Queen before Don's basketball game. I can't sleep worrying that the team might lose to the Outlook Blue Jays. I hope Harry comes home from Vietnam. His mother is so worried about him. He's flying helicopters."

"Don't worry about those things, Mom," I said. "The war is over, Harry is fine, and we won the basketball game. Other than that, you haven't missed much."

✑ TWENTY ✑

BEING THE CURIOUS TYPE, I headed for the dam after our get-together at the cemetery. The northern Montana summer days of my youth were Arctic in length and blisteringly hot, and the heat would mirage off the water. One summer when I was ten years old, my mother left for Florida to visit her mother and sister, which meant I fished from sun-up until midnight. The rainbow trout ranged up to twenty-four inches and gave quite a fight, but by the time Mom came home in August, I filled the basement freezer with those silvery trophies, freezing them in milk cartons filled with water to make them taste as good as a fresh catch. Unfortunately, the warm lake temperature caused the fish to taste foul so they weren't fit to eat. She threw them all out, but told me she appreciated the effort.

Our family friend, Shorty, had three sons: Craig, Joel, and Gary who were like brothers to me. Craig and Joel received degrees in civil engineering from Montana State and eventually landed back in town to work on the dam project. Gary became a fly boy with the Navy in San Diego and returned only for hunting in the fall. Shorty was thrilled to have at least Craig and Joel home. I hadn't seen them since I was back in town, and this seemed like a perfect time to stop and say hello.

Together, we watched, awestruck, as the earthen dam was being built in the early 1960s. It was the biggest manmade structure ever built in the county. At the time, it looked huge. These days, it looked less formidable. As I drove on the dirt country road to the dam, I saw the temporary concrete retaining wall they were working on to hold back Devil's Lake. It looked like they were getting close to being able to blow out part of the dam and add the turbines.

The lake was one mile wide and six miles long and one hundred feet deep in the middle. It was home not only to trout but blood-suckers, horse flies, and mosquitoes. We never swam in any lake with fish because we knew we'd be pulling suckers off our skin all day.

The Army Corp of Engineers constructed a security check point at the side of the dam. It was manned by old classmates of mine, Skippy Grover and Bully Bennett, who directed me to the portable construction office. Large cranes had lowered concrete panels into the water that would serve as the temporary dam, and scuba divers then bolted them together. The dam was a godsend. It provided the community with recreational skiing and fishing and picnic facilities. Unfortunately, a flash flood in 1946 swept away the smaller Carroll dam along with telephone lines, homes, and railroad tracks. It was the great flood of 1953, however, that devastated the community.

The *Cottonwood Herald* described the catastrophe: "this quiet little city of 2,000 people Wednesday was a grim picture of death, destruction, and misery following a flash flood in mid-afternoon Tuesday which killed two people, sent 400 fleeing their homes, and did damage estimated at over a half-million dollars."

Since the River of Doubt came right down the middle of the old town site, buildings there were hit the hardest. Some say the river was given that name as a tribute to Teddy Roosevelt who a few years after his Presidency traveled down the River of Doubt in South America. Others say the name came from the uncertainty of when the next flood would hit the area.

The Riba Mansion had water up to the second floor and was the only home built well enough to survive the flood waters. At the time, the owners lived upstairs and ran the most exclusive restaurant in town. They were found dead floating in their back yard. After the flood, their relatives boarded up the house and left it uninhabited. Neighborhoods were moved to higher ground, and no one ever lived in the old town site again. As children, we were all convinced that the house was haunted. No one played anywhere close to it.

It was great seeing Craig and Joel again. They were all grown up now, professional-looking in their hard hats and directing the cranes. I waved at them from the parking lot as they climbed down from their perches. Although it had been several years since I'd seen them, we connected again as easily as we did when we were kids.

As we talked, I could tell that they were proud of the dam project. They welcomed me into their mobile office where blue prints were spread all over their work table. Empty cereal boxes, half full coffee cups, and dirty microwave dishes cluttered the counter. They were known for their dedication to their work and not for their tidiness.

The long process of putting a temporary dam into place was coming to an end within a month. They would blow a hole in the dam big enough to install hydroelectric turbines. Partially subsidized by the Trinity Project, the hydroelectric plant was only part of Trinity's green movement that also included wind powered turbines west of town.

A recent aerial view tacked on the wall showed that the old Riba House was the only structure of any size downstream from the dam. The image was so sharp that I could detect satellite dishes on the roof. What's that all about?

After finishing the dam project, Joel and Craig were commissioned to help install the wind turbines. With a constant northwest wind blowing, I couldn't think of a better place to build them, especially when the power was going to be consumed locally. Between the two sources of energy, Cottonwood would be self sufficient and heating oil would no longer be needed.

Craig and Joel were a few years older than me, and their youthful builds were replaced with beer bellies. Of German stock, they still had rugged, good looks. They told me that dynamite charges were all in place for the expected detonation in a month and showed me where they still needed to place panels to hold back the reservoir water.

"Joel, why don't we take Don out in our fishing boat?" Craig said. "We can throw the lines in while we show him the retaining wall being built."

"Let's do it," Joel said. "Don, do you have time?"

"You bet," I said. "I haven't been out on the lake in years."

Shorty's eighteen-foot aluminum boat with a Mercury outboard seemed smaller than I remembered, but the gas and oil fumes were as foul as ever. We motored to the center of the lake and looked back at the earthen dam. Steep, grass-covered hills surrounded the lake. A few scrawny trees dotted the landscape.

"Fishing's been kinda slow lately," Craig said. "You should have been here a month ago."

"I've heard that one before," I said. "Hey, where'd Devil's Lake get its name?"

"It has nothing to do with God or being anti-religious, thankfully," Joel said. "Back in the twenties before the dam was built, the lake was more like a big pond that by the end of summer got stagnant. A rancher's cattle drank out of the pond and died. The rancher thought the devil had done it. More likely, it was a blue-green algae bloom. That stuff is deadly."

I had never heard Joel utter the word, "God," before. I wondered what they thought of the Trinity Cornerstone Church. I knew the Project had subsidized the construction. Growing up, they never set foot in a church, but enjoyed the gift-giving of Christmas.

"You mentioned God," I said. "Shorty said you two are going to church and loving it?""I hope the roof didn't collapse."

"I think it's something the community as a whole has embraced," Joel said. "Pastor Luke has presented the concept of church in a whole new and refreshing way. Nothing against Pastor Tim, but earlier in life, we just weren't interested. Mom and dad didn't go to church so we didn't either. It's that simple."

"Pastor Luke taught us that just hearing the word of Christ isn't enough," Joel said. "That's internal. You also need the external through good deeds. The best deed we can do for this country is the Christian gift of universal health coverage. For us, it's almost easier to grasp his message since we didn't have the baggage of going to church. That will probably be true for many Americans when the church expands nationally."

"Are you happy with your health care?" I asked. I couldn't believe they were parroting the party line.

"The health care provided by Doc Dennis is good and very affordable," Craig said. "That's something this country has needed for years. We think, brother Don, that you doctors should be on a salary just like the rest of us. We did all the right things. Dad wanted us to get a college education. We worked hard, did well in school and stayed in Montana to be close to our parents. What's our reward? It was job uncertainty, unemployment and low wages. That is—until the Project came around."

"You rebelled, Don," Joel said. "Your dad wanted you to stay and run the store like he did with his father. He never understood why you left and didn't come back."

"Tell me something I don't know," I said. "He made that clear to me more than once. I thought I could make amends with him by someday coming back home, but I got back too late."

"That might be genetics," Craig said. "You have lots of crazy relatives. I hope you don't think we're being too tough on you, but you know brothers have to tell it like it is."

I smiled and shook my head approvingly. But I was seething. However, this wasn't the time or place to get into an argument, and I didn't want to anger two of my closest friends. We landed the boat and came ashore and walked back to their office.

"When we push this, a quarter of the dam will be leveled," Joel said with a gleaming face as he showed me the red detonator button. "If we did our job right the water should hold. If not, dad will kick our butts, and we'll be sent to a new project in east L.A."

"What's your safeguard to prevent an unplanned detonation?" I asked.

"We have to enter a six-digit code first, and then we can start the fireworks," Craig said. "We've got it programmed to detonate using Joel's birth date as the code, but that's a secret."

"I don't know," I said. "Joel used to beat me up so many times that maybe I'll get my revenge by tying him to a stake in front of the Riba House and pushing the button."

With that we laughed and said our good-byes.

✐ TWENTY-ONE ✐

I T WAS STRANGE coming home without Anne there. I fed the horses and cleaned their stalls before fixing myself a tuna fish sandwich. The dogs swarmed around me, happy to see me. I was sitting down for a night of reading. Tonight, maybe I'd reread Teddy Roosevelt's *The Strenuous Life*. Teddy Roosevelt was my favorite President mainly because of his courage, taking on big corporations and preserving millions of acres in national parks and forests. One of Roosevelt's idols was Charles Darwin whose theories centered on survival of the fittest. Roosevelt thought Americans were getting too soft living in urban areas and needed to revitalize themselves by getting out in nature. He believed that there was room for God in evolution. Teddy embraced the statement of the great naturalist, John Burroughs who stated natural selection may "account for survival of the fittest, but not for the arrival of the fittest."

Anne called me from Regina on my cell phone. She had a great time at the horse show and found some new tack. An old girl friend from Oregon was living in Regina, and Anne was visiting her tomorrow and coming home Wednesday. She reminded me to check in on Ray. She was worried about his drinking and paranoia. I didn't tell her, but I was starting to share his same concerns. Because we had both lost our fathers, Ray had become like a surrogate dad for us. I wished her a goodnight and headed off to check up on him.

It was a dark night. The gravel road in front of me was hard to see. Suddenly, I noticed bright headlights in my rear view mirror. A car was closing in rapidly. My heart raced. A cold sweat broke out, and I jerked the steering wheel and my car plunged into the ditch. The mystery car never slowed down, and the red tail lights disappeared within seconds. As the dust cleared and my heart settled down, I drove back up the road to Ray's ranch.

As I approached, I could see Ray's prized twenty-five-year-old quarter horse, Wild Fire, standing in the paddock area over a body. It was Ray. He was lying on his back in the mud. I quickly braked, jumped out of the car, and ran to him. I checked for a pulse. He was still warm. There was none. It looked as if he was killed by a blunt blow to the chest. Most of his ribs were fractured. It was hard for me to believe that Wild Fire would have knocked him down and stomped him. He was an old horse that had never acted up before.

I used my cell phone to call the sheriff and told him what I'd found. I asked him to contact Roger, Ray's older son, an attorney in Kalispell and Bill, a teacher in Chinook. Both would be devastated. I couldn't contact them because there was no cell service past the county line due to cell tower damage near Froid. The sheriff said that he'd be out in about twenty minutes. Boy, did I feel isolated.

While waiting for him, I walked inside Ray's home to see if anything was disturbed, but nothing seemed out of place. Lying on the kitchen table next to an empty whiskey glass was the pamphlet distributed at his wife's memorial service many years ago. It was titled, *A Witness to the Life of Jeanne Koler*. There were songs, *Majesty, The Power of Love, There You'll Be*, and *The Lord's Prayer*, and a Bible passage from Isaiah 40:28-31. Most touching were the words he wrote at the bottom of the page. "As I came across and reviewed this in the deep silence of this house, I sat down and wept (as no real 'man' is supposed to do). The weeping was not so much from sorrow, but for—thankfulness for all the wonderful things granted to me by God during my life-time. My entire life began to pass before my eyes including things for which I am not proud. However, I cannot help but believe that my family can be compared to any other without serious competition. No one knows better than I that this beautiful lady was so much responsible for it all. RRK."

I paused, staring at the table. At least, he was now reunited with Jeanne in heaven. I locked the door to the house and headed back to the paddock. Just then, Sheriff Butch Boone drove up.

"I told Ray he was too old to be riding those widow makers," Butch said as he spit out a wad of chewing tobacco. "He was a damn fool. This was probably for the best. He was plain paranoid. I took calls from him almost daily that were plain loco. He ranted and raved about his phone conversations being bugged and that the government was out to get him. That's preposterous. He wouldn't have wanted to end up in the care center, anyway. His productive life was over."

"I don't think you should be the one to determine when a man's productive life is over," I said. "How do you know it was an accident? Wild Fire would never trample him. He didn't have a saddle on. From my exam, I think it's entirely possible that someone could have beaten him to death."

149

"No one can predict the actions of horses," Sheriff Butch said. "I think you spent too much time with him. Are you getting paranoid too? Good thing that you're here so we don't need to call the county coroner. He's probably down at the bar tanked up by now anyway. Most of the time he's called out to pronounce some-one dead he has enough booze on board to get a DUI, but he knows I don't give tickets for too much drinking. How's a guy sup-pose to get home from the bar? This looks pretty cut and dried to me," Butch said. "Though I suppose a medical doctor can assess the situation better than the gunsmith. He's been our best coroner in years. That bartender who had the job in the seventies should have stuck to mixing Tom Collins. A few live ones jumped off the table at the funeral home. Help me put old Ray in the body bag after I take a few pictures."

It was a waste of time arguing with Butch. I said my farewells to Ray. First, it was Doc Peters, Banner, then Steve, now Ray. This place was looking more like the killing fields than my home town, and no one seemed to care. All I could do was shake my head and go home. Anne would be devastated at the news, even though she'd only known Ray for a short time.

Tomorrow was going to be a challenge. The Trinity Project ran a morning clinic twice a month in Poplar on the Indian reservation. Ray's death didn't exactly put me in the mood to work the clinic. It was decided that Dennis and I would take turns manning it, and unfortunately, it was my turn. It really wasn't part of the Trin-ity Health Plan, but more of a public relations effort to reach out to the underserved on the Indian reservation. Dennis asked me to run this week's clinic since he was trying to finish the final review of the health plan before he left on Friday. The clinic was open from nine in the morning to noon.

Initially, the reservation health agency balked at having the Project's doctors run the clinic, but after pressure from Senator Bo Hart, they relinquished and published a big article in the *Poplar Chief* stating that it was all their idea to bring off-reservation doctors to the clinic twice a month. I was comfortable letting them have the positive press as long as I could help those in need. One of the government doctors told me that he was thrilled. It meant fewer "Injuns" for him to see.

∽ PART FIVE ∽

REVELATION

Tuesday
September 25, 2020

✍ TWENTY-TWO ✍

CATTLE AND HORSES grazed peacefully together alongside the highway, a sight that filled me with a sense of the common unity of nature's people. A certain freedom reigns through the image of them on the move in a setting unfettered by civilization.

With uncertain futures, they are satisfied and blessed being able to live life under the Big Sky, a sky that this Tuesday was Maui blue. The combination of God, animals, the garden, and sky made for a memorable moment. The wheat fields produced a lot of manna.

When Montanans changed their license plate from "The Treasure State" to the "Big Sky Country" in 1967, it marked a change in their consciousness and self-image. There was a change in focus from resources to be exploited to a focus on a place to be valued and nurtured. The great author, A.B. Guthrie, who wrote *The Big Sky* in 1947, is credited with this enduring Montana moniker. A few years ago "The Treasure State" logo made another appearance, but that didn't last long.

Eastern Montana is ground zero for appreciating what it really means to be in Big Sky Country. Those living in the Rocky

Mountain West from their lofty perches only get a partial view of the great vistas we enjoy every day. Turning west off Highway 43 onto Highway 2, I looked forward to enjoying the solace of the thirty-mile drive to Poplar on the Fort Peck Indian Reservation. The early morning sun was at my back. The highway paralleled the Missouri River the entire way. It was littered with towns of lost opportunity. They looked like exhibits in a dust bowl museum. Stretches of the Missouri, nicknamed the Big Muddy, were over a mile wide. I could almost envision the buffalo, symbols of the American West, crossing the river by the thousands seeking prairie grass. Steamboats belching black smoke from their twin stacks on their way from Fort Benton north of Great Falls to St. Louis were often halted for hours by those great herds.

A few miles east was Fort Union, an old military fort close to the Montana–North Dakota border, where the Yellowstone River, coming up from Yellowstone National Park, marries the Missouri River. That's where Clark rejoined Lewis on their way back to St. Louis. Southeast of Fort Union is Medora, North Dakota, the frontier stomping grounds of a youthful Teddy Roosevelt.

It's no wonder that James J. Hill, the empire builder, ran his railroad tracks on the north side of the Missouri where gullies and coulees sloped into a gently undulating earth. The groves of cottonwoods and poplars stayed close to the water's edge. The grassy plateaus of high buttes kept their distance from the river providing level terrain to lay the tracks. Their only obstacle was the deep rooted sagebrush now colored burnt yellow from the summer sun. Hill built the Great Northern Railway with private finances, a poster boy for American capitalism, but couldn't have completed his great rail line without a right-of-way issued after the United States government in 1888 eliminated the enormous Blackfeet and Gros Ventre reservations that encompassed all the land in Montana between the Missouri River and the Canadian border.

Karl Marx called it "the annihilation of space by time." The commercial culture that was initially fur traders, horses, and steamboat capitalism was transformed by the railroad into a mining and agricultural economy. By the time the last spike was driven in a mountainside in Washington State in January 1893, the full blown advertising of this dessert country as a Garden of Eden was underway.

The Great Northern Railway promoted the northern plains with slogans like "wonderfully fertile Montana valley," "go to the land of opportunity," "room for thousands more today—millions," and "winters are pleasant and healthful." With less than ten inches of rain a year on the northern plains, the farmers and ranchers soon realized that thousands of acres were really needed to make a living in a desert environment. In Big Sky Country one cow might need hundreds of acres to survive through fifty-below winters and hundred and ten-degree summers. One thing was for sure: the relentless wind. To address the problem, the Enlarged Homestead Act of 1909 expanded the grant of free land from 160 to a measly 320 acres. Still, between 1909 and 1919, Montana homestead entries increased from five million acres to thirty-five million.

The Great Northern Railway reached out to northern Europeans who couldn't wait to come to the northern plains, a region that reminded them of their Scandinavian homeland. My Swedish Grandpa Len took the bait.

Another was the family of Pulitzer prize winning author, Wallace Stegner, who called Saskatchewan when he left it as a youth "the capital of an unremembered past." But still, like many who grew up on the northern plains, he found his identity there saying "if I am native to anything, I am native to this." I was too. I still remember his words that I read on one cold winter night in the library at Montana State: "Some are born in their place, some find it, some realize after long searching that the place they left is the one place they have been searching for. But whatever their relation to it, it is made a place only by slow accrual like a coral reef." All the promotion of the plains proved quite successful until after WW I.

Drought conditions led to a slow exodus from the region until, by the 1970s, the population was one-fourth the size of its peak in 1920. Large government subsidies and the soil bank, where farmers are paid not to plant, backfired leaving main street commerce in a shambles. The farmers moved to warmer climates and bought homes with pools on golf course resorts.

Poplar, like most reservation towns, was the home to a broken race. Highway 2 trenched the town in half. The Indian plight is known by many but essentially forgotten by all. Most now lived in tar papered shacks that dotted both sides of the highway. Rusting, forty-year-old Cadillacs lying in heaps on side yards were yet another testimony to the greed of the white man. In order to wrestle away oil rights from the Indians, speculators included these transient symbols of wealth to make the deals more enticing. Based on trust, the Indian's agreements with outsiders were always broken.

The Assiniboines of the Fort Peck Indian Reservation were Sioux-speaking plains people. Two smallpox epidemics in 1781 and 1837 brought by white explorers and settlers decimated the Assiniboine populations. They contracted the last outbreak at Fort Union, an American Fur Company trading post established in 1829. In some cases coats rubbed on open small pox sores were traded with the Indians with the expected deadly outcome. Once they lost most of their land in 1888, the tribes were even more dependent on promised federal funds which usually never arrived, were embezzled by crooked agents, or were way less than promised. Apathy persisted with both political parties showing little concern for their plight. They didn't represent enough votes or money.

Tuberculosis was the biggest concern on the reservation around 1900. Back then, there was no treatment while today our current medications aren't working on an increasing number of bacterial resistant strains. There haven't been any new drug treatments in fifty years.

Native Americans have received federally funded health care for decades. Low cost or free health care is administered by The Indian Health Service (IHS). It runs forty-eight hospitals and 230 clinics on the reservations around the country. The tribes can also receive funding from the IHS and make their own decisions about what services to provide. Not surprisingly, the present federal program hasn't worked well in Montana. Heart disease and lung cancer are much higher than the American average across all IHS regions. Average life expectancy is 58 on the Fort Peck Indian Reservation. Alcoholism on some reservations is over fifty percent.

The common wisdom on the reservation is "don't get sick after June" because that's when the federal funding usually runs out. Canadians can relate to that one.

The IHS Clinic was where I would see patients this morning. A nurse and receptionist from the community were paid by the Project to assist me. Unlike the modern clinic buildings in Cottonwood, this one was seventy-five-years-old and run down. Ten-year-old, tattered *National Geographic* magazines were the only reading material in a waiting room dimly lit by a sixty watt light bulb that dangled from the ceiling. The exam rooms were also poorly lit, and the wooden tables wobbled with gentle pressure. Water-stained ceilings indicated ongoing roof problems. Even so, by nine in the morning, the waiting room was packed. The schedule was meaningless since some never showed up and most appeared randomly.

I was introduced to Comenha, the Sioux nurse, my clinic assistant. She was thirty-seven years old and stood six feet and one inches tall. She was striking with her coal dark hair and almond eyes. Unlike most of the women her age on the reservation, she kept fit. I heard she was considered one of Montana's best girl's basketball players in high school. She was a big hit with the male patients. Perhaps, she was the reason they showed up. That was fine with me.

As the morning progressed, it was clear how much patients appreciated that fact that I took the time to see them for free. At the end of the clinic, I filled my trunk up with bacon, cookies, a chicken, and even a pair of moccasins. I felt more gratitude in one morning than in years practicing on the coast.

Almost all the children and adults were obese and had a poor understanding of health care. One after another had tuberculosis, rotten teeth, strep throat, ear aches, diabetes issues, and high blood pressure. As much as possible, we urged them to follow up with their IHS family practitioners. However, they resisted the suggestion since they regarded them as apathetic government employees just putting in their time until they could retire.

At eleven o'clock, we had a lull. I noted that six of the twenty-five patients had tuberculosis, five of them with the resistant type.

"Comenha," I said. "About a quarter of the patients have tuberculosis. Aren't they normally seen in a regular clinic in town?"

"No," she said. "Doc Dennis worked hard to direct all of them to this clinic. He told the IHS here he would manage them. They didn't care. He takes sputum samples from each one of them home with him. Once I asked him what he was doing with the samples. He told me that he was experimenting to find a cure for the resistant type that we're seeing more of here all the time."

"That's interesting," I said.

"We noticed the vans driving through town from Cottonwood taking patients to Galen for treatment, but we never see anyone coming back," she said. "It's a joke around here that if that's the

Project's idea of quality health care, then we don't want it. Doc Dennis doesn't send any of our patients to Galen. Old man Lightfoot made the mistake of living in Cottonwood. We saw him on the bus to Galen, too."

"I saw him at the Trinity Hospital last week," I said. "He had just enough life in him to hit me, and then he collapsed and died. It was a shocking experience. That's how I got this gash on my thumb."

"That wasn't like him to get angry," Comenha said in disbelief. "He was one of the gentlest men I've ever met in these parts."

"Dennis never told me he was doing research on T.B. patients in Cottonwood," I said. "I'll have to ask him about it next time I see him."

"Well, we have some patients waiting now, so I better get them in the rooms," she said.

"Yea, I need to be done by noon," I said looking at my watch. "I'm going to visit Mrs. Lightfoot to give my condolences and also see my friend and ranch foreman, Two Moon, who's down here visiting his sons."

The three hours went by fast, and fortunately we got through seeing all the patients on time. I tried hard to never run behind. I promised Two Moon I would join him and his sons in their sweat lodge around one o'clock before we headed over to Mrs. Lightfoot's home.

∽ TWENTY-THREE ∽

Two Moon was spending the week with his two sons. I thought it was wise to have him along with me when I visited Mrs. Lightfoot

Two Moon was married long enough to have children, but his wife was unhappy living on our ranch so she headed back to Poplar where she drank herself into oblivion. One January she froze to death in front of one of the taverns. These days, their two sons lived together in a three-bedroom, doublewide rusting trailer with their wives and children. The women worked at the local convenience store, and the men were unemployed. Green tarps covered the roof where Arctic winds long ago tore the shingles off. I walked to the back yard after a knock on the front door didn't rouse anyone's attention.

The three men were naked and ready to enter their sweat lodge. From my days in the history department at Montana State, I was familiar with the ritual. These tiny huts were around four feet tall and made by covering a circular frame of bent willow branches with animal hides. The small opening faced east, towards the sunrise and the future, but right now it faced a broken

down, rusty barbecue. Originally, sweat lodges were used to prepare for vision quests, ceremonies, raids, hunting, and therapy for
a variety of ailments. Wisdom and spiritual strength were also
gained. Today, my friends were just going to relax and use it as a
sauna and drop a few brewskies.

I stripped my clothes off and entered. It reminded me of the
time after a high school basketball game in Poplar when dad and
I joined them in the sweat lodge. I didn't remember much about
that experience, except it was the first and only time I ever saw my
father undressed. During our games with the Poplar Indians we
battled, but afterwards we were friends again. There was a close-
ness there that we never experienced with the other white teams
in the conference.

Lonnie, the younger defiant son, devoted himself to acquiring
knowledge of the Indian's spiritual life that greatly differed from
Christianity. He didn't want any part of our modern society or
Christianity.

In contrast to the book of Genesis, where God created man
in his own image and gave him dominion over all creatures, the
Native American legends reflected the view that humans were
no more important than any other thing, whether alive or inani-
mate. Death was seen not as something to dread, but as part of
nature's cycle. It was a stage like puberty that all creatures must
pass through to complete the circle of life. As the four of us sat
cross-legged around the steaming stones, talk eventually came
around to religion.

"You Christians have always been burdened by the sin of
Adam and Eve," Lonnie said. "That burden is only equaled today
by your silly desire to hold onto this pain-ridden, earthly life when
you are promised eternity with your maker. We don't understand that."

"That's not true for genuine Christian believers," I said trying
to act like I knew what I was talking about in my new missionary role.

"Your genuine believers must be as rare as a white buffalo roaming free," Lonnie said. "Your funerals are full of crying and remorse."

"That's crying because of the pain of loss," I said.

"Where was the crying for us when our people were exterminated?" Lonnie pleaded. "You white men have what I call the pain of relativity. You only have pain if it's a friend or relative. Perhaps, there might be a few seconds of emotion for the earthquake victim or a murder victim in another state or city. You have fleeting grief while we have eternal joy. We honor even the death of a coyote. I believe that God is in every animal and every plant."

"There's no excuse for Christians who watched as genocide of your people was carried out by the U.S. government," I said. "I admit they were guilty and ask for your forgiveness as I ask for forgiveness from God for my sins."

Maybe, this missionary stuff was going to work for me after all.

"You are a good man," Lonnie said. "You and your family have been wonderful to my father. You don't need my forgiveness. You have no sin against my people."

"Lonnie, don't offend Dr. Lewis," Two Moon said. "He is our guest. You need to get off religion. My younger son has always been the rebellious one."

"Dad, explain to Dr. Lewis what you told us all our lives about sin and the arrows in the quiver," Lonnie said.

"Don came here to relax, not be attacked," Two Moon said.

"No. Please tell me. I value your opinion," I said.

"I am a Christian, but still value our Indian traditions," Two Moon said. "I think there's room for both. Every human has a quiver full of good arrows and bad arrows. When you have a bad thought or emotion you are pulling a bad arrow out of the quiver. Put it back or better yet, don't even pull it out. Pick out only good arrows. Those bad arrows are from Satan who wants to destroy your faith. He controls sin and evil spirits. Life is all about picking the right arrows."

"That's a great message," I said. "I've heard the analogy that sin is like missing the mark with an arrow. I think Pastor Tim taught me that many years ago."

"Yes, he did," Two Moon said. "I was in church with your family when he spoke about it. That is a good way to think of it. We start life with no bad arrows, but Satan adds them the longer we live. Adam and Eve didn't have bad arrows until Satan deceived them. Jesus was tempted by the Evil One but never pulled out a bad arrow. Unlike Adam and Eve, he always made the right choices. He is the second Adam and the only human to walk this earth whose quiver never had a bad arrow in it."

"Satan deceived the Indian just like he did Adam and Eve by tempting us with alcohol supplied by the white man, his helper. That deception ruined us as a race," Lonnie said.

"Do you think Adam and Eve would have sinned if Satan hadn't tempted them?" I asked.

"Only God knows for sure, but I would say no," Two Moon said hesitantly. "Satan wants to break our faith by using his favorite persuader, sin. If God is love, then Satan is sin."

"Pastor Tim would second that," I said.

"Today's pastors are reluctant to preach on sin," Two Moon said.

"That's what Pastor Tim says," I said. "What's your take on it?"

"Either they fear Satan or underestimate him. Both are dangerous," Two Moon said.

"They'd rather talk about socialized medicine at the Trinity Cornerstone Church," Lonnie said. "I think Christian pastors are frustrated mathematicians. They're obsessed with the number of church goers. They like to count numbers, not true believers. Big numbers bring in big bucks and big egos."

"Yea, we don't understand the Trinity Project," Willie said. "Our Trinity is earth, fire, and water. It seems like the Project is experimenting on yet another way to control society. It didn't work here. We don't trust the Feds. They want to make everyone in the country dependent on them just like we are dependent on their promises. Those are promises that were never kept. You would think the white man would learn from our plight, but they totally ignore us."

"Now you are hearing from my cerebral older son," Two Moon said. "Sorry."

"I agree with you, Willie," I said. "I have only been here a few days, and I certainly don't have the whole thing figured out, but it's odd that everyone seems so accepting of the Project's vision for the future. One of the things I'm trying to figure out is how Mr. Lightfoot ended up at the hospital in Cottonwood. I have a feeling that he was there to settle things with Doc Dennis and found me there instead. I need to get to the bottom of that."

"Outsiders have always been able to enter Eden and change it, and it's never the same afterwards," Lonnie said. "Lighfoot's wife is a good woman. She's had to deal with an alcoholic husband just like our wives have had to put up with us, but Lightfoot did a lot of good in this community. On weekends he came down here and chopped wood for all the widows in town."

"He also gave quite a bit of his meager salary to the widows so they could buy food for their children," Willie said.

"Yea, Lightfoot didn't need some white preacher pleading for ten percent of his money in order to do good," Lonnie said. "He did good himself."

"Let's stop talking," Two Moon said. "All this chatter is giving me a headache. Let's meditate."

As the heat intensified, we all bent over to breathe in any cool air that was still present. They prayed to God and for me while quietly chanting. My body and mind felt like it was going to be smoke dried if our session didn't end soon. It was hard to meditate after awhile when all I could think about was getting out into fresh air. Finally, Willie motioned for me to exit through the air tight flap. The cool autumn air was refreshing and breathed energy back into my core. The boys lit up cigarettes and drank a beer as Two Moon and I waved good bye. He had contacted Mrs. Lightfoot a few days ago about stopping by when I was in town. Maybe, she could help me start unraveling the mysteries of the Trinity Project. Lonnie threw his beer can on the ground and waved as we drove away.

∾ TWENTY-FOUR ∾

RS. LIGHTFOOT was hanging wet towels on the clothes line as we drove up. I hadn't seen her since high school, and I hoped she wouldn't remember me. After a basketball game my junior year, several teammates and I raided her garden. I was crawling on my stomach, pulling carrots when she pinned my head to the ground with her foot. Dennis Anderson, of course, was the ring leader, and he escaped. I thought my goose was cooked, but she didn't tell our coach. If she had, my high school basketball career would have ended. Instead, the end came the next year in Poplar when I blew my knee out on a fast break. Every time it aches, I think of Poplar.

Mrs. Lightfoot looked weathered and tired. If there was any pinnacle to her life it was long gone. A heavy woman, she suffered from emphysema and back problems and moved slowly, as if she knew there was nothing in life to hurry up for.

"Hi, Mrs. Lightfoot," I said. "I'm Don Lewis from Cottonwood. It's nice meeting you. Thank you for letting me come over."

"We've met before when you were sneaking around in the garden stealing our carrots," she said in a husky voice. "It looks like you turned out okay. Nice to see you, Two Moon. Come on in, and I'll pour you a cup of coffee."

Her singlewide trailer couldn't have been more than six hundred square feet. The white wash on the walls had disappeared years ago. Worn *Life*, *Look*, and *Reader's Digest* magazines were strewn everywhere. The orange shag carpeting was right out of the 1960s.

"I'm sorry about your husband," I said. "I was with him the night he died. By the time I got to the exam room, he just had a few moments left before he passed on. He didn't suffer. I was hoping to see you there."

"We've been separated," she said. "I am at peace with his passing. There was no work in Poplar so he moved up to Cottonwood to work as a janitor at the school. He found a painful lump on his chest and was diagnosed with breast cancer. We were shocked. We didn't know men could get that. He called me and told me about it. He was prepared to have surgery, but Doc Dennis Anderson told him that the treatment was expensive and that it might be best at his age to do nothing. My husband then took a butcher knife and tried to cut the lump out himself. By the time he got to the hospital, he was a bloody mess. Then, quack Anderson told him he also had tuberculosis and needed to be hospitalized at Galen. Last I knew he was shipped off for treatment."

"I'm so sorry," I said. "I was also at the Trinity building when your son died."

"He was not my son," she said as she looked down. "He was from my husband's first marriage. We were never close after he was beaten up by those white men. As a child, he was passionate, free, and loving, but after his face was scarred, he was a different man. He was angry, paranoid, a drug user, and hopeless. His father's death made him crack."

"I'm committed to getting to the bottom of this," I said. "When was the last time you saw your husband?"

"When I got home from the grocery store last Thursday, I could tell that he'd been here," she said. She lit up a cigarette and took a deep draw, exhaling a cloud of smoke. "I wasn't gone that long. His gun was missing, and I didn't know where he was until I got the call from the hospital. I don't understand why he ended up there. I knew that he was angry that Doc Dennis wouldn't treat his cancer. Doc just sewed up the wound from his butcher knife cut. He must have escaped from Galen because I had calls from them, and some federal agents stopped by to question me."

"He was a good man and my friend," Two Moon said.

"He was a fine man, but he had many demons," she said. "He was so generous with his time and money with the needy in this community. Even though we were separated, we were still friends. I always loved him."

"I'm very sorry it ended like that," I said. "Do you remember what the agents looked like?"

"They were Chinese," she said. "They said they were on special loan from the Chinese government to run the border north of Cottonwood. Why were they here drilling me about my husband? Why weren't they up at the border doing their job?"

"Good question," I said. "They seem to be show up every time someone dies."

"You should know that after Doc Peters was found dead in the river, our nephew, Billie Red Dog, told us that earlier he saw several uniformed men down there arguing with him," Mrs. Lightfoot said. "And no surprise—they were Chinese. Billie was fishing and heard the ruckus—but he didn't tell me for several weeks after Doc died. Billie thinks Doc was murdered. The car the men drove away in was a border patrol car. What were they doing, down here forty miles from the border? Then Billy talked too much at the bar. Next thing I knew, Billy's arrested for arson and murder and convicted two months later. I've visited him, but he could barely talk. I've heard they keep him sedated. Johnny Thunder should be down at the Palace bar right now. He almost never leaves. He is Billie's best friend, and he might know more."

I thanked her for her time. As I headed for the door, I noticed a shiny piece of metal lying on the bookshelf. Sitting there on top of a magazine was a bracelet inscribed with a number and Galen Tuberculosis Hospital. On the inside of the bracelet were inscribed the Latin words, *simul justus et peccator*. As I picked it up, she told me that her husband had left it behind on his way to Cottonwood. It was similar to the bracelet fragment that Steve found in the cave. There was some dried blood on the bracelet. I remembered in the emergency room that Lightfoot had cuts on his wrist. He must have used a knife to free himself from the bracelet.

Was Dennis sending patients to Galen that cost the health plan too much money? Maybe, they didn't return home because they were murdered and dumped in a cave.

"I think we'll head down to the bar," I said. "Thank you for your time."

"He left one other thing," she said. "A brief note."

She handed it to me. It read "Pain is unmasked, unmistakable evil. I'm filled with evil because of the Trinity."

Was it possible that Dennis was diagnosing resistant tuberculosis when he wanted those who consumed too many of the Trinity's precious health dollars to be permanently removed from the insurance roles? That was one way to save health care dollars and come in on budget. I'm sure that they didn't want Chen pulling the funding carpet from underneath them. Who needs death panels when one man can do the job?

"What causes tuberculosis?" Two Moon asked me as we drove downtown. What is Galen all about?"

Tuberculosis, I explained, was caused by a bacteria. It was the leading cause of death in America throughout the nineteenth century and by the early twentieth century, nearly eighty percent of the population was infected. Once called consumption or phthisis and thought to be a constitutional weakness or inherited, tuberculosis was found to be caused by a tubercle bacillus in 1882 by Robert Koch. It is a cousin to leprosy, a malady made infamous in the Old Testament. The truth about the origin of T.B. led to the development of state health departments and sanitariums.

By 1900 one-quarter of those settling the American West moved there to find the cure for the disease. States like California, Colorado, Montana, and New Mexico with their fresh mountain air, unsurpassed water supply, and serene settings were especially popular for treatment centers. An added benefit of these treatment centers was their isolation. If patients were separated from their family and community, they posed no further threat to the public health. Galen, the Montana State Tuberculosis Sanitarium, was founded in 1913 to meet the hopes and needs of the sick and minimize the fears of the healthy.

At the time, there was no antibiotic treatment available so doctors relied on happiness, food, and rest for treatment. In addition, fresh mountain air was essential. Rules stated that "patients should be in closed rooms only when dressing." They slept in open porches that were provided with canvas screens and were closed only during storms. Cold weather didn't deter them from sleeping in the open. Supposedly, sufficient covering and properly made beds provided adequate protection from the harsh temperatures. Some survived and were eventually released, but most never found the cure or saw home again.

All of these measures were only palliative, and not until the 1940s were antibiotic treatments developed. By the 1950s, doctors were convinced that tuberculosis would be a thing of the past in the next thirty years, and they were almost right as there were declining rates until 1985. Then, the increase in HIV created a population particularly susceptible to T.B.

In 2020 the world's faced with a new strain of T.B. that was resistant to modern antibiotics. About the time the Trinity Project came to Cottonwood, Galen was reopened after being boarded up for fifty years. Today, tuberculosis is the top killer in the world. Nine million people are infected, and over two million die a year from it.

From my limited time practicing in Cottonwood, I was surprised by how common the diagnosis of resistant T.B. was, especially in the elderly population. Clinic staff told me that over the last five years thirty percent of the seniors over the age of seventy were sent to Galen, and none so far had been released. They were told that the disease spread into the community from custom wheat combiners that brought it up from Texas. Epidemiologists tracked the resistant strain to illegal immigrants from Mexico.

"Wow," Two Moon said. "You've learned a lot since leaving Cottonwood. I didn't understand all that you told me, but I've learned enough."

"I probably said more than I should have, but I get going and can't stop," I said. "Sorry. Anything else you want to know about it?"

"No," Two Moon said. "Your dad always said you liked detail. Now, I know why he said that. You have quenched my thirst."

∞ TWENTY-FIVE ∞

POPLAR'S MAIN STREET made Cottonwood's downtown look like the Las Vegas strip. The only businesses still open were several bars and a gas station. Before we parked the car, I asked Two Moon about Red Dog's problems.

He said that Billie Red Dog was behind bars because he had been accused of burning down a vacant, ramshackle house in Poplar. Sometime after leaving the Palace bar, he was found unconscious next to the collapsed house. The arrest was shocking because he was one of the few in town who wasn't a binge drinker. Red Dog claimed that he only had a couple of beers and that someone came up behind him and hit him on the head. Next thing he knew, he was in handcuffs. Curiously, police didn't obtain a blood alcohol level.

Unfortunately for Red Dog, a transient was inside the house. Because Billy was a tribal member, he was tried in federal court. He was charged with felony murder, a first-degree murder charge that carried a mandatory life sentence. If the same crime had happened off the reservation, it would have gone to a local prosecutor and the worst charge would have been deliberate homicide with a penalty as low as ten years with the chance of parole in as little as two years. He denied setting the building on fire, but there he sat.

It was only three in the afternoon, but the Palace Saloon was crammed with patrons and thick with cigarette smoke. There was a constant dinging from the video poker machines, where every seat was taken. It was a familiar setting for Two Moon who used to come down to take his father home at closing time.

Sitting right where we were told we would find him was Johnny Thunder, slumped over and peering at a line of his empty beer glasses, next to an ashtray heaped with butts.

"I can still see you making that thirty-footer against Wolf Point to win the game," Two Moon said. "Pistol Pete Maravich had nothing on you."

Johnny looked up but said nothing. His eyes were glassy, unfocused, as if his mind was elsewhere or gone. It was hard to tell.

I stayed quiet. I'd decided to let my friend work his magic.

"Too bad about Red Dog," Two Moon said. "I heard that he said he didn't burn down the building."

"I don't want to talk about him," Johnny said. "I'll end up like him in jail or like Doc Peters. Who's your tag-along?"

"Dr. Don Lewis," Two Moon said. "He's my friend."

"Nice to meet you," I said as I held out my hand.

"Right," Johnny said turning his head away from me.

"We've heard that Red Dog was drunk and ranting about Doc Peters getting beat up down at the river the night the house burned down," Two Moon said.

"He told me a lot more than that," Johnny said. He looked around and back at us. "He wasn't drunk that night. Someone whacked him over the head and then started that house on fire. He was framed. I have to be careful. There were strangers in this bar every night for weeks. They overheard Red Dog that night talking about Doc Peters."

"What did he say?" Two Moon said.

"He told us that he was fishing downstream from Doc Peters when he heard arguing," Red Dog said. "Through the cotton-woods, he saw them beating him up. They were yellow men in police uniforms. They knocked him down and threw him in the river. This sort of crap has happened on the reservation forever, but it's usually one of us. Whether it's lying or killing, the Feds gets a pass. The Feds never admit no guilt so they should receive no forgiveness. Where's the justice?"

"Two Moon and I are friends from way back," I said. "I want to help your friend get out of this mess. I agree with you. I think my friend Doc Peters was murdered and Red Dog was framed."

"He tells me his jailers want him to change his story," Johnny said as he blew smoke in my face. He paused, burped, and then started up again. "And they will reduce the charge to ten years. His only guilt was being in the wrong place at the wrong time and telling the truth. He told me that his only choice was to say he made it up in a drunken stupor. He's a proud man, but I told him to go along with it. They have him drugged up most of the time now. But enough. It's time for you to leave me alone."

We thanked him and left. As we walked out of the Palace Saloon, I shook my head. Two Moon told me he was staying in Poplar for the rest of the week and would continue to see if he could find anything else out. I told him to call me if he did.

I looked at my watch. It was five o'clock. My clothes reeked of smoke. Although I wasn't in the mood, I had promised Bull Berg that I would stop by and see him on the way home. Our paths hadn't crossed since we canoed through the white cliffs of the Missouri, ten years ago. Bull was a straight-shooting cattle rancher and a voice of reason. The kind of voice that was pretty much absent in Cottonwood.

❧ TWENTY–SIX ❧

BULL'S 100,000-ACRE RANCH stretched along the Missouri for fifteen miles, one of the largest in Montana. Full of dinosaur bones and fossils that studded the sandstone, the terrain looked like a blasted-out Grand Canyon on a smaller scale. From the porch of his house you could see badlands, wind-ravaged ponderosas, sandstone pillars, and abandoned pioneer homesteads. Silvery hills were the final resting place for piles of fossilized sea shells that, on a sunny day, reflected the sun like millions of tiny mirrors. The essence of eternity, Bull said, was in the fossils of ancient fish and odd-shaped buttes.

Bull was a self-made man who grew up twenty miles from Cottonwood in Scobey. During high school he made a name for himself all over Montana and North Dakota as a rodeo bull rider. After a few broken bones, he headed off to Concordia College in Morehead, Minnesota to study business, then to Omaha to make millions in the computer world. At fifty, Bull decided to head back to Montana to become a cattle rancher. That was years ago now. He'd slowed down some after an angry bull trampled him and landed him in the ICU for a month. The broken ribs, back, and pelvis and a punctured lung only added to his legend. When he got out of the hospital, the first thing he did was to shoot the bull, which was the main course at their next July fourth barbecue.

His favorite hunting spot was adjacent to a huge lake in northern Canada where he and Choteau almost drowned in a storm while pulling a moose they shot behind their leaky canoe. Knowing they couldn't make it back to camp, the two of them spent the night on a rocky ledge with no food or sleeping bags. Bull, Choteau said, stayed up all night with his face directly into the wind and freezing rain.

He was no friend of the Feds. While the Missouri River swept through his property, the government wouldn't allow him to use any of its water to extinguish fast moving wild fires that frequently erupted on his sun-scorched, prairie soil. Two years ago, a fire burned down most of his outbuildings and ponderosa pine and cooked five hundred head of his cattle. By mistake, the Feds dropped fire retardant on him and his truck. He had to pay for the new paint job. Also, they didn't allow him to use the river for drinking water for his cattle or personal use. Wells might cost $250,000 to drill, and there was still no promise of striking the aquifer.

Candy, Bull's wife from Chippewa Falls, Wisconsin, was out in the round pen breaking a wild mustang. Her Dorothy Hamill hair style belied her years, but her Fargo accent was authentic. We chatted for awhile. Bull rode up on his four-wheeler after rounding up cattle all morning.

"Don," he said in his gruff voice giving me a bear hug that nearly crushed me. "Great to see you! I was hoping you'd stop in. How's God's country been treating you since you've been back?"

"Well, it's a mixed blessing," I said. "Anne and I love being out on the family ranch, but the whole scene in Cottonwood is troubling. Between you and me, I'm a little suspicious of the Trinity Project. There are lots of unanswered questions. It's like Ringling,

Montana in Jimmy Buffet's song. It's a dying little town in more ways than one."

"How so?" Candy asked.

"Dying in the sense that some of my best friends, Doc Peters, my paleontologist friend, and Ray Koler, are dead," I said.

"Holy shit, Don!" Bull said. "I only knew about Doc Peters. I'm sorry to hear the bad news. That Trinity Project is a bunch of crap. I go to the doctor in Omaha and pay cash. I'm one of the few that does that. I'll spend my last penny before I'll join that commie health plan. I'm independent. The only thing I'm entitled to is a hard day's work."

"You know, I always agree with you," I said. I felt flooded with relief. Someone, finally, was making sense.

"Listen, it's another bullshit government program," Bull said. "I call the head guy, Bruce 'Bad' Deeds. He and Senator Bo Hart are buying up all the oil rights around here along with the prime ranch land. Hart just bought his uncle's ranch. I'm convinced Deeds is behind some of my cattle being poisoned, that bastard. Where'd he get all the bucks? Bad boy stopped here a few times trying to buy us out, but I won't budge. We're smack dab in the middle of the Bakken Shale Formation where the dinosaurs left their calling card. It's one of the biggest oil deposits in the country, and I'm going to make sure that the oil coming out of here will make us less dependent on those damn foreigners. It'll end up over in China over my dead body."

"Your dead body would make them happy," I said.

"I've heard that Deeds is getting his money from the Chinese," Bull said. "They want the oil. I'll never sell, and it's not about the money. If I can't work the land, they might as well shoot me. I told Deeds to get the hell off my property. The land he and Hart own has been ruined. To get the oil out of the shale they have to inject water under high pressure. It takes a lot of water, and that's something that's scarce around here as an honest politician. Check out the Little Muddy Creek. It's just full of mud now from the oil guys siphoning off all the water. It's interesting the Feds give them all the water they want, but won't give me any. Don, if you took your Chevy down to the levy you'd find the levy is dry. Them good old oil boys who work for Deeds are the reason."

"It's nice someone thinks the way I do," I said. "Almost everyone up in Cottonwood, including old friends and Anne, seem to be thrilled with the whole thing. They even have God on their side. If Pastor Luke up there told the townspeople to leap off a buffalo jump, they'd do it."

"That community is the perfect nest of zombies that makes the Trinity Project look successful," Bull said. "I know better. The rest of the country is ready to follow the music too. The Republicans aren't any more financially responsible than the Democrats. They're all out of the same barrel, a barrel I'd like to blast and send 'em all to North Dakota. You're going to have to flush more than twice to get all the crap out of Cottonwood. I told you that you should have grown up in Scobey."

"Please," I said. "Scobey was our biggest rival. I hated to set foot in your one-horse town."

"Look," Bull said. "We've known each other since we were kids. Don't look the other way and don't buy into that shit. Evil is everywhere, and there's a constant battle against it. But who am I to tell the doctor anything? I'm just a lowly dirt-pusher."

"I value your opinion even if you are from Scobey," I said. "I totally agree with you. Your words are exactly what I needed to hear. I'll never give up."

"You're a good man, even if you grew up in Cottonwood," Bull chuckled. "Let me know if I can help. We Scobey Spartans kicked your ass in sports. Now I'd like to go up to Cottonwood and kick some more."

"I don't remember it that way, but I know you're a good ass-kicker," I said.

"Hey, why don't you stay for supper?" Bull asked. "Bob Drewman, my art dealer friend, is visiting from Coeur d' Alene. His nickname is 'Genius.'"

"Thanks, but I have to get home and check on the recipe for kicked ass," I said.

We laughed. It wasn't hard to convince me to stay. While Candy prepared supper, Bull took me on a tour of their home. It was filled with wonderful western art and photography. I especially appreciated the images by L.A. Huffman. Bull said he bought all his photographs from Gene and Bev Allen in Helena.

Candy was a great cook, and the roast beef with potatoes and vegetables were a whole lot better than a burger at Knutson's Drive-In. Bob Drewman, who Bull said was one of the country's top art dealers, told one story after another about different art deals.

"Genius," I asked. "How'd you get your start?"

"Well, I used to be a medical supplies salesman," Bob said. "Thirty years ago I was coming from Cottonwood after visiting with Doc Peters. He was one of my favorite doctors. I stopped at the Elks Club in Wolf Point and noticed a little oil painting on the wall. I offered the owner $25 for it, and he took it. The painting was a real dog, but at the time what did I know? I drove to Glasgow and sold it to a cowboy in the Moose Club for $75. After that, I figured there was easier money in art than medical supplies."

"Sounds like the rest is history," I said.

"Sure is," Bull said. "He sells Charlie Russell oil paintings for millions now. He's sold me almost all the art hanging on the walls here at the ranch. Believe it or not, Bob is honest too."

"That's true," Bob said. "I'm not a little weasel like some art dealers. Mike Obey, the good guy that took over my route, says Doc Dennis up there hardly ever buys anything from him anymore.

All of it comes directly from China. Mike says the quality is real shitty. He says Doc Anderson's an ass and a weasel. He won't talk to Mike even after he's driven seventy-five miles out of his way to go to Cottonwood. You're going to have fun working with that jack ass."

When supper was over, we all shook hands and said our goodbyes. I was relaxed and happy for the first time in days—what a breath of needed fresh air this had been.

"I'll be up on Friday morning," Bull said. "With the help of some of my friends on the reservation, I'm loading a few hundred head of cattle on boxcars at the train station in Cottonwood. We're sending them to Chicago to be slaughtered. Maybe, we should round up some of those Trinity people too."

"We'll have you for dinner," I said. "Anne and Candy will hit it off. Give me a call after you've loaded them on the train."

Driving down a straight-as-an-arrow highway is great for sorting things out. As I drove that ribbon of gray, it was clear that Doc Reynolds was murdered down by the river. He was killed because he must have not gone along with the Trinity's guidelines. Steve was killed because he was nosing around the cave where they were burying the Galen patients, and Ray's death certainly wasn't from horse kicks. What about Pastor Tim? Was he next? The cell tower between Poplar and Cottonwood was damaged and not operational. That made it impossible to contact him. He had an appointment with Doc Dennis. Would he wind up on the bus to Galen? Not a pretty thought.

∽ TWENTY-SEVEN ∽

WHEN I RETURNED TO COTTONWOOD, it was dark. I drove by the care center to check in on mom and Pastor Tim. Mom was asleep, so I headed to Tim's room. The door was locked. The desk clerk said he was transferred to Galen. I jumped in my car and sped back to the clinic. Dennis had a lot of explaining to do. If he was in his normal routine, then he should still be at the hospital making rounds.

As I drove up, he was getting into his car. He wasn't thrilled to see me.

I rolled down the window.

"Where's Pastor Tim?" I demanded.

"Did you check the church?" He asked. "Maybe he's at the altar confessing his sins."

"Very funny," I said with a grimace.

"He saw me yesterday afternoon," Dennis said. "He's got resistant T.B., and we shipped him immediately to Galen. It's protocol. You better get used to it."

"That skin test takes forty-eight hours," I said. "How do you know he was infected?"

I got out and walked over to him. We stood and faced each other.

"Trust me," he said. "Remember, I won an award for being the best family practitioner in America. I can smell tuberculosis. Besides, T.B. patients have a particular cough. I'm really good at picking it out. I'll try teaching you, but I doubt you'll master it."

"You're an arrogant ass," I said and grabbed him.

"I'm the most humble person I know," Dennis said. He glared at me. "Now, take your hands off of me. Don't you know who you're dealing with? I'll have the sheriff over here in two minutes if you don't get your hands off of me right now. "

"Your sincerity is touching," I said as I let go.

I knew they'd love to throw me in the slammer.

"I've been meaning to talk to you," Dennis said. "Deeds wants to chat with you tomorrow. We are having our final summary meeting before we present the results in Minneapolis. You need to be at the Trinity office at three o'clock. He wants to button things up before we leave on Friday for the Twin cities. That's a big day. Now get out of my way. "

My hands dropped to my sides. The confrontation was going nowhere. I just watched Dennis drive away.

I was boiling mad and not in the mood, but I had promised Shorty I'd stop by. I appreciated him staying up past his normal seven o'clock bedtime. Even though he was over ninety, he was as sharp and witty as ever. If the Project had their way, he would have been eliminated a decade ago. His long and strenuous life was certainly something they frowned on.

Munchie and Hook, Shorty's younger brother, were drinking with him at the table. When I arrived, Shorty heartily welcomed me in and fixed me a wall-banger.

"Where the hell have you been, Donnie?" Shorty asked. "Those God damn doctors are always late, even when they're mooching booze. I got about ten more minutes in me before I hit the hay."

Shorty had enough vim left to spin several off-color jokes, but my mind was on the Project. Finally, when I thought it was appropriate, I asked Shorty about his take on the changes in Cottonwood.

"After World War II, we were a great nation," Shorty said. "We suffered through much pain durin' the war, but pain is tolerable when you have a formidable opponent. There were few government entitlements and people understood they needed to work hard to make it. We didn't dwell on the war but moved forward."

"I'm so proud of you," I said.

"In terms of all this Trinity stuff, I've never gone to church and won't start now," Shorty said. "Too many hypocrites. Your Dad went and that was okay with me, but don't force it. The Trinity has brought a lot of prosperity to town. I don't know how long it will last and who is footin' the bill, but I'm an old fart and won't have to worry about payin' the piper. The pain I suffer now is from arthritis. That's a pain that isn't noble and much harder to deal with. I like the fact that the boys are around with the dam project, and they're going to church for the first time. They seem to be happy and love Pastor Luke. That's their decision. The bad thing is that they don't like comin' around for drinks like they used to do. They said they're gettin' high on the Lord. I'll stick to gettin' high on Jack Daniels and rye until the day that I die. He always delivers. Hey, it's way past my bedtime. During bird huntin' season, I get up and hit the fields by six o'clock. I've won the award for the biggest pheasant shot every year for the last thirty."

"That's 'cause thirty years ago you shot the biggest pheasant ever seen in these parts and kept his tail feather," Hook said.

"Yeah, Shorty, show Don what's in the box on the table," Munchie said.

Shorty opened the long narrow oak box, and there resting on red velvet was the biggest tail feather I'd ever seen.

"What a specimen!" I said.

"I kinda think the judges know I enter the same feather every year," Shorty said. "At my age, they don't want to ruin my fun. I do get my picture in the *Herald* every year. Well, I need to get to bed. Craig and Joel are going to go out huntin' with me for a couple of hours in the morning before they have to get to work at the dam. I'm glad I was a plumber and could call my own hours. Good night."

"Good night," I said as Shorty abruptly headed out the kitchen for his bedroom.

"That Shorty's like a father to me," Munchie said, looking toward Shorty's bedroom door. "I adore him. My dad left us when I was twelve. Shorty and I both have just an eighth grade education, but look how successful we are. Shorty built his house himself for $6,000 and started saving $25 a month back in the 1950s. Now he gives scholarships to high school graduates here. I got $1,000 saved up myself. I don't have a singlewide. I have a double-wide trailer. Who needs more than that?"

It was just as well the visit ended early because I needed to get home and feed the horses and dogs. I felt very alone that night, driving away from Cottonwood. It seemed as if I would have to take on the Trinity single-handedly. Where's Gary Cooper when you need him?

∽ TWENTY-EIGHT ∽

RIVING OVER MILES OF GRAVEL ROADS on a moonless night made me uneasy. The night was quiet as sleep. Then it happened again. In the rear view mirror, two headlights rapidly approached. This time, however, I stopped. So did the other car behind me. I opened the door and waited. My heart raced, and I broke out in a sweat. My jaw dropped when I saw who it was.

"What the hell are you doing here, Abigail?" I asked. "If you found a gift for Anne, you could have told me during normal business hours."

"Kiss me and hug me right now," Abigail said as she approached me. "They're watching."

I awkwardly embraced her, much like I did during our high school days. Half-concealed under her coat was a briefcase. She whispered to me that we needed to get in the back seat of my car. I didn't know what she was up to, but her voice sounded urgent.

"I tried to get you in the back seat of my dad's station wagon during high school and never could," I said. I smiled. "Now, you're pulling me in. Isn't modern maturity great?"

"Very funny, but this isn't the time," Abigail said, her voice low. "We have to make this look like a tryst, nothing more. Dennis doesn't care about me, but he wouldn't hesitate to take a pound of my flesh, or yours, if he knew what I was giving you. The Trinity is not what it seems."

"You're preaching to the choir," I said.

"Dennis and I haven't shared a bed for years," she said. "We are quite indifferent to each other. Ever since the Project started, its success has been his passion. I overheard odd conversations between Dennis and Deeds about their concerns with patients over-utilizing health care and screwing up their bottom line. They talked about people like they were cattle. If they didn't meet budget, they were afraid the Chinese would pull the plug on the Project. Dennis and Bruce were promised powerful positions at the national level. In time, I started going through his briefcase that he kept in the library."

She paused, straightened up, and drew a breath.

"It's clear that the Trinity set up a death panel where those who were a strain on the system were eliminated," she said. "Dennis accomplished this by infecting his patients with a resistant tuberculosis strain. He hoped for a quick, inexpensive death, but if there was any lingering, then they were shipped to Galen. Others, like Mr. Lightfoot, were conveniently misdiagnosed with resistant T.B. and sent there too. Cost containment was achieved by elimination of those who were the neediest."

"Eugenics," I said.

"Indeed," Abigail said. "Eugenics is alive and well. More shocking is the fact that many of the patients were murdered within a few months of arriving at Galen. Those with the mildest cases who were expected to live had a triangle cut on their abdomen and marked for death. Dennis didn't want his problem patients coming back to Cottonwood and screwing up the bottom line. They weren't dying of T.B. but of lethal injections. Their bodies were ground up and buried in caves in Hell Creek!"

"That's why they had to eliminate Steve," I said shaking my head. "He found out the truth." They must have gotten the idea to grind humans up from the movie *Fargo*.

"Exactly," she said. "He was exploring in the wrong place."

"I hate to bring it up, but is Pastor Luke in on this?"

"It's unclear, but I do know that the Trinity Cornerstone Church is critical to their plan," Abigail said. "The Project is using the Church to brainwash everyone. They want Cottonwood and the rest of the 'SEN' region to be shining examples of prosperity in America through socialistic control of people's lives."

"That's been the goal of the damn progressives for the last hundred years," I said. "After that, the Chinese take over."

"That's right," Abigail said. "The Chinese government wants total control of America. Once everyone has health care insurance subsidized by the Chinese, there is no turning back. It's like any big government entitlement. To seal the deal they wanted one spiritual voice to lend full support to universal health care and socialism."

"You sound like Dr. Chen," I said.

"Look," Abigail said. "I haven't told you the most frightening thing about the church. Even with Pastor Luke heading the church, attendance wasn't reaching their goal of ninety percent. They needed that level to achieve a 'wow' factor. Necessary steps were taken. An experimental mood elevator developed at the National Institute of Health, code named 'joy juice,' was secretly added to the weekly communion wine. There's no taste or smell to it."

"I've read in my medical journals that researchers were working on several variations of the most commonly prescribed antidepressants, the serotonin uptake inhibitors," I said.

"'Joy' must be one of them," she said. "But what does serotonin do?"

"Serotonin has calming and submissive effects on human personality," I explained. "According to the journals, the National Institute of Health is testing a new generation of antidepressants in mice that also stimulates the expression of the MAOA gene that regulates the production of serotonin. Several studies show that an ineffective, mutated MAOA gene leads to increased gang participation and increased criminal behavior. With an increase in serotonin from 'joy juice' you get the opposite effect, a person who behaves like an angel and has the will of a zombie. The newer drugs also have hypnotic and confusing affects on human personality. They also work like a diet pill."

"Isaiah 9:16 says: 'God sends confusion to the wicked,'" Abigail said.

"I didn't know you were such a Biblical scholar," I said.

"There are many things you don't know about me," she said. "The Trinity Cornerstone Church is delivering to God the joy and submission he desires through drug manipulation along with a good dose of confusion. No wonder the church members feel so good after Sunday functions. One of Dennis's notes said that through a time release formulation, the drug's effect lasts seven to ten days, basically, which keeps it effective until the next service. The Trinity Cornerstone Church has proven that Marx was right. The opiate is coming from religion."

"Damn, now I know why Anne is acting so different," I said. "Most of my friends were making comments I didn't think they would make. And the junior high and high school students are behaving like angels because they're getting a good dose of 'joy juice' at the Sunday communion. It must make the high school athletes more attentive and focused. I thought I was going crazy. I feel somewhat relieved, but I'm still not sure I'm not crazy."

"If you and I weren't crazy," Abigail said. "We'd be insane like everyone else in this damn town. All my old girl friends are snowed under from 'joy juice,' and they probably love the weight loss."

"I'd sure like to know what Pastor Luke knows about all this," I said. "If he does, Anne will be devastated."

"I'm not sure," Abigail said. "Here's a briefcase full of copied notes that will prove what I've told you. There's more incredible information in these papers about how the Trinity Project manipulated people in the 'SEN' region, but you can read that later. Now that you have these notes, I feel safer. I can't wait to get the hell out of here. Time is running out. Secrecy is so important to the Project that all the statistics compiled over the last five years have been kept on computer hard drives in the Riba House. They didn't trust sending the information over the internet because of piracy."

"That's ironic," I said. "It seems no one was concerned about sending electronic medical records over the internet, and the Feds want us to believe that patient's records won't be stolen."

"I've got to go," Abigail said. "I'm sure Dennis will know about our meeting within the hour. Be careful. He is an evil, vengeful man. But I'm not telling you anything."

"That's for sure," I said.

"Our only chance is to keep the notes safe and out of the hands of Trinity," she said. She leaned over and kissed me on the cheek.

"What's that for?" I asked and then looked into her eyes.

"That's for what could have been," she said. "I made the wrong choice not loving you, but it's too late. Go now and be careful. I'm not sure we'll see each other again. I'm sorry it turned out like this."

With that she ran to her car, slammed the door, and the taillights faded into the darkness. Was this a dream? I pinched myself, half-expecting to wake up, with my dog, Beau, licking my face. I needed to find a safe place for these papers. According to Dennis's day planner, Bruce Deeds was picking the hard drives up at eleven in the morning on Friday from the Riba House and then taking them with him on the train to Minneapolis. I had two days until the showdown at high noon on Friday.

Abigail was leaving on the westbound train at 7:30 in the morning. I wanted her to get out of here for her own safety. Suddenly, everything made sense.

While I listened to Abigail, I wrestled with telling her the truth about her father's death. It was clear to me that he was murdered, since he wasn't buying into the program, and Dennis had called the shots on that one. Perhaps, I would tell her another time if there was one. She told me to look through the documents, but not in the ranch house, which had audio and video bugs everywhere. Ray was right.

When I arrived at the ranch, I headed off to bed with the briefcase cradled in my arms, Beau and Lexy swarming my feet. The hoot owl outside my window kept me awake with his relentless calling. First thing in the morning I had to find a safe place to hide the briefcase. I needed to let someone I trusted know about the evidence. I was probably next on the hit list.

∾ PART SIX ∾

CAPTIVATION

Wednesday
September 26, 2020

∽ TWENTY-NINE ∽

SEVEN IN THE MORNING was a great time for a ride into the coulees north of the ranch. The cool morning air scented with sage and prairie grass lifted my spirits. As a child, these ravines were my back drop for imaginary shootouts with bad guys wearing black hats. Now, they provided a quiet respite to digest the cold facts within the briefcase Abigail had given me.

Quarter horses love to move out, and Big Sky was no exception. A cloud of dust rose up behind us. If only I had the energy of Big Sky, the courage of Teddy Roosevelt, and the wisdom of Ray, I thought.

Years ago I made a bench out of cottonwood branches in one of the coulees a half mile from the ranch. It was near the wood cross that was erected by Ray and my dad for an Easter service. The grave of my brother, David, who died during delivery, was right next to it. The cottonwood bench seemed like a safe place to sit and go over the copied notes.

When I arrived, I tied up the horse, sat down, and began to read the copies of Doc Dennis's meticulous, handwritten notes chronicling the whole charade. Abigail copied what she deemed the most important entries.

Pastor Luke initially was confident that he could attract the majority of citizens in Cottonwood to his new church, Dennis wrote, but after several months, Deeds became impatient. The sheep weren't flocking to Church on a regular enough basis. Even adding more financial incentives didn't help.

That's when Deeds and Doc Dennis added "joy juice" to the communion wine and weekly attendance grew to more than ninety percent. When everyone felt "joy," Dennis wrote, any grumblings about the quality of health care melted away. Surveys showed how pleased everyone in Cottonwood was with the Trinity Cornerstone Church and their health care insurance. Unfortunately, I couldn't tell from the notes if Pastor Luke knew about the plan or not.

However, the health care expenditures in Cottonwood were disappointingly high after the first few months. If that wasn't corrected, Dennis noted, then the planned expansion of the Trinity Health Plan in 2016 to the entire SEN region wouldn't take place.

Not surprisingly, analysis showed that the budget was going in the red because the elderly were over-utilizing health care. Dennis came up with the idea to falsely misdiagnose patients over the age of seventy with resistant T.B. so he could have the patients shipped to Galen Hospital and removed from the health plan. Who would know? He also infected some with the resistant strain with sputum samples he gathered from the reservation. He knew that T.B. bacteria could remain living in sputum stored in a test tube for over a week. He hoped those infected would quickly die and not eat up more health dollars.

For the Trinity Project, Galen was a dumping ground for those deemed unworthy to live. Originally named the Montana State Tuberculosis Sanitarium, Galen had been reopened for the increasing numbers of tuberculosis patients. For the Trinity Project, it was a modern day Auschwitz, their final solution to America's health care problems. If they weren't killed outright, the

Galen patients were used as guinea pigs to determine the human dosage that provided the perfect level of submission with the least side effects. Initially, the higher doses proved to be lethal, so the dosages were tapered until the desired effects were achieved.

When the Cottonwood ward filled up at the sanitarium, Dennis made a visit and told the Galen officials that some were ready to return home. The patients were then overdosed with barbiturates and "joy juice," loaded on a bus, and driven to the Hell Creek. Their bodies were ground up in a brush chipper, and the remains were dumped in the deep recesses of the caves.

According to the notes that Dennis had scribbled, the NIH required experimental drugs, such as "joy juice," to be sent directly to a pharmacy. The hypnotic arrived at Neil's drug store. It appeared Neil didn't know what was inside the packages. He was instructed to call Dennis when it arrived, and then Dennis delivered it to the church kitchen where an unnamed accomplice added it to the communion wine. This, the good doctor noted sarcastically, was his community service for the week.

As I read the notes, I was disappointed that Neil didn't question the contents of the packages. They paid him commissions for handling the boxes so I figured that dulled his interest. Shortly after the first package arrived, he probably received the tainted communion along with everyone else. Still, I needed to find out what he knew.

With local success, in 2016 the Trinity Health Plan was expanded to the entire SEN region, but the Trinity had a problem. It was easy enough to keep patients submissive by adding "joy juice" to the communion wine in Cottonwood, but how would they handle several million disgruntled patients in the entire SEN region? The goal of one national church, the Trinity Cornerstone Church, was still years away. Doping communion wine in hundreds of regional churches was impossible.

Deeds came up with a solution. Corrupt officials at the Food and Drug Administration were bribed by the Trinity to quickly approve a new "preventative treatment" developed by Trinity scientists in Bismarck for resistant T.B.. Modeled closely after the old polio vaccine administered on sugar cubes, the "preventative treatment" consisted of sugar cubes that were secretly laden with "joy juice" in an extended time release formula that lasted eight weeks. A second cube that had a rare, virulent strain of T.B. imported from China was given to anyone over the age seventy. Death occurred in a matter of days after ingestion.

In informational advertisements that ran in every form of media, the Trinity reminded citizens that there wasn't a cure for resistant tuberculosis. Prevention was the only answer. They emphasized that more than two million people worldwide were dying from it every year and resurrected the old "check up and a check" campaign that ran in the 1950s and 1960s to combat tuberculosis. Kiosks in every town in the SEN region from Great Falls to Fargo and south to Rapid City and Cheyenne were set up to administer the sugar cubes. Panicked citizens eagerly lined up every two months for their free dose of vaccine.

How would the Project keep over utilization down in certain areas? By an additional "booster" dose. Needless to say, business at Galen, other state tuberculosis hospitals, and the mortuary was brisk.

To complete the charade and "comfort" a panicky population, technicians in mobile Trinity vans tested everyone with tuberculosis every two months. As the number of positive skin tests rose to a desired level, the number of tainted sugar cubes was adjusted downward. There was a fine line between eliminating enough patients from the Trinity Health Plan and over-populating the tuberculosis hospitals and stirring the ire of state officials.

The stakes were high. If Deeds succeeded, he would assume the directorship of the National Trinity Health Care Plan and

Doc Dennis would be nominated for the Surgeon General position after Bo Hart was elected President. Pastor Luke would not only head the national Trinity Cornerstone Church and champion universal health care coverage, but also train pastors at his Minneapolis institute. Finally, the Christian's dream of everyone united under one roof would be realized. Amazingly, all the Project data was stored in the basement of the old Riba House on hard drives that would be heading east on the train on Friday. Where's the Dalton Gang, I wondered, when you needed a train robbery?

Several notes indicated that the Project had the full support from the politician who would stand to gain the most from its success: Senator Bo Hart from Great Falls, Montana. He was running for President as an Independent. President Obama's victory in 2010 came close, but ultimately failed to hand the progressive wing universal health care run by the government. Hart made the Trinity Health Plan the centerpiece of his presidential run and stressed that he was a fiscal conservative with compassion.

Hart was six feet, seven inches tall, tanned in a sun-chapped sort of way and handsome (Senator David Melick joked that if he had Hart's face he would be President today). He was unfailingly genial, modest, and nice. A high school basketball star, he had idyllic small-town manners. Some said he emerged into the twenty-first century from a more wholesome time.

After high school, he attended George Fox, the same small Christian college in Newberg, Oregon that Anne had attended. He then received an M.B.A. from the University of Montana and spent his adult life ascending the political ladder—congressional staffer, Montana Democratic Party chairman, a member of the U.S. House and now a Montana Senator. He was head of the powerful Senate Finance Committee that controlled the purse strings of the federal government.

Hart liked to talk about economic issues: job creation, balanced budgets and small-business-led growth. That's just what independent voters and conservatives wanted to hear. They liked his small-town values. He was on board from the beginning as Chen and Deeds together formulated the Trinity Health Plan which touted fiscal responsibility.

It was clear from Dennis's notes that the Senator didn't have a clue about how the Project achieved its spectacular results. Like most politicians, he thrived on power and outcome. He didn't question the process.

There were more notes to go over, but I figured I'd look at them later. My secret hiding place was a wooden box under a fallen tree trunk, not far from the cottonwood bench. I used to hide my coin collection there. That would be as good a place as any. Time was running out.

✥ **THIRTY** ✥

I DROVE INTO TOWN to talk to Neil Odegard to find out if he knew anything more about the "joy juice." I looked at my watch; it was eight in the morning. Shorty didn't hold court in the diner on Wednesday mornings so Neil was most likely still at home. I headed that way. His wife, Sharon, answered the door. She greeted me quietly, although she was usually quite hospitable.

"He's not here," she said, her eyes down. "He went out hunting, and I don't know when he'll be back."

"Thank you," I said. "I'm sorry I bothered you. Please let my friend know I was here."

I knew she wanted to say more but she was afraid. As I drove down the street, I saw Neil heading down the alley in his Plymouth in the opposite direction. Should I follow after him? It wasn't worth it. He knew that if he told me anything he would end up like the rest who crossed the Project.

Just then I got a panicked call from Anne, who'd been stopped at the border.

"Come quick, honey," she said, her voice frantic. "They've detained me here after a strip search. They've accused me of trying to smuggle a pound of marijuana into the country. I'm scared. Hurry!"

There was a sudden click. Then the call ended. It was hard not racing to the border, but I knew they would like nothing better than to stop me and throw me in jail, too. Approaching the border station, I saw more of our government money at work. The red brick building looked large enough to house a small company. I was taken from the entrance to a back conference room. Lit by more than 10,000 watts, the room had the warmth of a gulag interrogation cell. I waited alone for thirty minutes, anxious, my body twitchy and nervous.

Finally, Captain George Chang entered. With his slicked-back black hair and an overbearing hubris, he addressed me. "Dr. Lewis we have detained your wife on very serious charges," he said. "We found over a pound of marijuana in her trunk. That might be as common as a bag of groceries on the west coast, but here it means dire consequences. Five to ten years of jail time in a federal prison may be in order. Chief Chow wanted to be here, but he's down talking to Bruce Deeds right now about what happened."

My heart sank. The marijuana was planted in Anne's car to bring me to my knees. It did.

"There is no way Anne would have marijuana in her car," I said, my voice trembling, indignant. "Someone planted it there."

"We hear that all the time," he said. "Before we press formal charges, Bruce Deeds wants to chat with you this afternoon at his office. I think it's a meeting you won't want to miss. It could determine whether your pretty wife ever gets to ride her horse again."

"I'll be there," I said. "Dr. Anderson already told me about the meeting. Now, can I see Anne?"

"She's in the room next door," he said. "You have ten minutes with her."

Anne was visibly shaken. She looked the worst I'd seen her since her father died. Tears flowed down her cheeks and her hands shook. I entered the room. We ran to each other and embraced.

"I brought you your Bible," I said handing it to her.

"Thank you, honey," she smiled, looking at my face. "I can lose everything, but I still have the most important thing in my life. How is your hand? Are Big Sky, Sunny, Beau and Lexy all right?"

"You're amazing!" I said. "Here you sit in jail, and you're more concerned about us. What happened?"

"It's just so frightening," she said as she shook her head. "They pulled me out of the car at gun point after they realized who I was. One of them slammed his hand into my sun glasses, and they shattered. Then he pushed me to the ground."

"Assholes," I said. "I'll get you out of this. I'm going to meet with the one who's behind this charade this afternoon. You'll be free after that. I promise."

"Call Pastor Luke," Anne said. "He's the one who can get me out of this. He is a powerful man in this community who can make anything happen."

"Deeds is calling the shots on this one," I said.

I didn't know whether Luke was friend or foe, but I didn't want at this point to alarm Anne. Besides, I knew the room was bugged.

"I believe God will clear this up," Anne said. "Christians must have tribulations. I'm going to pray that this all will get resolved."

"I'm sure praying to God is good, but he gives us the tools to help ourselves," I said. "Sometimes, prayer isn't enough."

"You've always doubted the power of prayer," she said. "That's really disappointing. Pastor Luke has told me to look to the teachings in Job in times of trouble. Satan roams the earth and God is eager to use our lives as a battlefield. If there wasn't pain, then you wouldn't long for redemption. I'm not going to focus on the temporary, but the eternal. I know that God owes me nothing. I release the feeling of entitlement. I understand part of life is chaos from the sin of Adam and Eve."

"I don't think this is the time to get into Christian theology," I said impatiently. "You pray, and I'll work on the earthly matters. I love you." I bent down and kissed her.

"I love you too," Anne said. "Call Pastor Luke. Please call Pastor Luke."

✎ THIRTY-ONE ✎

USTICE OF THE PEACE, Crash Bastar, hopefully, was my ally. He deserved the name. Three years older than me, Crash got his nickname from crashing the backboards during our neighborhood pickup basketball games. The first time I met him, he told me if I called him bastard he would beat me up. After law school at the University of Montana, Crash came home to run a private law practice and preside over the local court. Ray Koler and Crash had some much publicized run-ins over the years. Ray said he was arrogant and didn't mind bending the law to get his way. With a name like Bastar, he demanded respect.

The County Courthouse was a 1932 Works Project Administration project, a concrete eye sore that greeted everyone looking north on Main Street. Dolling it up with white paint every ten years did little to improve its appearance. The interior was slightly more appealing with dark maple paneling, although the dim lighting was similar to that seen at the local bar. The clerk told me the judge was in his office.

Crash had a penchant for bow ties. When he shook my hand, he had a mischievous twinkle in his eyes. Along with yellowing diplomas, his office walls were adorned with personal photos of Crash and other notables: politicians, coaches, other judges, and regional news personalities. Crash's father was a respected area wheat farmer, but Crash had inherited none of his father's genteel manner and instead demonstrated a certain farm yard crudeness.

"Hell, Don," Crash said as he spit chewing tobacco into a spittoon. "It's great to see you. I heard you were back in town to make sure we didn't end up at the funeral home sooner than later, but until my shit stinks you won't be seeing me in your office. I hate doctors. Everyone I know that goes to the doctor ends up dying. That's not a good proposition."

"Crash, everyone dies," I said. "You're a living example of the saying, the good die young. You should live to 120."

We laughed.

"Crash, old buddy, I need your help," I said in my most charming way. "The border patrol has Anne locked up and accused her of trying to smuggle a pound of marijuana into the country. Someone planted it on her, and between you and me, I think it was them."

The twinkle disappeared faster than a falling star. He rose out of his chair and slowly walked to the window, where he gazed south down Main Street to the downtown. That was not a good sign.

"Don, I've always liked you, but this is not in my jurisdiction," Crash said. "I just have a couple of years left until I can start receiving my pension. It isn't much, but it will allow Peggy and me to travel. The judge that stood up to the Red Scare in the 1920s got two bullets in his head for his valiant efforts."

"Crash, this isn't what I wanted to hear," I said.

"This isn't the same situation as when the warden gave you a ticket for shooting ducks too early in the day," Crash said. "You were lucky back in high school. I know the game warden was pissed when he heard that your dad called me, and I said just forget about the ticket. You'll need to talk to Bruce Deeds regarding this unfortunate situation. He's the real justice in this town."

"I have a meeting with him today, but I'm worried that nothing good will come out of it," I said.

"He's headed up a very successful program here," Crash reminded me as he spit again. "The town feels like someone is on their side. We feel important. He and I are working on the final architectural plans for a remodel of this worn-out building. The Project is going to fund it. They've even interviewed me for their documentary on the Project that will be aired nationally in October on all major TV channels and internet sites. The airing is only a month away, and I'd be rocking the boat if I got in the middle of this fracas. Look, I'm the Justice of the Peace. If I got into this I would lose reelection this fall. It would be political suicide and would affect my pension."

"You mean to tell me your reelection is more important than what's right?" I asked.

"You're naïve, justice isn't important. It's agenda," Crash said.

"I've heard that one before from someone who didn't need a law degree to figure it out," I said. My voice grew louder. "I think you and your Project people are a bunch of bastards who are going straight to hell."

I slammed the door as I left his office. Has there ever been a more effective drug than "joy juice?" Its only flaw was its weight loss affect. There were still lots of overweight folks around town including Judge Bastard. I guess they'd be even heavier without it. Cottonwood had turned into the epicenter of hypnotized zombies, but no one seemed to get it or care. Time had slowed like a walk in gumbo.

Heading to my car, I was gripped with the soullessness of Cottonwood. The railroad tracks that crossed Main Street seemed like the arms of an apathetic stranger who welcomed the good, the bad and the ugly. Soon, the tracks would send the bad and ugly eastbound, and the good in the opposite direction.

✂ THIRTY-TWO ✂

HE TRINITY OFFICE was the last place I wanted to be. The fact that Deeds framed Anne meant that he saw me as a serious threat.

This time, I was shown immediately into his office. Deeds silently grimaced as he pointed to a chair for me to sit in. He paced in front of me, slamming his fist against his leg. His demeanor had changed from that of a salesman trying to close the deal to a prison camp commandant.

"This meeting was supposed to be about the health plan, but you need to have Anne released," I said. "You're the only one that can do it. All I can think about is her safety."

"Look, asshole, you're out of your league," Deeds said in voice that resembled a bark. "If you want Anne home, then you'd better focus on the next 'finger up the butt exam,' and leave worldly matters to me. I haven't sacrificed my life to make sure universal health care is a reality in this country to have it all screwed up by some two-bit Sherlock Holmes. I know you've been nosing around Hell Creek, Poplar, and everywhere else. What the hell are you doing having a tryst with your partner's wife in the back seat of your car? You've seen what's happened to others around here who caused problems. You're getting close to the salvage pile yourself."

"There are lots of crazy things happening around here," I said.

"Look, doctor of democracy and capitalism, I live for health reform," Deeds said. "It's all I think about, whenever I'm not sleeping, and sometimes I even dream about it. I'm running this meeting, and I will address Anne's situation when I damn well please. This is the last time I'm going to explain to you the importance of our health plan. Don't you get it?"

"At this point, I don't give a shit about your health plan," I said. "I'm not going to listen to another minute of your raving. Anne needs to be released right now and have this bogus marijuana charge dropped."

"Not so fast," Deeds said. "We can't just drop something like this. I might consider some leniency or plea bargain if you start acting like one of the team instead of the enemy. Dennis said you never really got team sports and were a pussy."

"That may be the nicest thing he's said about me since I've been back," I said. "Are you going to give us the kind of leniency that you gave Doc Peters, Lightfoot, Steve Thompson, Ray Koler, and Pastor Tim?"

"Accidents happen," Deeds said. He paused and walked to the window, gazing outside. "As far as Lightfoot and Pastor Tim are concerned, they had resistant tuberculosis and needed treatment. We can't have them running around our community like Typhoid Mary."

"I have documents that prove murders were committed," I said. "If anything happens to Anne, Abigail, or me, they will be sent to every national paper. That should put an end to your Trinity Project."

"Oh, so you and Abigail were exchanging more than body fluids in the back seat," Deeds said. "Dennis has been showing signs of being overly stressed. We know he's drinking too much, and you know when you drink too much your mind can wander. Things are written down that are pure fantasy. There's no proof of any wrongdoing. We have the bases covered. With your good behavior, I may have Anne released Friday. Without your cooperation, I will personally make sure she doesn't ride her horse for at least twenty years."

"You're telling me that you'd put away an innocent person for years?" I said.

"I wasn't only talking about jail time," Deeds said. "I was talking about a few serious fractures our Chinese border patrolmen would love to inflict on her, but only after they take their turns giving her a little affection, if you know what I mean."

"You're beyond evil," I said.

"That's no way to talk to your boss," Deeds said. "What if we found cocaine in the car too? Or terrorist connections? It's amazing what you can come up with when you keep investigating. Look, I need to get back to work. We have to wrap up our data by tomorrow before I leave on Friday's noon train. The officers will be with me. I'll have them release Anne before we board, or she'll accompany us to Minneapolis. I think you can see the IDS tower from the downtown federal prison. You decide."

"Release her, and I'll hand over the documents," I said although I knew I wouldn't give the papers up until all other avenues were exhausted.

I felt sick inside as if I just made a deal with the devil. There was no proof of the murders. The dead were buried, and they don't make good witnesses. I'm sure by now the human remains were removed from the caves. Dennis could make up some excuse. The government, Senator Hart, Deeds, Pastor Luke, Dennis and the community would unite to have me lynched in the town square. It would be a scene right out of *Lonesome Dove*.

"Good. Anne should be your priority," Deeds said. "We all have our priorities. Now go out and be a good citizen. Do the right thing. Get ready to take care of patients. You doctors make poor politicians. You let your emotions and morals get in your way of seeing the big picture. I'll be gone soon, and Cottonwood can live happily every after and bask in the stardom of knowing it was the site for the beginnings of a new America. Anne will make a wonderful pastor."

I was shown to the door.

∽ THIRTY-THREE ∽

T HE SWEET SMELL OF HAY was better than a tranquilizer.
The horses were glad to see me, since it was their feed-
ing time. They didn't care about health care, murder,
or manipulation. They just wanted some chow. I was petting Big
Sky's back when something smacked the side of my head and it
rocked forward. It was a basketball. Turning around, I saw Dennis.

"Catch the basketball, Junior," Dennis said. "Put a saddle on
him and get out of town. You scared?"

"Yes and more," I said bewildered.

Dennis pulled the saddle off the rack and threw it on the star-
tled horse's back. "You never had good hands, Junior," he said.

"You hit me in the back of the head," I said.

"Oh, yeah," Dennis said. "You never had a good head, either.
One thing you still have is the hots for Abigail. That bitch. They
showed me the infrared photos of you two the other night. Now
get on that damn gelding. You're trying to screw up our mission."

"What's that?" I asked defiantly. "Come in on budget by killing the old and weak? And where in the hell do you think I'm
going to ride? No horse can take me that far."

"Canada or hell would suffice," Dennis said. "What I've accomplished is called sensible health care rationing. It has to happen. Eugenics makes sense. Do you want to spend $100,000 on an old fart so he can spend the last six months of his life shitting in his underwear or do you want to provide care to a thousand children who have their productive years ahead of them? Easy call, I'd say."

"Who said you could play God—Pastor Luke?" I asked.

"We had to make tough decisions," he said. "Your hero, Teddy Roosevelt, would be on board. He was a Progressive and believed in social Darwinism. You know—survival of the fittest."

"Roosevelt said natural selection may account for the survival of the fittest, but not for the arrival of the fittest. He had a deep belief in God," I said.

"Professor, you're always so full of bullshit," Dennis said. "I believe in evolution. Any good scientist does. "

"Your evolution is lowering the standards of human behavior to nothing more than that of animals," I said. "That's why you believe in it."

"I didn't come out here to take Religion 101 from a prick like you," he said. "I came out here to kick your ass."

With that he grabbed me and pushed me into Big Sky. I threw a punch but missed. His didn't.

When my head cleared, I looked up at the barn clock. It was ten in the evening. I'd been out for hours. I limped into the house, my head and left hip on fire. Three Advil and a glass of scotch put me out for the night.

∾ PART SEVEN *∾*

DETONATION

Thursday
September 27, 2020

∽ THIRTY-FOUR ∽

THE MORNING BROKE with the lilting song of a meadowlark. I felt inspired, but I didn't know why. After chores, I was on the road and headed into the Elgin Café. The towns-people needed to know what was going on before it was too late and on my way into town, I rehearsed what I was going to say. As I reached for the Elgin's door knob, Bruce Deeds almost knocked me over as he came out. He just stared at me as he brushed past me and walked down the street.

The place was packed, every table humming. There wasn't an empty seat at the counter. I sensed Deeds beat me to the unofficial town meeting, and the crowd was in no mood to hear from me.

Jim Pesci, the owner, had his back to me as he spewed forth. "I agree with Deeds that Lewis and his wife have turned into real trouble for this town."

Everyone nodded. The rumble of voices halted when they realized I had just entered the room.

"I didn't know you were here," Pesci said. "That's quite a shiner under your left eye. We heard Dennis needed to inflict a little western justice on you for screwing around with his wife. Deeds just showed us photos of you two together in your car."

"Folks, I've known most of you all my life," I said. "You know I'm honest. Nothing was happening between Abigail and me. She was sharing information about the Trinity."

I heard a few snickers break out.

"That crazy woman was sharing more than information," a voice yelled out.

"That's not true," I said. "I hate to tell you, but there are some bad things going on in this town. The Trinity Project is not what it seems. They've lied to you and manipulated you. I have proof they're behind some recent deaths. They're drugging the communion wine. Now, they have Anne up at the border on bogus charges. I need your support."

There was silence. I looked to see if Shorty was there, but he was missing. Coming to the Elgin was a big mistake.

"You must be crazy," Pesci said. "You'll try anything to get your new wife out of a fix. She's not one of us. For all we know she is a west coast hippie with a dope problem, and Dennis tells us that Abigail needs shock treatment. We hear she's leaving town tomorrow because she couldn't stand the shame. The sooner she leaves the better. Anyone that doesn't go to a church is plumb loco. You should have never come back here. We don't need another doctor that bad. The Trinity will find us another pill pusher."

With that, several people laughed and shook their heads in agreement. I looked around the room into lots of apathetic eyes. I hoped the drug was to blame for their lack of action.

"They were grooming my son to be the next pastor here after Luke left," Harv "Great Falls Select" Mann, owner of the Orpheum Movie Theater, said. "It wasn't fair that your wife got the spot instead. My wife, Lucky, and I are sure you negotiated that as part of the deal to come back. Well, if I wasn't such a good Christian, I would beat the shit out of you, but I don't act like that anymore."

218

"Look, there were no deals regarding Anne," I said. "You've got to listen to me. Tomorrow they're leaving on the train with information that will support a universal health plan that is just a bunch of smoke and mirrors. Worse yet, it will lead to the Chinese takeover of this country. I can't believe you want that."

"When are the Martians arriving?" Hook asked. "I always thought Shorty should have stayed clear of your family. He's my brother, but he's made some bad calls. I've done everything to get him to go to church, but he won't. I pray for him every night. Who do we believe, Pastor Luke, Doc Dennis and Bruce Deeds, the three who have united us though Jesus and brought prosperity and good health to Cottonwood, or the irrational ranting of someone who was caught with his pants down? He must have smoked some pot before he came in here. Get the hell out of here."

Others shouted for me to go. With that I turned and left. The last comment really stung coming from Shorty's brother, Hook. I hoped Shorty didn't feel that way. Where was he?

✌ THIRTY-FIVE ✌

I DECIDED TO CHECK ON SHORTY, who lived two blocks from the Elgin. I knocked on his back door where a sign above it said "Welcome to Shorty's bar, Come on in." I walked through the family room that was still decorated with the same 1950s furniture of my youth. Even though it was a little more tattered, the recliner still looked like it could support three boys eating ice cream and watching *The Lone Ranger*.

I looked through the door and into his bedroom, and there Shorty was lying on top of the covers with only his underwear on. He looked horrible. Sweat rolled off his feverish body. The skin that covered his once muscled torso sagged over his sides. His face was flushed.

"Shorty, you okay?" I asked. Then I noticed his hearing aids were lying on the night stand.

I handed them to him.

"Shorty, are you okay?" I asked. Fortunately for him, the Project wasn't using the quick acting and more deadly T.B. strain from China in Cottonwood. Dennis's notes said that they reserved that for the rest of the SEN region.

"Every day is Christmas," he said with a weak smile. "I got an appointment to see Doc Dennis this afternoon before he leaves tomorrow. He said I've got T.B., and they're going to put me on the next bus to Galen. I feel like crap. I hope they can help me there."

"Shorty, trust me on this one," I shouted frantically. "Don't get on the bus to Galen. Promise me you won't. Patients don't return from there. They're killing them. You can do just as well staying here. This fever will break in a day or two. Most folks recover without treatment. I will get you over this. I'll even make house calls."

"Doc Dennis said if I'd gone to church like everyone else, then Satan wouldn't have kicked my ass likes he's doin'," Shorty said. "I didn't know what he was talking about. That talk might work on all the religious types, but it has about as big effect on me as someone pissin' on my leg. They're both off target."

"Don't trust Dennis," I said.

"That kid always was full of himself," Shorty said. "I'm in my nineties. I lived to play, and I'm still playing. I have my own God. He's the God of good morals, hard work, beautiful prairie sunrises, and loving family and friends. All the religious types never can explain why there is pain and sufferin'. They whine and rationalize. Hell, the answer is easy. God is saving a pain-free life for heaven. The Devil's kickin' our ass now. We're in his country."

"I'm back to stay and will never leave," I said. "I'm going to rid Cottonwood of the curse of the Trinity. You're going to be just fine. Drink plenty of water and stay in bed."

"Dennis told me not to take anything for the fever," Shorty said. "That doesn't seem right."

"That should prove to you that he's up to no good," I said. "If your fever gets too high, you could have a seizure. You need to take Advil. Where is it?"

"The medicine cabinet," Shorty said.

"Take three every four to six hours until the fever breaks," I said after retrieving the pills. "I'll have the boys check in on you later today, and I'll come by tomorrow afternoon. Take care, dad."

"I aint goin' nowhere, son." Shorty said in a weak voice and fell to sleep.

✑ THIRTY-SIX ✑

THE DRIVE TO THE BORDER seemed to take hours, miles upon miles of miles of nothingness. My mind was half-numb and half-searching for some kind of answer, a solution to this mess. I simply had to see Anne.

The officer on the other side of the bullet proof glass window told me that, Sam Chow, the head of the border patrol, wanted to talk to me before I could see Anne. He, no doubt, was Deed's henchman who was responsible for killing Doc Peters and Ray and for trying to kill Steve.

"We finally meet," Chow said in perfect English. "Have a seat. We have a few matters to discuss. You've been a big disappoint-ment to the Project since you returned."

"Feeling's mutual," I said, my face flushing. My hands clenched in a fist.

"Look, I am the law enforcer around here," Chow said as he grabbed me by the collar. "I take orders from only Mr. Deeds and ultimately, Dr. Chen."

"So the Chinese government doesn't trust Deeds either," I said. "I knew you guys were smart."

"Very funny, Dr. Lewis," Chow said and pushed me down into a seat. "It's our culture not to trust you Americans. We call it 'defensive nationalism.' Since schoolchildren we were taught that China was humiliated for centuries by foreign powers, and that unrelenting support of the Communist state is the only way for China to regain its greatness. Chinese know that foreigners who talk about human rights are doing so only to bash us. We know that human rights are only relative. What's more important to us now is having healthy comrades."

"That's where the Trinity Health Plan comes in," I said.

"Right," Chow said. "It's important we keep an eye on the Trinity's bottom line."

"You seem quite familiar with our American sayings," I said.

"We Chinese have studied you Americans closely, while you arrogant Americans don't have a clue what makes us tick," Chow said.

"That's right," I said. My knuckles whitened as I gripped the arms of the chair. "Where does the murdering come into play?"

"You have no proof of that," Chow snapped. "Change your tune if you want to see your pretty wife at home again. If I was in China now, I would have you arrested for talking like that. Someday, we'll have that power here, and we'll ship all you American doctors to China to take care of our brothers and sisters."

"What about her Miranda Rights?" I asked.

"There isn't a lawyer around here that would represent her," Chow said. "So there is no need for her to make a phone call."

"Especially after you killed our friend, Ray Koler," I said.

"Unfortunately, he didn't know his horses well enough, or he might have been around to help Anne out," Chow said with a wry smile. "It must have been painful to lie there in the paddock gasping for air with those broken ribs. Nasty. Besides, don't you know that those linked to terrorism don't have rights? They're tried in a military tribunal."

"Terrorism?" I said incredulously. "What the hell are you talking about now?"

"We found notes in her possession outlining her attempt to smuggle suspects living in Regina with known terrorist links across the border," Chow said. "We Chinese are much better at finding the terrorists than you Americans. Your state department is already praising our work here uncovering this ring."

"Unbelievable bullshit," I said.

"Anne may not have told you, but she hung out with some anarchist at Reed College in Portland," Chow said. "Remember the movie, *Reds*? That was set in Portland. I thought Warren Beatty did a great job."

"I'm not interested in a movie review," I said as I stood up. "This is a frame job if I ever saw one. Can I see Anne now?"

"Sure, but only for a few minutes," Chow said as he walked out of the room. "Remember, she has no rights. If you'd only taken communion like a good Christian, you wouldn't be in this predicament."

"Yeah, I'd be walking around Cottonwood like the rest of the zombies," I said as Anne was escorted into the room.

She looked horrible. We embraced and cried. At this point, I didn't care if they were eavesdropping on us.

"Everything's going to be okay," I said. "I talked to Deeds, and he said you'd be released tomorrow."

I didn't mention the latest terrorist charge.

"I hate it here," she said trembling. "Why would they hold me here and plant pot in my car? Your face looks like hell!"

"Dennis and I had a little dispute," I said. "There's a big misunderstanding, but everything's going to be alright come Friday."

"They showed me a video of you and Abigail in the back seat of your car," Anne said looking me in the eyes. "They told me that they have audio tapes of heavy breathing and love talk. Chow said they may entertain the idea that the pot was planted by Abigail if you'd stop stirring things up and sign some disclaimers. Don, I can't believe you did this."

"I didn't do anything wrong," I said. "Abigail gave me copies of notes that Dennis wrote proving that they're killing people on purpose to make their health plan successful. They're drugging the communion wine, Anne. That's why everyone, including you, has been in a submissive fog. They're trying to portray Abigail as some wacko. She's not. The notes she gave me are the only reason the two of us are still alive!"

"I'll try believing you Don, but it will take prayer," Anne said.

I kissed her forehead. "I'm working to clear things up. I wouldn't be doing this if I didn't love you," I said.

"Have you talked to Pastor Luke yet?" Anne asked

"I'm going to talk to him this afternoon," I said.

"Does he know about the communion wine?" Anne asked.

"I'm not sure, but I hope not," I said.

"I can't imagine him knowing," Anne said.

"Well, we're all sinners, but I don't think his sins include murder," I said. "Hang in there. I love you, and I promise that you will be out of here by tomorrow."

I didn't know if that would calm her, but I needed to say something to cheer her up.

∽ THIRTY-SEVEN ∽

As I DROVE BACK TO COTTONWOOD, a speeding car zoomed by me headed north towards the border. As it passed, I watched in the rear view mirror as the car spun around and closed in on me. I slowed down and pulled off on a side dirt road. The car came to a screeching halt close behind me. I let out a breath. It was my old friend, Choteau. We pulled the cars up, side by side, to visit.

"Howdy!" Choteau said. "Thought I'd take Fran's Cadillac out for a spin and heard you might be up this way. What in the hell have they done with Anne? Those sonsofabitches."

"They have Anne locked up on bogus charges, and they're trying to blackmail me into not uncovering the Trinity charade," I said.

"What the hell's going on?" Choteau asked

"The Trinity Project is killing people," I said. "When they deem someone undesirable, Deeds and Dennis have them killed. That's what happened to Doc Peters, Steve, and Ray. Others, like

227

Lightfoot, were falsely diagnosed with resistant T.B. or infected with it and sent off to Galen."

"Holy crap," Choteau said. "Dennis always was a shit head. And Deeds struts around town with his bleached blonde slut wife. I can tell you she likes cowboys. She's half Deed's size and a fraction of his conceit, but I hear she's quite a bucker."

"You have the descriptive powers of a poet," I said. "Look, it all boils down to eugenics. They believe it's the only real way to control health care costs."

"Eugenics?" What's that? Choteau asked. "Is that where you took your pre-med courses in Oregon?"

"No, Choteau, that was Eugene," I said.

"I know," Choteau said. "I just said that for a little shits and giggles. We can't get too dark here."

"You're so right," I said.

"Me and you are like old cowboys cleanin' the town up of the bad guys wearin' black hats," Choteau said. "I hate them cocky, city slickers that makes fun of us cowboys. To me, the cowboy stands for self-reliance, friendship, honesty, hard work, and doin' the right thing. Those city folks don't know shit."

"We're the two amigos," I said.

"I can bust Anne out of that tin can of a cell," Choteau said. "I installed the sprinkler system in that jail. I knowed the weasel contractor that they brought in from Denver to build it. He got paid by the Project three times what it cost to build. He left out rebar and cut corners. The hell if they cared. They ain't friends of mine so I didn't care either. My old Chevy pickup has more than enough horses to pull the bars out of the window in that shit can. Just give the word, and she's done."

"I know I have a friend in you, but let me think that one over," I said. "Choteau, I'm not sure what to do. It's just you and me against the world or at least the world created by these crooks."

"I know Munchie's on board," Choteau said.

"Let's leave Munchie out of this," I said. "He isn't sober long enough to be of any help. Joel and Craig might help, but if I get them involved, they'll lose their jobs."

With that, we shook hands.

"I'll come over later today," I said. "I'm sure they have my cell phone bugged."

"I'll be home sharpenin' my pecker ax," Choteau said. "Isn't retirement great?"

∽ THIRTY-EIGHT ∽

PASTOR LUKE was the one member of the Trinity I thought might not be part of the conspiracy. Surely, he had a higher calling than to use religion to scheme with Deeds and Doc Dennis to get the Trinity Health Plan adopted nationally. If he wasn't involved, I figured he would be devastated to realize that his high church attendance rate was the courtesy of spiked wine. He was my last, best chance. Pastor Luke was the one voice that could move the town to action. When he found out that his partners were killing off patients, he would halt this holocaust. I drove to the church. Outside, the parking lot was relatively empty. Inside, employees were everywhere packing boxes for the move to Minneapolis.

"Is Pastor Luke in?" I asked his secretary as I rushed through the door.

"He's busy, Dr. Lewis. Can I help you with something?" She asked.

"This is something that can't wait," I said, impatiently. "I need to see him now."

I moved past her and opened the door to his office. The timing was perfect. He was just finishing a phone call. He smiled and motioned me in.

"Dr. Lewis," Pastor Luke said. "Please have a seat. It's nice to see you again. Are you doing your Bible study on your time off this week?"

"Pastor Luke," I said. "Please. There's some important information I need to share with you. Deeds and Anderson are doing bad things."

"Now, now," he said in a reassuring voice. "Nothing is more important than the Bible. Where's the passion? God hates lukewarm."

"Please!" I said.

"No, no, no," he said emphatically. "Before we go any further, it's Bible study time. I want to see what kind of man Anne married. I'm sure Anne has told you about my spiritual exercise."

"Yes," I said in a defeated voice. I figured I better not annoy my last best hope.

"Here we go then," he said, his voice high, excited like that of a child. "I can't be all things to all people. The Project is a great success, and for you to cast the first stone is unholy. You have seemed like a doubting Thomas from the beginning. I want the townspeople to enjoy themselves on Sunday. I want them to eat, drink, and be merry but stay away from the forbidden fruit. Deeds is a man after my own heart and is the salt of the earth. This 'woe is me attitude' of yours will get you fired. Don't you see the writing on the wall?"

"You just quoted nine sayings from the Bible: 1 Corinthians, John, Luke, Genesis, 1 Samuel, Acts, Matthew, Job, and Daniel," I said. "Those were the ones that you wanted us to memorize for this month to demonstrate how Bible sayings permeate our society."

"I'm impressed," he said. "I was testing you to see if you were taking your Bible study seriously. You are. That gives you more credibility. Proceed. "

"Deeds and Anderson are evil," I abruptly said. "They've killed your members when they've consumed too many health care dollars and ruined the Project's bottom line. They're so desperate to secure money from the Chinese that they'll do anything to make their financial bottom line better to impress their financial backers."

"Don, you must be under tremendous strain moving back here," Pastor Luke said with a grimace, and then he forced himself to smile. "I know change can be stressful. Anne told me you have been up almost for a week straight. What you're saying is pure fantasy. I'm shocked. Bruce and Dennis are Godly men who share my vision of a socialistic nation with quality health insurance for everyone and that has a unified vision of Christianity. To suggest that they are murderers is absurd. Satan has grabbed hold of you."

"Listen to me," I said breathless. "They've grabbed hold of Anne at the border and accused her of being a drug runner and having terrorist ties. I'm sure you've heard. Everyone else in town knows about it. You know Anne on a deeply spiritual level. She would never do those things. Deeds was behind her arrest."

"No one told me that," he said. "No one has told me. Sometimes, the last one to hear the confession is the spiritual leader. I have total confidence in…."

"Anne, right?" I blurted out.

"Bruce Deeds, one of the brightest and most spiritual men I have ever met, the head elder of the church who possesses a vision not of this earth," Pastor Luke said. "No, He's why I'm here and why I will be leading the national church. Anne is Judas. I've been waiting all my life for Judas to appear and ruin me and my career. I preach that we are all sinners, but I have always wondered when my worst sin would appear. I sinned by having faith in Anne, but God will forgive me for that. I was deceived by Satan just like Adam and Eve. In God's eyes my slate is clean. "

"What?" Anne? Judas?" My skin grew taut, my face hot. "Anne is not Judas," I said. I thought it was time to burst his bubble. "Look, you were right when you said religion isn't an opiate, but your communion wine is. They've been drugging your communion wine with an experimental drug that makes people submissive and artificially happy. I hate to tell you, but your high attendance rate was only achieved by drugs."

"Blaspheme," Pastor Luke said. "I don't believe a word. I'm not going to let you ruin my send-off on Friday or the accomplishments of the Trinity Project."

"I thought you would help me uncover this charade," I said. "I'm very disappointed."

"God has uncovered someone who is unfit to head our church here," he said. "I'm disappointed in Anne, although I suspect she may have done this to support your drug dependency. Bruce Deeds told me this week that you were dependent on marijuana and prescription drugs. He said you obtained marijuana legally in Oregon for a back injury, but after you were over it, you increased your usage to handle the stress of your medical practice. He said you essentially had a mental breakdown in Oregon, and Deeds and Doc Dennis were doing you a favor by hiring you. They were trying to give you a chance for redemption."

"Hog wash," I said. "I don't smoke dope. Listen, they had Doc Peters killed. It was no accidental drowning. He found out about Dennis faking false tuberculosis tests on patients so he could have them removed from the health plan permanently. Dennis is your devil's helper."

"You're getting more absurd by the minute," Pastor Luke said. "Get the hell out of here. I'm calling the guards if you don't."

"I hope you take that picture of the prodigal son with you and stick it up your holy ass," I said.

He slammed his Bible down and shook his fist at me. I thought I'd better escape before I was handcuffed and sent to jail. I wasn't sure if he knew what was going on, but I chose to believe he didn't. Still, his crazy acceptance of Deed's bullshit was bizarre. Maybe, he was on the "joy juice" too.

I headed to the parking lot, determined to go straight to the Riba House to destroy the hard drive with all the Trinity Project statistics before they took it back East. That was my only chance. It was stored in the computer room of the Riba House, but there was high security around the building.

Still, a closer look at the Riba House was in order. It was almost a half mile to the Old Town Site from the Cottonwood city limits. The drive alongside the River of Doubt was picturesque with poplar and cottonwood trees thick along the banks. Their sparse leaves were quaking in the wind. The river itself barely moved this time of year and was muddy. There was prime real estate along the river, but after the big flood and people moved out of the low lying areas, the land was made into a park.

The Riba house sat about one hundred yards off the main road surrounded by a twelve-foot, 30,000-volt barbed wire fence. Security cameras were strategically placed so if I scaled the fence, I would be noticed. The entrance was gated with a security guard stationed just outside it.

I parked my car a few hundred yards beyond the entrance and climbed up a hill that overlooked the house and the valley. To the south was Cottonwood, and to the north I could see the base of the dam. The next hill over was the cemetery, and across the river was the care center.

Maybe, I thought, Choteau and I could pull the gate down and rush the guards. His Cadillac had about as much steel in it as a Panzer tank. I figured we may get to the front door before they mowed us down with machine gun fire.

An hour or two passed. My mind was numb as I tried to figure out what to do: reverse course or move forward into the unknown. I decided I needed to move forward.

I walked down the hill and headed home. My latest plan was to retrieve the notes Abigail gave me and share them with Stu at the *Herald* newspaper. His family fought against communism, and I was confident he would publish those damning papers in the Friday morning edition.

✎ THIRTY-NINE ✎

I SADDLED UP BIG SKY, and we headed to the coulee where I hid the papers. Thankfully, the box looked undisturbed. About one hundred yards away a coyote scampered away from me as fast as he could. As I reached down to grab the notes, I heard a voice from behind.

"America is full of spiritual pollution. It is partly sex, drugs and rock 'n roll, but also democracy and human rights. The Trinity Project will put an end to pollution more toxic than a thousand Chinese coal-fired plants. The Trinity Cornerstone Church will spread the message of socialism across the globe. China will have the last word and no white coated doctor is going to screw things up. Now hand over those papers. Dennis was sloppy, and I don't tolerate sloppy."

It was Chief Sam Chow from the border.

"I'm not going to let that presentation in Minneapolis happen," I said. Boy, was he a big dude.

"That presentation doesn't matter," Chow said. "Do you really think the Chinese government is stupid enough to dole out trillions of dollars based on a study conducted in this shit hole?

Deeds, Pastor Luke, and Anderson are testimonies to the arrogance and self importance that highly educated Americans possess. My Chinese bosses can't wait to get Americans hooked on universal health care. It's the final nail in the coffin of capitalism after Europe fell into our control in 2016. At least we didn't have to deal with religion in Europe. We just promised them more entitlements. The Chinese government doesn't care about the study results, but we know it needs to look successful to the American politicians and voters. "

"Appearance is everything, I guess," I said.

"That's right," Chen said. "Now, hand those papers over."

"You're going to have to shoot me and then explain how it happened," I said. "No accident or tuberculosis is going to explain my death."

"I've got a better idea," Chow said. "Listen, we've kept you alive so we could locate these stolen papers. I'll either take them from your corpse or from you while you're alive. It doesn't matter to me. One dead American is what I call a good day."

"Go ahead, shoot me," I said.

"That would be too easy on you," Chow said. He smiled. "The penalty should match the crime. In your case, I'll use my horse whip until there's enough blood loss that I can stake you to that cross over there. How fitting that the cross you all made for Easter will be the place you take your last breath. Where's your savior when you need him?"

"He's with me all the time," I said. My voice sounded shaky.

"We'll know shortly that's not true," Chow said. "Our investigation will show that your friends, Choteau and Munchie, did this horrible deed in a devil worship ceremony. That won't surprise church members. Those two are already on their shit list. I attend the church every Sunday. Pastor Luke preaches that if you're not worshipping Jesus, then you're worshipping Satan. This will just prove it."

"Talking about Satan worship, what's the deal with the goat head in the toilet?" I asked. "I'm sure that was your creation."

"You're so perceptive," Chow said. "I was reading the Old Testament where it explained atonement. One goat was sacrificed to remove sins and another, the scapegoat, was spared and sent off into the desert with the sins of the nation. I sent a warning to you that if you behaved, you wouldn't have to be sacrificed. You two just didn't get it. See where Anne is because of your sin? You were the scapegoat, and now you've forced us to make you a human sacrifice for your sin. This is your hour of atonement."

"That's a bizarre analogy," I said.

"The problem with you modern Christians is that you don't spend enough time absorbing the Old Testament," he said. "I did enjoy chasing down the goat and strangling it. Chopping its head off was somewhat disagreeable. I got a little blood splattered back in my face."

"You're sick," I said as I shook my head.

"It was my idea to have *simul justus et peccator* inscribed on the Galen bracelets," Chow said proudly. "We know you saw Light-foot's bracelet at his home in Poplar."

"What was that all about?" I asked.

"Again, you need better religious and medical training. This confirms education in America is crap," he said. "It was a phrase that fed Martin Luther's theology. We are all saints and sinners. Some are more comfortable being saints, and some are more comfortable being sinners. Didn't you learn Latin in medical school?"

"Only the dermatologists did," I said.

"Forgive me Lord, for I know not what I do," Chow said. He threw his head back and laughed as he started whipping me.

The burn from the leather sliced my skin. I gasped. Big Sky went berserk. In one quick motion, he reared up and thrust his front right hoof into the back of Chow's head and rolled on top of him. Who said horseshoes aren't worth the expense? He was dead.

The horse was panting, whinnying, and shaking its mane as it shifted from foot to foot over Chow's body.

"Well, boy, he should have worried more about the Sky falling," I said. "I guess the Chinese don't know about Chicken Little, but there are a lot of things they don't know about America."

I grabbed the notes and jumped on the back of Big Sky and headed back to the ranch. Blood was all over my shirt, and dizziness washed over me. I cleaned the wounds with hydrogen peroxide and rubbed some antibiotic ointment on them. I drank four glasses of lemonade and ate some pickles. The salt would keep my blood pressure up. Then, I rested for about an hour before I felt like I had the strength to go on. Publishing the notes in the *Herald*, I figured, might be my last chance.

✑ FORTY ✑

ANDERSON AND DEEDS needed to be stopped before they got on the noon train. The Chinese would have to withdraw their support if all the bad deeds of the Project were revealed. I was convinced if I showed Stu the notes he would publish them in the *Herald*. The *Herald* office was buzzing with the deadline for the Friday edition looming. I walked through the outer rooms and directly into Stu's office. I could tell he was editing text for tomorrow's edition.

"Stu, I need to talk to you" I said. My voice was low and quiet and serious. "This may be the most important information your paper has ever published."

Stu peered at me from over his reading glasses. "I'm already editing the most important edition this paper has ever published," Stu said. "The whole issue is dedicated to the Trinity Project. Pastor Luke, Dr. Anderson, and Bruce Deeds have all written guest editorials. We're also adding wonderful testimonials by many folks on the success of the Project over the last few years! Sorry, but we had to move the article about you out a couple of weeks. Our online edition will reach the entire world!"

"Stu, it's a hoax," I said. "They killed Ray, Doc Peters, my friend Steve, and lots of others and they're drugging the communion wine. Look, I have papers from Dennis proving everything. They need to be published tomorrow so everyone in the county and the country knows the truth. For the sake of America, we can't let the Project succeed."

I threw the papers on his desk. My cell phone rang. It was Abigail.

"Hi, Abigail, hold on," I said. "Stu, I'm going to step out for a minute. I'll be right back."

"Fine," Stu said not hiding his annoyance with me.

"Abigail, what's wrong?" I said talking from outside the *Herald* office.

"Dennis said they're going to kill you. He told me he drugged the coffee I drank twenty minutes ago," Abigail said in a slow but frantic voice. "Then, he stormed out. I'm feeling unstable and dizzy. I called Delia, and she's here with me now. "

"Look," I said. Then, I heard a crash as her phone hit the floor.

There was a pause, and then Delia got on the line. "Don," she said. "It looks like she's passed out. What should I do?"

"I'm sure Dennis gave her just enough to knock her out until he can take her on the train with him tomorrow," I said. "Just watch her respirations and her pulse. If there's a big change in either, call me."

"Don," Delia said. "There's a bottle of sleeping pills on her night stand. I think she took some of them. Dennis wouldn't drug the coffee. I don't believe this paranoid stuff about the Trinity. Good bye."

I was overcome with frustration. I had to get those papers published. I went back to convince Stu.

"Don, why did you have to come back to town and cause all this trouble?" Stu asked. "Your wife has disappointed everyone around here. And you and Abigail are the talk of the town."

"Abigail met with me to give me the notes I just gave you," I said. "She's being framed. Abigail just told me that Dennis drugged her."

"You're a little too late trying to pull that one over on me," Stu said. "We had our men's Christian luncheon today, and Dennis told us that Abigail is mentally ill, and that he will be sedating her before she leaves with him tomorrow on the train. We all prayed for God to forgive you. When they return from Minneapolis, he's arranged to have her committed to the state mental hospital. You took advantage of her when she was most vulnerable. Everybody in town knows you were trying to score one on Dennis."

"I'm not going to listen to this crap anymore," I said. "Where are the notes I gave you. I want them back."

"I shredded them while you were out talking to your latest poke," Stu said. "Now, get the hell out of here. You should have never come back. "

I stared at him in silence and turned around and left the office.

∽ FORTY-ONE ∽

VENTUALLY, I found myself driving on the road to the dam hoping to get help from Joel and Craig. It was late afternoon, and it looked like the construction workers were gone for the day. I hated to draw them into this mess, but time was short. Like the homes in Cottonwood, the construction office was unlocked, and no one was inside.

A chill came over me. The thought of the dam breaching always scared me when I was a kid. It became clear what I needed to do. Dynamite was already in place to blow out a section of the dam. Push the detonator button, and there goes the Riba House, the hard drives, the Project. If I pushed the button, Joel and Craig would be fingered for giving me the code. Their careers would be jeopardized as would our brother-like friendship.

I hesitated. The Trinity covered their tracks as far as the murders, and now the papers were gone. No proof existed of any wrongdoing, and it looked like Dennis and Deeds had everyone convinced I was having an affair with Abigail. I opened the cover on the detonator button and entered the six-digit code: Joel's birth date. Sweat poured down my forehead. My finger shook as

I moved it in the direction of the button. I sat down next to the button and spaced out for I don't know how long.

"What the hell are you doing?" Joel shouted as he shook me. "Have you lost your mind?"

"Man, don't scare the shit out of me like that," I said in a daze.

"We've been trying to talk to you, but you've just been staring off in space," Craig said.

"Lack of sleep, I guess," I said. "Look, I need to flood the Riba House where the Trinity computer records are kept. They're taking them back east tomorrow on the noon train, and then there's no turning back for this country. They've killed Doc Peters, Ray, Pastor Tim and others who have gotten in their way of making this Trinity Project charade a success. I've got proof, or I should say, I had proof before Stu shredded it at the *Herald* office."

"Shit!" Joel said with an incredulous look.

Dennis infected your dad with tuberculosis," I said. "He's home in bed burning up with a fever. Get over there. If you don't, they'll have Shorty on the bus to Galen, and then it's all over for him."

"Wow!" Craig said. "That's a lotta jerky to gnaw on. Hold on there. We need time to digest this. Is dad going to be all right?"

"I think so," I said. "The fever needs to be controlled right now so he doesn't have a seizure. He's taking Advil."

"What are the chances of him dying?" Joel said.

"Fairly low," I said. "Fortunately, he isn't infected with the quick acting, Chinese strain."

"That's good news," Joel said. "Are you sure Dennis infected him?"

"Look, I've never lied to you guys before," I said staring back and forth at both of them. "I am positive he did this to your dad. The Project is spiking the communion wine with a drug that makes you feel good and submissive. Look, you two used to argue all the time."

"We did," Joel said. "I thought we were getting along so well because we were back in town with a job and had matured."

"I did too," Craig said. "But you know in the last week we've started arguing more. I pegged that to the stress of getting close to D day, detonation day. Joel even pushed me against the wall the other day."

"Now that sounds like the old Joel," I said. "Remember, he broke most of my front teeth out when we were kids. Tell me something. Did you guys have communion last Sunday?"

"Come to think of it," Joel said. "We haven't had communion the last four weeks but don't tell anyone."

"Yeah" Craig said. "Shorty insisted that we go pheasant hunting with him. It's peak season. We've never missed four Sundays in a row, and we're ashamed of that. Pastor Luke demands that everyone in the congregation attend every week, and if you miss, you should stop by during the week to take communion. They even installed a drive up window, but we were so busy we never did. "

"Communion to go. Unbelievable," I said.

"If you miss two weeks, and he finds out, then you have to take a special course." Joel said. "Kinda like I had to do when I got a speeding ticket erased from my record."

"We both felt horrible for missing church, but we watched it later on the internet," Craig said.

"Thank the Lord for hunting," I said. "It may have saved this town and country. So, are you ready to help?"

"We're on board, brother," Craig said. "Tell us what we can do to help?"

"There's no time," I said. "Anne's in jail up at the border. They planted dope on her and are holding her on bogus terrorist charges. That could mean big jail time."

With that, I pushed the button. Nothing happened.

"We change the code every day," Craig said with a disappointed look. "Today, it's my birthday, not his. You're lucky, anyway.

We've got the temporary dam almost completed. If it would have blown, only a small trickle of water would go down the river."

"Then it's over," I said and dropped into a chair slumped over. "We're doomed."

"Don't give up," Joel said. "I said we're almost done. We still have the last panel unsecured. Lift that piece with a crane, and you'll flood the computer room at the Riba House with ten feet of water. Through each step of construction, we calculated a worst case scenario if the dam failed. Part of doing a thorough job is covering your ass if something bad happens."

"I love engineers," I said. "How long will it take to get the crane in position and lift the panel?"

"I need to get the keys from the crane operator," Joel said. "He's probably in the bar at the Golden Wheel in Culbertson. That's forty-three miles away. Craig has some experience operating the crane. I have none. Let's see. It's six o'clock now. We can be back by nine tonight.

"That's halfway to midnight," I said.

"Yeah but look at it another way. Halfway to midnight is also high noon," Craig said with a smile. "That's when the Trinity leaves on the train for good. Hopefully, they won't be carrying the files. If they would do something like that to dad, then they are capable of doing anything. They don't know Montanans. We're brothers. I'm grateful for that. Besides, we were going to blow the dam up next week after the final inspection. Craig can lift the panel for a couple of hours, and that'll be enough to flood the computer files. Then, we can drop the panel back down, and we're back to baseline. We'll say the crane operator left the keys in the cab, and some kids who were partying got in there, lifted the panel and pushed the button. I'll throw a few beer cans out there. We'll say the security system on the detonator failed. After all, it's made in China. The dam construction will be done on time. The Project can't make a big stink about it because they would have to reveal what the Riba House was really being used for. We'll blow up the dam at nine o'clock sharp."

We gave each other high-fives and then parted. Finally, I had some allies. I was gaining some traction, but what about Anne? There was no way they would release her on Friday. I needed to get her out of jail. I figured I might take Choteau up on his offer.

❧ FORTY-TWO ❧

CHOTEAU'S HOME was about three miles from the dam and sat on a hillside on the north end of town. Fran greeted me at the door and pointed me to Choteau's hobby room. The walls were covered with Charlie Russell calendars from the early 1900s and Montana memorabilia. Old wooden filing cabinets were stuffed with more goodies.

"Choteau, I need your help," I said from the doorway. "I want to take you up on the offer to spring Anne out of jail."

"Howdy, Kid," Choteau said. "Sounds good to me. I've been in enough jails and seen enough westerns that I should be able to have her back at the ranch in no time. Did I tell you about that time in Shelby when I spent two nights in jail just cause I punched a few fellers?"

"Yeah I remember that story," I said, pressing my hands against the sill. "Look, Joel and Craig are blowing up the dam tonight to destroy the computer files that are stored in the Riba House. I guess adding a jail break to my resume won't affect my ability to take some art classes at the state pen in Deer Lodge."

"I'm not as smart as you, but I think that might put us in the Fed's pen," Choteau said. "But what the hell. I'll pull the bars out of the window and have Anne out of there in no time. We'll be back to your ranch by ten tonight. They won't catch me. I'll be cruisin' down the road at 120 mph in my Road Runner, just like in high school."

"Good luck and be careful," I said. "The border guards may be on alert. Big Sky took care of the head Gestapo agent."

"You're a Cadillac, Kid," Choteau said. "You look a little peaked. When's the last time you ate?"

"I can't remember," I said. "I think I'm running on fumes."

"Then let's have some chow first," Choteau said. "Fran cooked a deer roast. We can't be the magnificent two on an empty belly. After we eat, I'll head up to the border. I wish I knew where Munchie was. I could use his help."

"Munchie's probably in some bar in Antelope or Westby hanging out for a few days," Fran said. "That wouldn't be anything new."

"Fran, I admire you staying married to this old coyote for so many years," I said.

"Well, Don we fell in love in high school and have been in love ever since," Fran said.

After a quick supper, we went our separate ways. I pulled my night vision binoculars out of the trunk. They would make it easier to determine the extent of flooding around the Riba House. Soon I was driving close to the River of Doubt.

⤾ FORTY-THREE ⤿

I DROVE DOWN RIVER ROAD and took an old dirt side road up a hillside that looked down on the Riba House. We used to search for agates up there, and I knew it would give me a good vantage point to watch the flood. It was 8:45 in the evening. The last fifteen minutes seemed to take forever. Crickets chirped. A coyote howled. It was a moonless night, but thankfully, security lights illuminated the grounds. There was no activity I could detect inside or at the guard station.

Suddenly, I heard an explosion and felt a sharp pain through my ears similar to a shot gun blast. It was followed by a violent shaking of the ground like an earthquake. The swoosh of rushing water grew louder and louder, over the next hour. Around 9:30, lights on the property flickered, and then all was dark. My night vision binoculars showed river water up to the ceiling of the first story. That should destroy anything in the basement. Craig and Joel called it right. Hopefully, by the time I arrived home, Anne would be there. I didn't know what we'd do next. I'm sure they'd be out looking for us. During the Vietnam War, the draft dodgers headed to the border to seek asylum in Canada. That might be our only option.

As I drove into our driveway, I sensed something was wrong. Things looked too quiet. The dogs greeted me at the front door, but there was no Anne. Choteau never answered his cell phone. I called Fran. She told me she hadn't heard from him and feared the worst. I could tell she was upset with me for getting him involved in this mess.

Just then I got a text message from Deeds:

> We have Anne in custody at the border. She will be accompanying us to Minneapolis on the train for obvious reasons. We shot the tires on your friend's car. He was running through a wheat field just before our Chinese sharp shooter killed him. Nice try, but we removed the computer files yesterday. You can run but you can't hide. You've failed and by the way, God bless America.
> Your ex-boss, Deeds.

∽ PART EIGHT ∽

REDEMPTION

Friday
Halfway to Midnight
September 28, 2020

✎ FORTY-FOUR ✎

I T WAS TWELVE HOURS BEFORE HIGH NOON, or halfway to midnight, as Craig called it. Grabbing a flashlight, my Stetson, and my Colt .45 revolver, I headed to the station wagon. Was there a locator device on it? I needed to hurry. It was probably only minutes before they would be here. They were too familiar with my whereabouts. I checked under the car and eventually looked under the back bumper, and sure enough there was a small homing device. I grabbed it and put it in my pocket. Maybe, I could use it to my advantage. I hooked up the horse trailer to my Silverado pickup and loaded Sunny and Big Sky. Beau jumped inside the cab. Poor Lexy was too old so she'd have to sit this one out. With my horses, dog, and saddle bags as my only companions, I headed north to the border on lonely back roads hoping I might lose any pursuers. Lexy barked from the front porch as we sped away.

I crossed the main highway leading to Cottonwood and continued north on a one-lane dirt road. Every road from here to the border was familiar territory to me ever since the first day I started bird hunting. The ruts shook the trailer as the dust spewed out from behind. After about an hour, we were at the border. I saddled up both horses and placed the homing device in a saddle bag strapped to Sunny's saddle. I slapped her on the butt, and she took off heading north towards Canada. That would keep them busy. I jumped on Big Sky and continued to the border station to find Anne. It was close to one in the morning.

After two hours, I reached the station. It looked like Choteau had successfully torn out the bars on Anne's jail window, but things must have gone wrong after that. The building was dark. I could see a group of guards drinking and playing cards in their sleeping quarters. The windows were open and loud talk and laughter boomed from their party. As I crawled toward the quarters, a prickly pear cactus tore open one of the whip wounds on my arm. Blood gushed out, but I had no choice but to keep crawling. Below the window I heard them talking.

"I'll be glad to get back to China," a guard said. "I would rather be caught by Russians and sent to Siberia for a year than stay in this place another month."

"Where's Chow?" another guard asked. "Maybe, he took off out of here without telling us. At least we don't have to deal with that woman. Deeds is taking her with him on the train. I'm glad he took her to town. We didn't take this job to plant dope."

"Or have some crazy American tear the side of the jail out," said another voice. "I usually try hitting the left back. I'm sure I hit my target. I always do. "

"Well, if you didn't, you have an excuse," another voice said. "It's darker than hell out there, and you were all boozed up."

"Yea," another said. "It looks like shredded beef after the bullet hits the heart. It makes me hungry for Chinese food. Where's the soy sauce? Pass the whiskey bottle. It's my turn."

"Hey, look at the grand Tetons on this blonde," one guard said. "Now I remember why we volunteered to come to this country. We can't get magazines like this back home."

"I can't wait until China makes this country a province," one said. "Each one of us can have as many blondes, hooters, and asses as we can grab. Now that's real socialism. I love sharing. We'll take over for the pro athletes and movie stars. The girls will flock to us because we'll have all the money. You know American women. They're horny and go where the green is."

"Yea," another said. "Right now, Kentucky Fried Chicken is the most impressive product from America that we have in China. Soon we'll be able to order American women on their value pack menu. Two thin thighs, no wings, and two big breasts."

They all roared with laughter. I'd heard enough. Their version of America's future was sickening. Chow and this clan certainly were poor representatives of the Chinese people. Every country has its scum.

I was too late to free Anne. It was devastating to think that Choteau was dead. I headed back to Cottonwood to find Deeds and stop him before he boarded the train. That's where I'd find her. By horseback it would take a few hours to get there. Beau kept pace a few yards behind us.

✍ FORTY-FIVE ✍

THE GENTLE, ROLLING HILLS made the ride easy. Only a handful of hunters visited this stretch over the last seventy-five years. The only sound was howling from a family of coyotes clearing their throats, just because they could.

An old abandoned homestead was my hideout. We sometimes passed it hunting. It was about halfway to Cottonwood and provided shelter from the cold. I could sleep there for several hours and then time my arrival at the train station for just a few minutes before high noon.

The roof was partially caved in and the gray board siding was tattered. It was close to freezing, and I brought my sleeping bag in to keep me warm. A few snow flakes floated quietly to earth. Beau settled in on top of me. Big Sky was tied up outside in an area where he could graze. As I lay down, I thought of the family who once lived here. They were nameless and faceless to me, but I felt a sense of communion with them. Their future was past, and who knows what their hopes were. No one cared now. Their earthly lives were like dust in the wind. Everyone's is. Time makes a lot of things not matter.

From half-asleep to half-awake, I jumped up. *Knocking on Heaven's Door* boomed from outside the shack. Just then an arrow split the skin on my left arm and blood started poring out. How much more could I lose? I was seeing way too much of it. I grabbed my bandana and tied a tourniquet around my arm using my teeth and right hand to tighten it. Holy shit! Now what? I held on to Beau as she growled and tried to lunge at the door.

"Junior, wake up," Doc Dennis shouted. "Don't you just love Bob Dylan? This game never should have gone into overtime, and you're going to lose big time. Welcome to Akeldama."

"This is Coyote Flats, shit head," I shouted back as I looked out the window. "You hit me in the arm with an arrow! Dennis, what the hell are you doing?"

"You need more Bible study," he said. "Akeldama is the Field of Blood. This time it's your blood, asshole. I guess my only sin is missing the mark with my arrow. I feel like John Ford directing the *Searchers*. You know the first scene where the Comanche kill everyone at the homestead. Do you feel like the wounded healer? You're certainly no John Wayne."

Three or four gun shots whizzed by me.

"Why don't you shoot at me with that Colt .45 you're packing?" Dennis said. "My Glock is just getting warmed up."

"How did you find me out here?" I asked.

"Easy," he said. "All cell phones send out a GPS signal, and my phone has an app for that. Welcome to the twenty-first century, cowboy."

"Why don't you come clean?" I asked.

"All right," he said. "Is there a shower in that Motel 6 you're staying in for the night?"

"Very funny," I said.

"I'll confess since you won't be here much longer," he said. "My conscience is bothering me. I need to cleanse it before

Minneapolis. What should I confess, father? That I didn't attend many of my classes at Stanford Med School? That everyone was doing it? That I went to only one lecture in my bioethics course?"

"Too bad you didn't go more," I said. "You might have learned something."

"I did," he said. "I learned that British preacher Thomas Fuller comforted sufferers with the reminder that 'it is always darkest just before the day dawneth.' How true that is for you, Junior, but there is no dawneth for you. Just darkness."

"We'll see about that," I said. "Look, you could start with your father-in-law."

"Doc Peters had to go," he said. "He was getting senile, slow at work, and nosy. Bad combo. He figured out that the bus to Galen was just like the freight cars full of Jews headed to the gas chambers in World War II. I figured a river needed to run through him. Chow enjoyed the process. Besides, I'm enjoying the inheritance. I just need to get rid of the slut."

"You're a lost soul," I said.

"Your old buddy Steve was at the wrong place at the wrong time," he said. "Deeds called that one. Chow and his troops screwed up so I had to finish him off with a nice cocktail. I did have a month to play around with the doses of 'joy juice.' He died for the advancement of scientific research."

A few more shots went over my head.

"Shit, Dennis," I said and ducked. "What about Ray?"

"That old fart?" he said. "Ray was nosing around too much. We knew he wouldn't get on the bus to Galen. Deeds called that one, too. Chow told me he knocked him down and then stomped on him. Chow loves beating the shit out of Americans. Chow even scares me. He's like a pit bull, only meaner."

"Well, you don't have to be scared of him anymore," I said. "Big Sky killed him."

"Good, no more Chow," he said. "The Project doesn't have to pay for his bus ticket back to China. Besides, he was getting sloppy. He loved to use his knife to cut a triangle on his victims while they were still awake before they were thrown in the grinder. After Lightfoot escaped, Deeds made him stop it."

"I hope you haven't killed Abigail," I said.

"You're always worried about that bitch," he said. "Not yet. She's drugged up for a nice train trip to Minneapolis. I regret she won't be able to enjoy the beautiful sights of North Dakota on the way. Those oil rigs are stunning at dusk. She'll be nicely sedated while the nurse and I are in the other sleeper room. Only we won't be sleeping."

"Is that all you can ever think about?" I asked.

"I have no choice but to send Abigail for treatment," he said, ignoring me. "She's been coughing a lot lately. It's the right thing to do. After Galen, she'll catch the next bus to the Lakota Gulch and then on to eternity. Because of you, we had to abandon Hell Creek. She misses daddy a lot. The least I could do is reunite them. Killing her in Cottonwood was too messy, a divorce too expensive and too damaging for my golden boy image."

Several more shots whizzed by my head.

"What about Pastor Tim?" I asked.

"Hopefully, by now his remains should be in a cave," he said. "Shorty is next. Anybody his age needs to go. He's outworn his welcome and health insurance."

"You're nuts," I said.

"Worthless patient minus no treatment equals a successful health plan," he said. "Any one with a brain knows that's the only way health care can work in the future. We just have too many pussy politicians. Senator Bo knows. He's a good salesman. Americans believe anyone with a baby face. I'm shocked the people in town didn't believe you."

"You're disgusting," I said.

"You sure are worried about the dead," he said. "I guess you want to know who you'll be joining. I've got a container of 'joy juice' with me. I want you to drink it. A suicide by overdose would keep up the family tradition, although I gave your dad a bolus of sodium pentobarbital. You know that's the drug they use for assisted suicide in Oregon. If it's totally legal there, then why shouldn't it be here?"

"I'm not drinking anything." I said.

With that I opened the door and unloaded several shots in his direction. To think he killed my dad almost made me charge him, but I knew that's what the bastard wanted.

"Getting feisty, are ye?" Dennis said, his voice mocking.

Beau barked.

"Shut that dam dog up. He's going first," Dennis said.

Several more shots came in our direction.

Suddenly, Beau broke my grasp and ran towards Dennis. As he stepped out from behind the outhouse, Beau leaped at him. It only took one shot, and Beau fell hard.

With Dennis's shadow in full view, I took two more shots at him, but at a distance of thirty feet I missed.

"Sorry, Junior," he said. "I have to tidy everything up so Chen will give me the dough and job in Washington."

"Does she know what's going on here?" I asked.

"Did she lean over on the table for you?" he asked ignoring me. "She does that when she's trying to close the deal. I wanted to get my hands on her sweet melons, but I figured I'd wait a while. No, she thinks everything is on the up and up. She's a bitch anyway. She doesn't give a shit about this church stuff. She thinks Luke is a dope."

"Pastor Luke told me she was touched by his message and fell to her knees," I said.

"She'll do anything to accomplish her goals just like the rest of the Trinity," he said.

He squeezed off several more shots.

"Your team is from hell," I said.

"You know Junior, the difference between you and me is that I'm bold, and I like to take risks," he said. "Christians need to be bold. That's the message in the Bible. You never had the balls to take the last shot in the basketball game. I did and always made it. When we were kids, I would jump off the bridge while you watched. Women love men that take risks. I know you too well."

I could barely see Dennis in the dim light. He said, "Every move you've made over the last week I predicted. I knew you'd enjoy the notes I left out for Abigail to copy. Didn't it dawn on you that the handwriting was just like yours? One of the Chinese border guards specializes in copying American handwriting. That's an important talent when you're a spy. The only DNA on the notes was yours and my soon to be ex. Deeds wasn't happy that I did it, but who cares. I was showing off. Besides, it's the only way I could get you here. Did you enjoy her kisses and embrace too? I humped her plenty when she was young, but she doesn't turn me on now. Any woman over forty-five is a turnoff, all that fat and sagging. Yuck. I gave you enough rope to hang yourself, and you did. The whole town thinks you're screwing around on your wife and using dope.

"I bet you'd like women over forty-five sent to Galen," I said.

"Why not?" he said. "They can't bear kids anymore. They're all crazy. And they're a bad screw. Send them all on the next bus to Galen. I'll wave good-bye as I'm pinching some ass on a twenty-year-old. Part of being a good socialist is making sure the needy are taken care of appropriately."

"You're dead wrong," I said. "Now I'm the next on your list?"

"Yeah, you need a bullet between the eyes," he said. "God, you're smart. At first I thought jailing you for the rest of your life would give me joy. No one would believe a word you said about the Project. We have everything covered. But I changed my mind. The dam fiasco was really amateurish. We'll make sure Joel and Craig are sent to a labor camp in Northern China for a few decades. I told the guards to move the hard drives out of the Riba House the day before when surveillance showed you hanging around the dam. You're so predictable. Killing you will bring me the most joy."

"I only want you to be happy," I said sarcastically.

"The most important thing I remember is that you always put five bullets in your Colt," he said. "My men tell me you left your gun belt back at the ranch. I do my home work. I always loaded six in my Colt, but you were afraid to do that for safety reasons. Keep the chamber empty and be safe is what you always said. Well, I counted five shots from your gun. You're out of bullets and out of time. I'll shoot you and stuff your ass down this outhouse crapper. You'll be found in about two hundred years when someone else is looking for dinosaurs. Until then, I'll mourn your disappearance. Maybe I'll even write a tribute to you in the *Herald*. 'Insanity Must be Forgiven' will probably be the title. I'll be sure to mention how emotional instability runs in the family. We'll speculate you headed to Canada because Sunny is up there wandering around right now. Maybe, you fell off a cliff or drowned in the Saskatchewan River. You'll be like D. B. Cooper who just disappeared in thin air. My next article in the *Herald* will be 'Legends of the Fall.' You'll be labeled another conscientious objector. Don't worry. Anne will be out of prison in about twenty years. Being your good friend, I'll fight for her early release in about nineteen. Maybe, I'll visit her in jail and show her what it's like to be with a real man."

With my heart pounding I stood up and walked out of the shack and headed toward Dennis.

"Got you mad?" he said chuckling. "Good. Come closer, Junior. I want to see your expression before you take your last breath."

264

Dennis stood, facing me, crouched in a gunfighter stance. His car lights cast long shadows. As I approached, I could see that he held his gun in one hand and a whiskey bottle in the other. He pointed his Glock at me.

"Anything else you'd like to say, dead man?" he asked as he staggered forward.

"Yes," I said as I raised my Colt and shot him in the chest. "Shooting me is one thing, but I won't stand for you shooting my dog."

"How could this happen?" He said in a gasping, weak voice as he fell to the ground.

"I learned to take risk," I said. "I loaded my Colt with six bullets, ass hole. Did Pastor Luke know about any of this? I need to know for Anne's sake."

"He, he," he blurted and groaned.

With that he took his last breath. Abigail deserved a lot better. Lust is the craving of a man who is dying of thirst. In every man, of course, a demon lies hidden. Dennis just couldn't keep his from ruining his life and so many others. I wish he had told me about Luke.

I walked over to say my farewell to Beau, but I noticed her chest was moving. She was alive! She groaned and lifted her head. The bullet hit her dog tag but didn't penetrate into her flesh. A huge bruise and welt were the only signs of trauma. Thankfully, she was just momentarily knocked unconscious. I gave her a drink from my canteen. After a few minutes, she was up and ready for action. We rested back in the shack and bided our time. Beau could use the rest. I didn't want to confront Deeds until right before he planned to leave on the train. There was safety in having a crowd around me when I got my last chance to stop him. I anxiously awaited halfway to midnight.

✣ FORTY-SIX ✣

I T TOOK SEVERAL HOURS to get to the outskirts of town. We were in no hurry. It was 11:30 in the morning. I left Big Sky and Beau at a friend's house and walked up back alleys of Cottonwood. All was quiet. The sun was intense. The streets were abandoned until I approached the front of the courthouse. Three blocks south on Main Street, a huge crowd had gathered in front of a large stage next to the train station. It looked like the Fourth of July. Brightly colored Trinity flags and American flags fluttered in the breeze from dozens of flag poles up and down Main Street. I heard the shriek of horns and pounding drums from the high school band playing patriotic songs.

How many western movies had I seen where it came down to this, a confrontation on Main Street? I glanced at the large clock at the train station. Fifteen minutes before noon. Here I was walking down the middle of town heading towards the bad guys and a shootout without a gun. I figured having a gun would give them a good excuse to shoot me.

Pastor Luke and Deeds stood on an elevated platform adorned with more flags. Behind them hung a huge banner adorned with a picture of Deeds looking down on a triangle. At the top corner was a picture of Doc Dennis with the words: Trinity Universal Health Plan. At the left corner was a picture of Pastor Luke with the words: Trinity Cornerstone Church. On the other corner was a picture of Bo Hart with the words: Progressive, Populist, and Balanced Budget. In the center of the triangle was a picture of Chen with the words: China Loves America. Deeds looked like a puppeteer working his marionettes. I guess the meeting in Minneapolis was just a formality. The Chinese were on board. It was the most obnoxious thing I'd ever seen.

As they spoke about their laudatory achievements, loudspeakers projected voices to a captivated crowd. By the time I got within fifty yards, Pastor Luke was done speaking, and Deeds had taken over.

When I moved into the back of the crowd, everyone turned their heads and began whispering. It wasn't a faceless mass. I knew every person there. Many were my parent's age. Many had affectionate nicknames like Chief and Glenda, Sundance and Dorothy, Roy and Dale, Great Falls Select and Lucky, Black Butte and Missy, Buffalo Bill and Annie, Duke and the Duchess, Padre and Madre, Gentleman Gene and Ambrosia, Honeycutt and Goldy. They all parted like the Red Sea as I made my way to the front of the stage. Deeds stopped his speech and glared down at me.

"Doctor Lewis, I'm glad you came to send us off to Minneapolis," Deeds said. "You're about the only person in town who wasn't here. Have you been at the hospital with Doc Dennis? Have you seen him? We wanted him on stage with us, but welcome, anyway."

"I'm not here to praise you," I shouted over the rumbles of the crowd. "I'm here to let the townspeople know this is a fraud. You all should know that Doc Peters and Ray Koler were murdered, and Deeds is responsible. They've also been sending your loved ones to Galen just to save money on their health plan. They're murdering them too! I've got proof."

The crowd jeered and laughed. People I'd known all my life turned on me, but I was desperate, and the truth needed to be told. If it cost me everything, then so be it.

"These are false accusations that you have leveled before," Deeds yelled back. "Everyone thinks you're crazy."

With that, several of my high school classmates grabbed me. Two armed guards stepped down off the stage to hand cuff me. I pleaded for help, but everyone just watched.

Just then, the sound of a bugle drowned out the clamor of the crowd. What a sight! Three to four hundred Angus cattle thundered down the railroad tracks heading right for the front of the train, driven by more than a dozen riders who were on horseback. The earth shook. As they got closer, I could see on one side was Bull Berg with six of his cowboys and on the other side were Two Moon, his sons, Johnny Thunder, and some of my reservation patients.

"This train isn't moving until our friend, Don, is heard," Bull said as he rode up to the stage. "Let go of him or we'll put some lead in that space between your ears."

"Don is a good man," Johnny Thunder said. "These Trinity men and their soldiers killed Doc Peters. My friend will testify to that fact."

"Jesus Christ!" Deeds barked. "Keep your mouth shut. Who wants to listen to a damn Indian?"

"Don't believe these cowboys and Indians," Pastor Luke shouted out. "They are agents of the devil. I have prayed to the Lord, and he is one hunred percent behind the Trinity Project. You all have been so obedient in good times. You are now tested like Job. Don't let this tribulation shake your faith. God is watching. Seek His approval."

The crowd seemed uncertain. That was a good sign. Some yelled out in support of the Trinity, but many looked confused. Then, Neil Odegard shouted "hold on" as he came out of his drug store and marched up on stage. He grabbed the microphone away from Deeds.

"You've been duped," Neil yelled. "I've been taking money from Deeds to keep my mouth shut. I'm ashamed. Please, forgive me. It's true about the communion wine being drugged. They had it delivered to my pharmacy store, and I was basically paid to look the other way. On one of the shipments a product insert was left by mistake. I didn't have the courage to come forward till now. It clouds your mind and will, and it makes you submissive. The last two services, I substituted water for the drug so you should be coming to your senses. Forgive me. But Doc Don is telling it straight."

"I forgive you, Neil," I shouted. "You were under the same spell, same as everyone else."

"I stopped taking communion a few weeks ago," Neil said. "The moral anchor of this country definitely isn't in LA or New York. It's here in the heartland. And as far as all this socialism bullshit, for Christians, the individual is incomparably more important because he is everlasting. The life of socialism is fleeting and only a moment in time."

"Look, the officer inside the train has called my agents at the border," Deeds said. "Ten of them will be here in a matter of minutes. Anyone that believes this trash will be arrested and put in jail up at the courthouse. If you resist, they will mow you down like ants with their machine guns."

"Not so fast," Judge Bastar said, emerging from the crowd. "It's about time I take control of this town again. I've known Neil and Don all my life. I believe we need to sort things out. Give us time."

"I agree," Sheriff Butch Boone said. "And it's about time I start enforcing the law around here again."

Suddenly, the two panicked guards ran toward their car and drove off.

"Don't believe them," Pastor Luke pleaded. "It's my word that captivated my followers. No drug could do that. It's my destiny to unite all Christians. I made a difference in this town and across this country. God wants me to go to Minneapolis and lead a national church. I am the third Adam, can't you see?"

"Somehow you don't seem as convincing when we aren't drugged up," Joe Pesci said.

"I agree with the Judge, Sheriff, and Pesci," Stu Bacon said. "You two need to stay here and answer some questions."

"Fine with me," Pastor Luke said throwing his hands up. "I will answer to you and God."

"I'm not going to put up with this bull shit," Deeds said as he pulled out a hand gun from under his coat.

Deeds grabbed Neil around the neck and pointed the gun at his head.

"Pastor, get on the train," Deeds yelled in a panicked voice. "We're leaving on time. We'll make hamburger out of the cattle and scum. You stupid shits aren't going to ruin a plan that will change America. No one is going to believe a bunch of hicks in this shit hole. I've got the computer discs, and that's all I need. I don't need any of you anymore. You're just a statistic. I hope I never set foot here again. My agents from the border should be here any minute. They'll put this rebellion down. This will look like another Wounded Knee massacre."

"Looks like you'll have to line up the coffins at the rodeo grounds," I said. "That's the only place that can hold all the people."

"Look up in the air," Festus, the town banker, said as he and several others pointed to the sky.

I figured it was one of the border guard's surveillance planes that flew along the border that was fitted with machine guns, but as it came closer I could see it was a crop duster. What was it doing flying around this time of year?

And, as if things weren't crazy enough, the plane looked as if it were going to land on Main Street! The wheels barely cleared the roof of the courthouse as it came to rest just short of the stage by a few yards. Yellow, oily fluid was dripping from the spray nozzles under the wings. The pilot and his passenger emerged from the two-seater. It's the closest thing to a miracle I'd ever seen. There was Pastor Tim and Munchie. Tim was helped out, and the crowd erupted in cheering.

"You're back from the dead," I said. "You have arisen."

"I have arisen, indeed, and we sprayed about one mile of corn oil on the highway to the border," Pastor Tim said. "The patrol cars are all in the ditch. They won't be joining the party. God, forgive me."

"It doesn't look like you'll be getting any reinforcements any time soon," I said to Deeds.

"Tim, you worn-out, blow-hard. I should have taken care of you myself instead of shipping you to Galen," Deeds said in disgust. "Those incompetent bastards let too many nothings escape from there."

"Don't blame it on them," Munchie said. "I kidnapped Pastor Tim out of the men's room at a gas station in Miles City. Gus in *Lonesome Dove* died in that town, but Tim was saved there."

"Howdy," Choteau said as he appeared on top of the Pullman car. "My deer rifle has never missed its mark unlike that Chinese hacker's pea shooter, and if you don't let Neil go, then you'll just be another notch on my rifle butt. I'm a little edgy after drivin' my motorcycle down from the border. Ground flying at 120 miles per hour ain't somethin' I've done lately. The trunk on Fran's Cadi is just big enough for my two-wheeler."

"We all need to fall to our knees and pray," Pastor Luke said. "Please, no violence. We need to do the right thing. If something has been done wrong here, then we need redemption."

"Shut up you jackass," Deeds said as he shot Luke in the right thigh. "Now you're on your knees. Don't you know you should pray in silence like the Desert Fathers? Hell, I know more about religion than you do."

Suddenly, Deeds threw Neil down and swung around to take a shot at Choteau. It was no contest. Choteau shot first and Deeds was blown backwards and fell off the stage. The next stop for Deeds and Doc Dennis were the gates of Hades. There, I was sure, Cerberus would welcome them.

"Are you okay?" I asked Pastor Luke, but all he could muster was uncontrollable crying.

It was just a flesh wound. Neil applied pressure to the site. Abigail and Anne, who were handcuffed together, stepped down the Pullman stairway, escorted by Choteau. Their guard surrendered and freed them.

Anne embraced me, crying uncontrollably.

For Abigail it was a different story. She grabbed the microphone. "I look at Dennis and see how evil can grip a man," she said in a slow, slurred voice. Although she was obviously still drugged, her voice had an odd steadiness. "He had so much potential and helped so many people. We loved each other long ago, but he turned to another lover, Satan."

"We all love you, Abigail," Delia, Korrine, Louise, Julie and Peggy shouted out from the crowd. "We're sorry. Please forgive us."

Abigail then turned to me and whispered. "I want to keep as much of this secret as possible. The kids loved their father. I don't want his sin to haunt them and their offspring. I'm going to catch the train tomorrow to be with them. I have nothing left here but memories."

"I killed Dennis this morning," I whispered back. "I had to, before he shot me."

"I understand," Abigail said, and put her hand on my arm, before she turned and walked away.

I still wasn't sure what Pastor Luke knew, and for Anne's sake I didn't want to know. Anne and I hugged, and as I held her close, she cried, her shoulders shaking.

"I'm ready to go to church on Sunday," Shorty said as he stepped out of the crowd. "And I want Anne to preach."

"Count us in," Choteau said. "Me and Munchie need some religion. The only religious music we listen to is *Ina Goda Da Vida* by Iron Butterfly. Hey, how 'bout we change communion to beer and pizza? I never did trust wine drinkers anyway."

"I'll be there too," Pastor Tim said as he was helped to the stage. "Don't let this destroy your faith. It should strengthen it. The evil one works in many ways. Never place your faith in men and their dreams. You'll always be disappointed. Put your faith in God, the only one who doesn't disappoint. God is enough. From the ashes, Cottonwood will arise. You are good people and live in a shining city. Feel blessed that you can live under the Big Sky. Anne, can I borrow your husband. I promise to give him back to you in less than an hour."

"Sure!" She said. She wiped her eyes and smiled. "But don't forsake me, oh my darling."

"Never have and never will," I said.

"I've got to get this plane off Main Street or Judge Bastar will give me a ticket for illegal parking," Pastor Tim said. "Come on, Don, jump in the seat behind me."

I shook my head, but the crowd cheered me on. Before I knew it, we were flying high above Cottonwood and marveling at the big, blue clear sky. The crowd below was waving.

"I'm not motion sick or scared anymore," I said with glee. "I forgot how beautiful everything looked from up here. I'm forever grateful to you and Anne for showing me the way to Christ."

"For Christians, gratitude is never the shortest felt emotion," Pastor Tim said. "After the original sin, God, through Jesus, gave us a second chance to join him in heaven for which we are eternally grateful."

"It seems so easy to understand now," I said.

"If Christians would open the gate and just get out of the way, the path to Him would be much easier for others," Pastor Tim said. "The Trinity Project lost sight of God. Without God, everything is permitted."

"Satan was sure in control of Dennis and Deeds," I said.

"He was," Pastor Tim said. "Unfortunately, they took greater risks to generate an ever diminishing satisfaction from the things they craved: sex, power, and money. That's idolatry."

"Look at how the sun shines down on our town," I said, looking over the orderly streets of Cottonwood. "I can close my eyes and still see the light. It's easy to find now.

"That's God's bright light," Pastor Tim said. "I pray that you remain in it, prodigal son."

"I promise you that I always will," I said. "Amen?"

"Amen."